Praise for Kristi...

THE FALLEN

RAZIEL

"A sexy and smart romp. . . . Packed with verbal sparring and sly shout-outs to Gnosticism . . . entertaining."

—*Publishers Weekly*

"Douglas stakes out her own fresh style of storytelling. . . . This story is edgy and darkly riveting as it follows two individuals struggling against destiny and insidious treachery. Terrific!"

—*RT Book Reviews*

DEMON

"Edgy and engrossing series. . . . Spellbinding reading!"

—*RT Book Reviews*

"The exciting second Fallen Angels urban fantasy is character driven though loaded with nonstop action."

—Genre Go Round Reviews

"Sardonic humor and characters who make no apologies for themselves."

—Heroes and Heartbreakers

ALSO BY KRISTINA DOUGLAS

Raziel
Demon

Available from Pocket Books

THE FALLEN

WARRIOR

KRISTINA DOUGLAS

Pocket Books

New York   London   Toronto   Sydney   New Delhi

Pocket Books
A Division of Simon & Schuster, Inc.
1230 Avenue of the Americas
New York, NY 10020

This book is a work of fiction. Names, characters, places, and incidents either are products of the author's imagination or are used fictitiously. Any resemblance to actual events or locales or persons, living or dead, is entirely coincidental.

First Pocket Books paperback edition May 2012

POCKET and colophon are registered trademarks of Simon & Schuster, Inc.

For information about special discounts for bulk purchases, please contact Simon & Schuster Special Sales at 1-866-506-1949 or business@simonandschuster.com.

The Simon & Schuster Speakers Bureau can bring authors to your live event. For more information or to book an event contact the Simon & Schuster Speakers Bureau at 1-866-248-3049 or visit our website at www.simonspeakers.com.

Designed by Jacquelynne Hudson

Manufactured in the United States of America

10 9 8 7 6 5 4 3 2 1

ISBN 978-1-4516-5591-9
ISBN 978-1-4516-5594-0 (ebook)

For Casey Casavant, a true Warrior,
who gave two of the greatest gifts anyone could give.
He gave me my adopted daughter,
and he gave his life for his country.
Rest in peace.

WARRIOR

BEGINNING

MARTHA, WIDOW OF THOMAS, moved through the predawn halls of the compound, hope, anxiety, and grief washing through her. She felt old at the age of thirty, old before her time. There was no role for a widow in the angel-centered order of Sheol, but she made herself as useful as she could. Were it not for her dubious "gift," she would have nothing to do, and that way madness lay. Not that she even had that choice. In Sheol there was no illness, mental or otherwise. Cursed with a longer-than-average life span, she would simply die of boredom. Eventually.

Martha had greeted her first vision, just three short years ago, with joy, even though it warned of trouble. Each succeeding vision had warned of more and more danger, though there had been the occasional happiness, a new mate joining them in Sheol, or a difficult situation they could avoid.

This morning was the same, good news and bad. And Allie would be waiting for her.

There were no children in Sheol. The women were barren, and they had all accepted it. But Allie, the Source, the wife of their leader, was secretly mourning that loss. Grieving it, hoping that, after all the millennia the Fallen had been relegated to earth, some miracle might happen. Rachel's arrival had started those vain hopes. Rachel, who was, in fact, the demon-goddess Lilith, providing comfort and hope for infertile women throughout history.

But Martha was bringing no good news to Allie's bedside. She had searched, done her best to force a vision, which never seemed to work, and she had seen nothing but new disaster on the horizon.

She climbed the many flights of stairs swiftly. Allie would be alone, awaiting her. Waiting for hope that wasn't coming.

But Allie wasn't alone. The door to their aerie was ajar, and Martha knocked before pushing inside. To her surprise, Raziel himself was sitting on one of the colorful sofas in the living room, a cup of coffee in his hand, a cool expression on his angelically beautiful face.

She had never felt entirely comfortable around Raziel. He had always been too stiff, too cold, though she supposed that leading the fallen angels didn't call for someone warm and fuzzy. They were an obstreperous bunch; there was a reason they had fallen. They had questioned, they had rebelled, they had done everything they were proscribed from doing, and done it flagrantly. In truth, her beloved Thomas had been the calmest of the bunch.

"Martha." Raziel's rich voice greeted her evenly.

"Alpha," she said respectfully, bowing her head, trying to hide her surprise. "I thought you would be gone by now." Raziel was usually up before dawn and flying over the compound to make sure all was well. Seeing the shadow of his iridescent blue wings overhead always made her feel oddly comforted. She'd feel a lot better if he were there now.

A wry smile flitted across his face. "I'm sure you did. However, I decided to keep my wife company a little longer."

Allie emerged from the bedroom, wrapped in a tie-dyed lounger that almost brightened her wan face. She put on a cheery smile, enough to fool most people. "Good morning, Martha. I'm so glad you could take the time to help me . . . learn to knit. I've been longing to."

Martha tried to keep the dismay from her face. There were half a dozen women who were master knitters in Sheol, and two of the Fallen themselves were no slouches. Logically, Allie would have turned to one of them.

Raziel's eyes were flitting between the two of them. "Yes, I'd be very interested in these lessons."

The Alpha adored his wife. He was, however, not above taunting her, and Martha decided to change the subject. "We'll show you the results," she said repressively, wondering at her temerity. "It's better not to have someone watching."

Raziel said nothing as Allie got coffee for herself and Martha. By the time his wife had taken a seat on the opposite sofa, she was entirely composed. "Don't you want to begin your morning duties?" Allie asked.

"After you tell me the truth." His voice was pleasant but inexorable. "Why is Martha here?"

Allie's composure crumpled. "It's my business."

Raziel's cold features softened. "My love, why are you shielding your thoughts? What is troubling you, and how is Martha supposed to help? And don't try to convince me that Martha can knit. She is a most estimable member of our society, but if she has any skills in that area I would be much surprised."

Oh, drat, Martha thought. It was never wise to try to outwit the Alpha. Raziel was far too observant. Husbands and wives shared thoughts easily, but if Allie was shielding her distress, Raziel would know it. And he was the kind of man who didn't let go of a mystery until he'd solved it to his satisfaction.

And how the hell did he know she couldn't knit? she thought belatedly. The first thing she was going to do when she left here was find someone to teach her.

"In truth," Martha prevaricated, "I must speak with you, Lord Raziel. I have had another vision."

Raziel was suddenly alert, all hard focus, and Martha could see the hope light in Allie's eyes. It broke her heart.

She gave Allie a quick, short shake of her head, one she could only hope Raziel wouldn't notice.

"It concerns the Archangel Michael," she said hurriedly, before Raziel could call her on it. "He has a mate."

Raziel looked dubious. "Michael has had only one mate in the two hundred years he's been here, and she was killed in a raid by the Nephilim just two days after they were married."

His casual words brought a wave of pain, surprisingly fresh, at the memory of Thomas, ripped into pieces and half-devoured by the foulness known as the Nephilim. She pushed it away.

"Nevertheless, there is a woman waiting for him, and if we are to prevail against the Armies of Heaven, she must join us. There's no choice."

She was just glad she wasn't going to be the one to break this news to Michael. Raziel was scary enough, but he was a pussycat compared to the warrior angel who wielded the flaming sword of justice.

"And who is it? I hope your vision was specific

enough to tell you how to find her." Raziel's voice was caustic. Her visions had been less than clear in the past, and this one wasn't a whole lot better.

"My lord, I can't control my visions, I can only report them," she said. She didn't like being bullied.

Raziel took the veiled reprimand well, reminding her that he wasn't, in fact, a bully. He was a hard man, but a fair one. "I understand, Martha. Do you know who and where she is?"

"I do. She is the Roman goddess of war."

He raised an eyebrow. "Fitting. Where?"

This was a little trickier. "I'm working on that. I know her name is Victoria Bellona, and I believe she's in seclusion somewhere in Italy."

Raziel nodded, rising. "I'll go talk to Michael. He won't like the news."

"No," agreed Allie, sipping at her coffee, "I imagine he won't."

"And later, perhaps, you'll tell me your reason for meeting with my wife," he added in a silken tone.

Martha felt a flush rise to her face. She couldn't lie directly—he would know.

"Leave her alone, Raziel," Allie said. "It's nothing important, I promise you."

He turned to look at his wife for a long, contemplative moment. And then he nodded. "Later," he said to her. "Martha, you will accompany me to speak to the archangel. I imagine he will have some questions."

She froze. The Alpha wasn't giving her any choice. "Yes, my lord," she said meekly enough. She cast one last glance at the Source, trying to give her the bad news as subtly as possible.

Allie nodded, her face impassive. She was a strong woman, and she'd been dealing with this a long time. Perhaps the next vision would bring hope.

CHAPTER
ONE

MY MOTHER WAS GOING TO kill me.

I looked out the window into the desolate countryside and I wanted to laugh at myself. How many teenagers had said that through the millennia? It should have been comical in a woman nearly twenty-five.

Except that Contessa Carlotta di Montespan seemed to have every intention of ending the life she'd reluctantly given birth to, presumably with the help of Pedersen, the teacher, the trainer, the guard who had haunted nearly my entire existence. They were going to murder me before my twenty-fifth birthday, and there was no one I could turn to. There never had been.

I pushed away from the window, looking around the lavish bedroom. The large bed was covered with the finest of Egyptian cotton; the rugs were ancient and beautiful, with soft, muted colors; the fresh roses were pale yellow, my favorite color. The walls were painted a soft cream, and the mullioned windows looked out over the mountainous countryside of what apparently was Italy. But the view was spoiled by the iron bars across the windows, and the door to my room was solid, ancient oak—and locked. I was a prisoner in a gilded cage, as I had been for almost my entire life, and now I'd been given a death sentence.

It shouldn't have come as a surprise. My cold, exquisitely beautiful mother was a woman totally devoid of maternal feeling, or any feelings at all, as far as I could tell. Even Pedersen, who was most likely her bed partner as well as her partner in crime, merited not a sign of warmth.

Pedersen had appeared, an enigma like everything else in my life, when I was about seven. He was a giant, six foot six at least, with heavy muscles, pale blue eyes, and the white-blond hair of his Scandinavian ancestors. I had no idea where he'd come from, and when I asked he wouldn't tell me. But then, Pedersen wasn't a man for talk except when he was instructing me. And those instructions had been endless.

My mother hadn't approved of schools. Even the most selective private academies held bad elements, she'd said, and I could learn everything I needed from Pedersen. She claimed he had a formidable intellect, and he was an expert in the physical training I would require.

The rest of my education came from the movies.

I never bothered to ask why the physical training was necessary. The contessa was even less inclined to answer questions than her henchman, and the time I spent in her presence was growing shorter.

So I learned, and I trained. We started with gymnastics, and I loved it, spinning on the bars, flying through the air to land smoothly on the mats. I was the Karate Kid, I was Bruce Lee. I felt . . . free.

Pedersen had moved on quickly. Tae kwon do, karate, and Shaolin kung fu came next, followed by more arcane forms of martial art. I had been an apt pupil, more for the love of movement than a need for approval. I was fast and strong, healing from Pedersen's brutal methods of teaching with preternatural speed, and I already knew there was no approval to be found.

Amazingly, they let me go when I was fourteen. I was small for my age, well before my ridiculous growth spurt, and my intense training had kept my period at bay, convincing me I'd never be a woman. The tiny private school in the Alps had been run by nuns, the half dozen students silent and cowed, but it had been human interaction, and I bloomed. For those three years I had no rigorous training, only the exercises I chose to do, and I'd made friends among the other exiles. And there'd been Johann.

The nuns would let me out to train in the meadows surrounding the remote convent, having discovered that my kicks and spins caused too much damage in confined quarters. I would move and swirl and dance in the sunlight, a lethal Maria von Trapp, singing "The Sound of Music" slightly off-key at the top of my lungs where no one could hear me. I would escape in the cold winter weather, in the soft spring air, and it was there that I met Johann.

But I didn't want to think about him right now. The memory still ripped at my heart seven years later; pain and betrayal still haunted me. When they'd dragged me back to my tower, I put all my rage into the endless training, determined on revenge—and even Pedersen hadn't realized when I finally became stronger than he was.

I kept that knowledge safe in my heart. I could best him in a fight. I almost had, during our sparring, but at the last minute I'd instinctively pulled back, not wanting him to see my strength. There were few enough weapons that could defeat the people who'd raised me, and Pedersen could be a dangerous man. I intended to guard any advantage I had.

As for Pedersen's impressive intellect, I'd outstripped that years ago, and no one even made the pretense that he could keep up with me. The library was endless, and they put no restrictions on my reading or the movies I watched. Unfortunately, there was no useful guidebook to tell me how to get away from my incomprehensible imprisonment, and escape movies didn't cover my situation. I could hardly tunnel my way out as they did in *The Great Escape*—I was surrounded by stone walls. I couldn't rappel down the outside of the building like Bruce Willis—I had no ropes and not enough sheets to make one. The only situations that even came close to mine were those of fairy-tale princesses locked in towers, and for me there would be no magic spell or handsome prince to rescue me.

This imprisoned princess had to rescue herself.

And I'd tried. For a few years I tried constantly, only to be hauled back by Pedersen before I got more than a few miles away. I knew better than to enlist help, after Johann.

He'd betrayed me—promised to love me forever—but all Pedersen had to do was flash money in front of him and he'd given me up like a bad habit, and I was once more a prisoner.

Now I had the strong conviction I was about to be disposed of by the woman who should have loved me. It sounded like a bad made-for-TV movie. I had no proof, of course, which made me seem even crazier. But I had learned early on that my instincts were infallible, and I'd always known she hated me, that she was just biding her time. That time was coming, and unless I got out of there I was going to be in deep shit. But I was locked in. All I could do was wait for them to come to me, and I wouldn't go down easily.

It wasn't until six o'clock that I heard the knock on my door. I started, calming the icy dread that rushed into my stomach. I could do this.

I rose, fluid though I'd been sitting for three hours, and went to the door.

The maid stood there with her usual stolid expression. This time she wasn't carrying a tray of food— evidently I wasn't going to be poisoned.

"The contessa says you are to dress in your finest clothes and come to the drawing room."

I stared at her blankly. I wasn't given free run of this house, and I had no idea where to find the contessa's drawing room.

"I will show you," she said, closing the door behind her. I didn't make the mistake of underestimating her. She would be child's play, but the two hulking men in the hallway were a different matter.

So I would have to use stealth and cunning. I could do that. I headed for my closet, withdrawing the shapeless gray dress I wore on the rare occasions I dined *en famille*, but the maid shook her head. "The contessa said you are to wear the black. And I will dress your hair."

I looked at her with surprise. I'd never worn the black dress, though I'd tried it on when it appeared in my closet one day. It was short and tight, sleeveless and cut low across the bosom. I usually counted on baggy clothes to disguise the tensile strength of my body, and that dress would reveal everything.

But I knew how useless it would be to argue. "May I shower first?"

The maid nodded.

There was nothing in the bathroom I could use as a weapon. The mechanism of the toilet was concealed, so I couldn't turn any of the working parts into a stiletto. I hadn't watched enough prison movies to figure out how they fashioned weapons from bars of soap and the like. And besides, my soap was in the form of geranium-scented gel. I hated geraniums.

I washed and dressed quickly, my nerves coming back, though I knew I covered them well. I sat still as the maid brushed my long black hair and fashioned it into six braids, wrapping them around my head in a style that made me look like an ancient Roman goddess. I stared back at my reflection bemusedly. For some reason they wanted me trussed and plucked before they killed me. Maybe I was going to be some kind of virgin sacrifice.

Too late, I thought with dark humor. Johann had seen to that.

The only pair of shoes that matched put me close to six feet, towering over the tiny maid. Could I take out one small female and two large, probably armed males? It was possible, but there were no guarantees. It would be easier if it were only Pedersen and my mother.

The moment I stepped into the hall, I was flanked by the guards. Four of them, not two. Good thing I hadn't attacked. They force-marched me through the stone corridors of the old *castello*, and for a moment I wondered if they were going to march me right off the cliff. I would take at least one of them with me if they did.

But they took me to a room I hadn't visited

before, knocking before my mother's voice floated out. I felt a meaty hand in the middle of my back propel me forward, and I stumbled into the room, graceless.

"Darling," my mother greeted me with a warm smile that didn't reach her cold, dark eyes. "What took you so long? We have a visitor."

She didn't need to tell me that—my mother never smiled at me without an audience. Pedersen was watching me, an unsettling expression on his face, and I turned slowly to face whatever had inspired the contessa to suddenly appear like a normal mother.

And I felt my heart slam to a stop.

CHAPTER
TWO

H E HAD TO BE THE MOST BEAUTI-
ful creature I had ever seen in my
entire life. He seemed to fill the
room, though physically he couldn't have been as
big as Pedersen. He had the face of a Botticelli
angel—high cheekbones, a rich, beautiful mouth, a
strong blade of a nose. His hair was close-cropped
to his perfectly shaped head, almost a military cut.
I'd always had a weakness for long hair on a man—
Johann had had extravagant brown curls. But this
man was . . . extraordinary.

He was very powerful, I could tell that from the
lean strength of his body, even though there was no
bulk of muscle beneath the sleek black suit he wore
with casual elegance. No tie, and the black shirt was
open, exposing smooth, golden flesh. The contessa
wouldn't approve of such informality, I thought,
looking him over. I tended to know instinctively

whether I could take a man or not. This one might possibly be out of my league.

I glanced back at Pedersen and the contessa. I could tell Pedersen wasn't as impressed as I was— he was looking at the beautiful newcomer with just the faintest hint of contempt, probably fooled by his almost celestial beauty into thinking him a light-weight. But then, Pedersen's intellect had never been as strong as the contessa had insisted.

"Tory, this is Michael Angelo. And this is my darling daughter, Victoria Bellona, affectionately known as Tory."

I snorted. Shouldn't have, I know, but I couldn't help myself. First, at his absurd name. Second, at the thought of my mother having affection for me.

"Are you named after the Renaissance master or one of the Teenage Mutant Ninja Turtles?" I asked before I could stop myself.

The man had been surveying me out of cool, distant eyes, eyes so brown they were almost black, but his gaze suddenly sharpened, homing in on me, and his mouth thinned. Clearly he didn't like what he saw.

"Tory, don't be absurd!" Her trill of laughter got on my last nerve. "Turtles?" No one ever accused my mother of being versed in popular culture. If they hadn't given me free run of the Internet, I might not have been either. "Pay no attention to her, Monsignor. She is young for her age."

Monsignor? Was the man some kind of priest? To

be sure, there was an ascetic tone to his beautiful face and eyes, but the mouth was far too sensual for a man of God. Then he spoke, and things got a lot worse.

"And what is her age, Contessa?"

Jesus Christ, his voice was indescribable. Rich and warm, full of music and life and powerful seduction, even as his face was cool and distant. The ugliest man in the world would have women instantly on their backs with a voice like that. It was obscenely unfair that God had wasted so many gifts on one human being.

The contessa stiffened but didn't let her smile falter. "You know as well as I do, Monsignor. She is almost twenty-five."

He stared at me like a farmer surveying a pig for the slaughter. "Almost too late."

"Indeed, Monsignor. If word hadn't come today, we were prepared to dispose of her."

I turned back, shocked at the calm boldness of her words, verifying everything. "Dispose of me?"

But the contessa had never paid attention to my questions. "If you think she is too old, we can wait for the next one."

Next one? What the hell were they talking about?

The man continued to stare at me, and I thought I saw dislike in his dark eyes. What did he have to dislike about me, apart from my smart-ass question about his name? He shook his head. "We cannot afford to wait another eighteen years. She will have to do."

Okay, enough was enough. While I might not be able to take on the newcomer in hand-to-hand combat, it was clear the gloves were off, and the contessa was no longer dissembling about whatever it was they had in store for me.

I walked across the room and sat down, halfway between my mismatched parental unit and the dark stranger. "Do for what?" I said. "Wait for the next who? Dispose of me?"

The contessa let her cold gaze drift across me like I was an unpleasant interruption, but for once she answered me. "You know as well as I do, Tory. You always were an intelligent child, despite your other failings. The fact is, you were bred and born for a purpose, and that purpose runs out when you are twenty-five. Fortunately, word came from Monsignor that you were finally to be called. It would have pained Pedersen a great deal to dispose of you."

I didn't even bother to glance at my hulking tutor. In all the years I'd known him, he'd never shown any emotion. I expected he was impervious to pain. But that brooding expression had grown even stronger, and he hardly looked like a man reprieved from an onerous duty.

"But . . . but why?" I said when I could catch my breath. "Called for what? Who am I?"

The silence in the room grew and stretched, and the contessa, the supreme hostess, shifted her bony ass uncomfortably in her seat. Pedersen said nothing either, and it was up to the stranger to enlighten me.

"I would think it is more a question of *what* are you?" the man with the voice of an angel said. "And the answer is that you are Victoria Bellona, the ancient Roman goddess of war, and—"

"You mean I was *named after* the ancient goddess of war," I corrected.

He wasn't a man who liked being interrupted. "No," he said. "You *are* the Roman goddess of war, or at least her newest manifestation. And you are my wife."

That took my breath away. Okay, so not content with just killing me, they were going to toy with me first by bringing in a beautiful lunatic to taunt me. "Yeah, right," I said. "Somehow I seem to have forgotten the wedding ceremony."

His gaze dismissed me, and he turned back to the woman who had ostensibly given birth to me. "You forgot to mention her indecorous tongue. Your job was to raise her as befits her rank. Her lack of proper deference is disturbing."

I opened my mouth to tell him where he could stuff his proper deference, but the contessa spoke first. "And she is no longer a virgin. I believe I made that clear. Indeed, she is more trouble than she is worth, Monsignor. I would recommend you wait until the next, more appropriate candidate comes along."

The next? WTF? But Monsignor shook his beautifully shaped head. "We do not have that option. The virginity is of no matter, as the arrangement is a formality only. And she will learn to watch her tongue. I will take her."

Wrap her up, folks, she's ready to go, I thought bitterly. I fastened my eyes on him. "And what if I don't want to leave?"

He glanced at me. "Do not be absurd, Victoria Bellona. Your choice is a quick death or life with the Fallen. Only a fool would choose death, and no matter what other defects you might have, you are not, I think, a fool."

He had me there. I had one last ounce of fight left in me, but in truth I'd go with Attila the Hun if it meant I could escape my mother and Pedersen. "My name is Tory," I said. "Not Victoria Bellona. And who the hell are the Fallen?"

For the first time that elegant mouth curved in a smile, though it was far from a pleasant one. "I'm neither some kind of turtle nor a Renaissance master, Victoria Bellona. The Fallen are fallen angels, and I am the Archangel Michael."

I could give long, assessing looks as well. Certain death at the hands of my guardians, or a future with a celibate madman? The choice was clear.

"Okay, Your Holiness. I'm in. When do we leave?"

He wasn't happy with me, but that was the least of my worries. "Now."

CHAPTER
THREE

THE ARCHANGEL MICHAEL STARED at the flippant young woman, steeling himself against the bleak despair that filled him. He didn't want this, he didn't want her. He wanted the simplicity of the life he'd carved for himself, and there was no room in that life for the creature who had been foisted on him. Ever since Raziel had told him of Martha's prophecy, three short days ago, he'd been dreading this. The sight of his future wife had only made things worse. This time the contessa and Pedersen had botched the job most thoroughly. They were called upon to breed and raise and train each new incarnation of Bellona, goddess of war, and over the centuries their work had been flawless.

Their job was a strange one. Most of the ancient gods and goddesses had vanished, no longer needed. Only the gods of war remained strong, and throughout the millennia the contessa and her henchmen had bred them, raised them until the age of twenty-five, and then disposed of them if they weren't needed. Victoria Bellona needed to be forever young, and there was no room for an aging goddess.

Gods and goddesses should be immortal, of course, but what kept them that way was the faith of their followers. There was no one left who believed in the ancient Roman and Greek pantheons. She was as vulnerable as a human.

A few of the incarnations had been called during the recent world wars, the fury of the Japanese assault on China, the battles that had raged over Europe and Asia during the centuries. The last few Victoria Bellonas had been effectively recycled, he thought with grim amusement.

Now this one had been offered for the use of the Fallen in their battle with Uriel and the Armies of Heaven, and he watched her, judged her. This was no shy young virgin with downcast eyes. This one had escaped with a lover when she was a teenager, though Pedersen had made short work of that. They still hadn't managed to tame her.

This was a disaster, from beginning to end, but Raziel had refused to listen to his protests, and Michael had been forced to agree with him. Uriel was preparing to attack, the détente that had kept the Armies of Heaven from the grounds of Sheol about to be broken as easily as a crystal goblet.

He had no doubt the Fallen would eventually prevail, but certain things were needed to make that come to pass. Michael would do his part, and he would ensure that this girl did the same. Anything to bring down the vicious rule of the last of the archangels, Uriel, and end his bloody war against the Fallen.

The girl rose—though he supposed she wasn't really a girl. Twenty-four. He could remember a time when women were ancient by the time they reached their twenties, their bodies worn-out by hard work and childbearing. This young woman didn't seem to have done any work in her entire life.

"It will take me a few minutes to pack."

"It's been taken care of."

A flash of annoyance danced in her clear green eyes, then flickered away. "All right. I'll need to say good-bye—"

"There is no one you need to say good-bye to," he said in the overpowering tone that allowed no contradiction. "I am ready. Come."

He could feel her resistance, surprisingly powerful in one so young. But he had to remind himself that her physical years had nothing to do with the years—no, millennia—of power that had been transferred into her at birth. She really had no idea how strong she was.

Which was how it should be. Perhaps that was why the contessa had been so eager to destroy her, jumping the gun by several weeks. Traditionally the candidate was destroyed on her twenty-fifth birthday, but that was four weeks away. If Martha hadn't had her damnable vision just days ago, then this young woman would be doomed, and the eternal contessa would already be carrying a new goddess to be passed along to servants to raise until Pedersen took charge. They were a chilling factory; the contessa put him in mind of a spider hatching her eggs.

He knew why the contessa had sped up the date of termination for her latest offspring. It wasn't the unruly tongue and lack of deference. It was the way Pedersen looked at the young woman when he thought the contessa wouldn't notice.

It would have amused Michael in other circumstances. Even immortals were at the mercy of their whims and emotions, and it appeared that the previously impervious Pedersen had fallen prey to his latest student. What would have happened to her if he himself hadn't entered the picture like a deus ex machina? Michael almost snorted at his own turn of phrase, but of late he'd lost his sense of humor.

He glanced at the big man. Pedersen probably would have tossed the girl over the cliff to join the bones of all the other young women. As long as no one else could have her, he would be content. Michael could read the thoughts behind that impassive face, sense the obsession, the stoic façade about to break.

If he did nothing, Pedersen might solve his problem for him. The idea should have been tempting, but it had been so long since anything had tempted Michael that he barely recognized the feeling. He had a duty to perform, and he would do it. He had to take Raziel's word on faith that it was a necessary evil.

"You should wait—" Pedersen began, as Michael had known he would, and he allowed himself a sour smile.

The contessa jerked her head up to stare at her lover. "Wait for what? The sooner she is gone from here, the better. At least for a while we'll be free."

"A while?" Michael said, ignoring the young woman who sat and watched them all.

"If she is the right candidate," the contessa said with a certain amount of satisfaction. "You yourself pointed out, Monsignor, that she lacks deference, respect, and virginity. I think it will not be long before we are called upon to shepherd another candidate through her childhood."

There were creatures in the natural world who bit the heads off their mates and ate their children, he thought. The Contessa di Montespan was one of these. Celibacy had been an easy choice for him with women like the contessa in the world.

"You will do as you see fit," Michael said.

The girl—no, woman—had risen, and he realized with an odd sort of approval that she was tall and lean, and there was strength beneath the skin that looked soft to the touch. Good. The life he was taking her to wasn't for the weak and gentle.

She knew she was trapped, and her eyes met his quite fearlessly. They were a bright, almost iridescent shade of green, startling with her very pale skin and inky-dark hair. Her shoulders were back, head erect. "I'm ready."

He caught Pedersen's instinctive move of protest out of the corner of his eye, but he ignored him. Pedersen was the past, no longer of consequence. If he had fallen in love with his charge, bedded her, then that was his problem and perhaps hers. It was no concern of his.

"You'll need to change. Something warm. We're flying, and you will be cold."

She nodded, all business. A moment later she was gone, without a single glance at her mother and Pedersen.

"That's gratitude," the contessa said, before eyeing Pedersen with disapproval. Then she turned back to Michael. "May we offer you something, Monsignor? Some of our excellent Italian wine, perhaps?"

He despised these creatures almost as much as the girl did. He shook his head curtly. "I am in need of fresh air."

"I'll have Tory sent to you."

"There is no need. I will find her." It was the simple truth, and he saw a flash of sheer rage flicker across Pedersen's face before it vanished. The man had never known how to find her, had never known the kind of link that immediately existed between Victoria Bellona and her mate, whether Michael liked it or not.

"Then godspeed," the contessa murmured.

Michael didn't laugh. God had nothing to do with it.

CHAPTER
FOUR

I T WAS STRANGELY UNSETTLING TO WALK through the deserted hallways of the *castello* alone, with no one to guard me. The man who thought he was an archangel must be very sure of me. He was a fool.

Anyone who thought I was an ancient Roman goddess had to be certifiable. I had had every intention of humoring him until I could find a quick escape, but it was looking as if I didn't even have to go that far. If I was truly unguarded, I could slip away before anyone realized I was gone.

I went straight to my room, stripping off the skimpy dress and pulling on dark jeans and a black turtleneck and sweater. I could imagine Angelina Jolie wearing something like this as she kicked butt and made her escape. I had money hidden in a place even Pedersen couldn't find, almost one hundred euros. It wasn't enough, but it meant I wouldn't be completely destitute when I got out into the real world. I hadn't much experience with money, but judging by the recent movies I'd seen, a hundred euros wouldn't go far. I would hoard it carefully.

Once I ditched the pretty, crazy man, I could finally begin my real life. There was a world I was missing, and I was more than ready to make up for lost time. I wanted to fall in love, I wanted to get a job, I wanted to have babies, I wanted to see the world. I was hungry for everything I'd missed during the long years I'd been kept in prison.

I even had a pair of black boots to complete my transformation. No ID, no passport, but I'd deal with that later. There were people who provided such things, according to the movies. The most important thing was to get away.

My door was unlocked but my windows were still barred. My escape route had been planned for years, and I knew exactly which direction I was heading. Pushing aside the priceless tapestry in the hall outside my bedroom, I reached for the knob of the long-hidden door and pushed it open, slipping inside before anyone could see me.

It was pitch-black, and I froze, waiting for my eyes to accustom themselves to the darkness. This was the oldest part of the *castello*, dating back to the time of the Borgias. I suspected the contessa was a descendant of that poisonous family.

Which made me one as well, I supposed, but from this moment on I was an orphan: no family, no ties, no genetic inheritance. I could make it up as I went along—I was thinking along the lines of an Irish princess. Not that Ireland had princesses, but I figured my pale skin, dark hair, and green eyes might work for Ireland. That would be a good place to start. I took a deep, calming breath, waiting for vision to reassert itself. The chamber smelled of mouse and mold and neglect. No one ever came up here—I think everyone else had forgotten it existed. I'd explored it once, long ago, when they hadn't watched me so closely, and I never forgot a thing. The short flight of stairs led up to a turret room, and then another, steeper set wound down inside the rounded tower to the cliffs outside. I knew exactly how many stone steps would get me up to the turret. The precise number of winding stairs that would then lead me down to the rough entrance overlooking the valley below. I had no idea who had used those stairs long ago. Armies seeking their way in? Cowards escaping? I was no coward.

The longer I waited, the more dangerous it was going to become. I began to move, carefully, trying not to stir the leaves that had found their way into the deserted stairwell, avoiding the crunch of what I expected were mouse skeletons. Or worse, rats. I held on to the cold, sweating wall and moved upward, concentrating on Pedersen's martial arts training to remain utterly silent.

I remembered the path correctly, reaching the landing when I expected. At last there was a faint shaft of light coming from one of the arrow slits, probably the portal the vermin had used to enter the *castello*, and I looked around me at the shadows. They would have started hunting for me by now, and I couldn't afford to waste time. I crossed the littered landing to the narrow, curved stairway, and started down.

It was a good thing I was essentially fearless. I didn't mind heights or dark enclosed places or even spiders the size of my fist. This was the way to freedom, and I couldn't afford to hesitate. Once I escaped, I would never have to see them again.

I wasn't crazy about the descent into total darkness, the stone steps slick beneath my feet, the sweating wall, slimy with moss and decay, providing a treacherous handhold. God only knew what lay at the bottom, but I had no choice. I had to move forward.

At least I would never again have to deal with Pedersen's obsessive eyes following me wherever I went. I'd never have to hear the contessa's contempt. I moved faster.

When I reached the dark, dank well that was the bottom of the tower, I was breathless. The door was still where I remembered it, but the years had been hard on it. When I pulled on the handle, it came free with a splintering of wood, leaving me trapped inside.

They would be far away, up in the main part of the *castello*. I would have to risk making noise. I spun, kicking at the door, and it splintered, a huge hole gaping into the night air. Another kick, and I could shove the shattered remains of the old door out of my way, stepping out into my first breath of freedom. There should be bright sunlight and triumphant music, I thought, instead of a cool, biting wind and darkness. But I would make do with what I got.

The door opened onto a narrow spit of land that overlooked the cliffs. The Italians tended to build their castles on mountains, to fend off marauders from adjoining city-states, and this one was no different. If I turned left and followed the pathway, I would end up in the courtyard, in full view of the inhabitants. I had no choice but to turn right and try to climb down the rocky outcroppings to a safer trail that would lead me away from my prison.

I moved out of the shadows, starting toward the rocks, when a thick hand grabbed my wrist, gripping so tightly I made a small, betraying sound of pain. Pedersen. He'd always enjoyed hurting me, and it had been a matter of pride that I never let him see it, never made a sound. Well, perhaps my cry would be my farewell gift to him.

"Where do you think you're going?"

I didn't answer. It was self-evident, but I had learned to watch my tongue around Pedersen. He had a vicious temper despite the creepy, obsessive watchfulness that suggested something far more disturbing than a wish to hurt me.

"You think you can escape your destiny?" He was clenching my wrist so tightly the bones ground together, the effect agonizing. For almost twenty years this man had tormented and tortured me, and I had had enough.

"I can escape you," I said unwisely.

"No." His denial was hoarse, guttural. "You aren't going with him."

"You're right. But I'm not staying here either. Let me go, Pedersen. Or I'll make you."

He hit me. I should have been expecting it; he'd done it often enough. He'd broken my cheekbone once, my jaw another time. I always healed with unnatural swiftness, and I'd never given it a second thought.

This blow made me see stars, but he'd smashed no bones. I blinked, trying to regain my equilibrium. I didn't have to let him do this to me, I reminded myself, shaking my head. Never again.

I looked into those pale eyes and knew that this time he was going to kill me. For whatever reason, he didn't like my reprieve, and despite the brooding looks and his tendency to flatten me whenever he could, he clearly wasn't envisioning a happy-ever-after with me. I glanced over the cliff. The rocks below were jagged, and with luck I would hit my head, an instant blackout so I wouldn't have to suffer.

I figured I had nothing to lose. "Why do you want to kill me, Pedersen? You were my mentor, my teacher. Why would you want to destroy all that?"

The bastard hit me again, and I stumbled, then

righted myself. He was even using his left hand. The right hand would have smashed my face in. "No one will have you," he said, and dragged me away from the sheltering wall.

"Not even you?"

It worked. He froze, the words so shocking that he couldn't move. But I could.

I kicked up, hard, hitting the soft place between his legs, and he screamed, releasing me, sinking to his knees on the narrow ledge. He was more resilient than I'd thought. I had barely taken two steps toward the rocks when his hand caught my ankle and I went down. He tried to pin me, but I'd been holding a few tricks in reserve. I moved, lightning-fast, bucking against his heavy weight, and I threw him off with all my strength.

He screamed all the way down to the jagged rocks below, and I heard the thud as he landed.

I lay perfectly still. It was too dark to see that far, and Pedersen was no longer making any noise. He was dead, and the thought was odd, unsettling. I had just killed a man. Someone who deserved it a hundred times over—but still, it was unnerving.

My face was numb from his blows. I'd sport some magnificent bruises for a few short hours, and then they'd be gone, thanks to my restorative powers. Not that I cared what I looked like. I scrambled up, stepped back from the edge of the cliff, and turned.

The man stood there, watching me. Michael.

"How long have you been there?" I demanded.

"For a while. You did a good job with that cretin. Did he train you?" His rich, golden voice sounded no more than faintly curious.

He'd been watching as I fought for my life? I managed to keep my voice cool. "Yes. He didn't realize I'd come up with a few tricks of my own."

"He did a decent job with you. We will continue when we reach Sheol."

I stared at him. "Why didn't you help me?"

"There was no need. You were more than capable of dealing with him."

I looked at him in disbelief. "What if he'd thrown me over the cliff before you could stop him?"

"Then I would have caught you."

Madman, I thought again, starting to edge away. I wasn't sure whether I appreciated the faint note of approval or resented it. "Look, we don't even know each other. You don't really want me to . . . to go away with you, do you?"

"No, I don't. It is, however, my duty." His voice was flat, uncompromising. "Whether I like it or not, you are the chosen one."

"I could fight you."

The crazy man laughed. "Do not waste my time, Victoria Bellona. The sooner we are back in Sheol, the better."

"Exactly where is this Sheol?"

"In the mist."

Oh, Christ. Not only was he insane, he was also cryptic. "Great. How do we get there?"

"We fly."

"And just which airline takes you into the mist?"

"No airline." He moved so quickly I barely had time to register what he was doing. He caught my shoulders, turned me, and pulled me back against him, snaking one powerful arm around my stomach to hold me against him. I had a momentary impression of overpowering strength, hard muscle and bone and heat all along my back, causing a strange, temporary weakness. And then, to my horror, he leapt off the cliff.

I closed my eyes, not wanting to see death looming up at me, but I didn't scream. The rush of wind was deafening, the darkness all around, but there was no sudden, sickening end on the jagged rocks below. We simply kept on falling.

Though it didn't feel as if we were moving down, as gravity dictated, but up, up into the sky, and I tried to open my eyes, to check the strange sensation, but my lids felt as if they were glued shut. I began to struggle, when I heard his voice growl low in my ear, "Stay still, you idiot."

Some stray bit of common sense compelled me to obey. The world had turned upside down, Alice through the looking glass, but if I wasn't dead yet I could wait until I was on solid ground before I started fighting again. It was getting cold, very cold, and it felt like ice was forming over my skin, my face. The air was thin, and I struggled to breathe, a little desperate in the cold, inky darkness. Maybe this was death after all, I thought dizzily. Maybe you didn't actually feel the impact, you simply slipped into some black, icy chasm where you were trapped for the rest of your life.

But didn't most people go to hell? I couldn't remember. Rational thought was becoming more and more difficult, and no wonder. I seemed to be moving through a bitterly cold night sky, without air to breathe. The lack of oxygen would kill me, that or the cold. I didn't need to smash my body against the rocks.

I stopped struggling for breath. Stopped breathing entirely. I could feel hot tears seep from beneath my closed eyelids. I had always avoided self-pity, but if I was dying I could allow myself this much. The tears ran down on my face, melting rivulets that froze over again. My eyes were frozen shut, my body rigid, the only warmth running all along my back.

I gave in.

I CAME TO with a sudden swoop of motion as the ground was jarringly beneath us, and I realized I was no longer cold. The arm around my waist released me, and the man stepped back, leaving me swaying slightly.

I opened my eyes. We were on a beach, surrounded by a soft ocean mist, and I sank to my knees in the sand and promptly threw up.

"It takes some people that way," that beautiful, hated voice said from above me. "I would have warned you, but you weren't in any mood to listen."

I hated to throw up. Even worse, I hated having an audience, and I tried to will myself to calm. Bile burned my throat, and I shut my eyes again. What had he done to me?

"Get up," he said. "They're coming."

Who's coming? I thought dazedly. *And who the hell cares?* I managed to look up at him, then saw a huge house behind him. On my other side was the ocean, the first time I'd ever seen it, and I stared in wonder, my misery temporarily forgotten.

I took a deep breath, inhaling the rich, salt smell of it. I could taste it on my lips, feel it on my skin, and for the first time in my life I fell completely and desperately in love. When I got away from here, I was heading toward a coast. The look and the sound of the ocean, coupled with its hypnotizing scent, was beyond seductive—it was downright addictive.

I pulled my eyes away reluctantly and saw a small group of people approaching us. The most beautiful men I had ever seen in my life—and, apart from my three years of semicloistered freedom, I was used to movie-star handsome. These creatures were like the one who had brought me here, almost eerily exquisite. There were three or four women as well, but they were ordinary women, not ethereal beauties. I racked my brain for an explanation, but none was forthcoming. The closer they got, the more glorious the men seemed, though none of them were quite as beautiful as the crazy man who'd kidnapped me. Surely these people would help me.

"Get up," the supposed Archangel Michael snapped in an angry whisper.

I would have, but I wasn't sure my shaking legs would hold me. Best to stay on my knees rather than topple over on my face in front of them.

I managed to look up hopefully as they stopped before me, and the gorgeous man in front, presumably the leader, with a soft, slightly rounded woman by his side, smiled at me.

"Victoria Bellona, Goddess of War," he said, "welcome to Sheol, the home of the fallen angels, and to your life as consort to the Archangel Michael."

I promptly threw up again.

CHAPTER

FIVE

ICHAEL LOOKED DOWN AT his bride for a moment, then met Raziel's steely gaze. "I told you this wasn't a good idea."

Allie was already kneeling by Victoria Bellona, holding his consort's black hair away from her face and murmuring to her. The girl was definitely not happy, and if he were the sort to feel guilt, he might let a trace of it bother him. He could have warned her. Could even have done things to mitigate the unpleasant effects flight often had on humans. The goddess of war wasn't exactly human, but right now her body was most definitely a frail, human vessel, and speed and altitude had had their expected effects.

"You should have warned her." Allie looked at up him with disapproval. The Source wasn't the type to mince words, and she'd been against this idea from the very beginning, which should have made them allies. But she'd caved first, and he hadn't been able to hold out against both her and her husband. Not when he knew they were right.

"She will be facing too many things to warn her about all of them," he replied coolly. "Are we ready for the ritual?"

The girl's head shot up. "What?"

Raziel gave him a fiercely disapproving look before approaching her. "Welcome to Sheol, Victoria Bellona," he said with great formality. "Welcome to the home of the Fallen, to membership in our family, to alliance in our war against the Armies of Heaven, to marriage with our brother Michael."

"Oh, hell, no," said his blushing bride, stumbling to her feet with Allie's help. "Nobody asked me whether I wanted to sign up for all this. I'm leaving."

Raziel didn't blink. "And where exactly do you wish to go?"

"Anywhere but here."

"Unfortunately, here is your only option. Sheol, or back with your mother and guardian for the few days remaining until you are twenty-five, at which point she will have you terminated."

"Pedersen is dead. She can't very well toss me over the cliff herself," the girl snapped.

"There is more than one way to kill you. The contessa likes ritual and enjoys the cliff, but she can just as effectively shoot you and have the servants dispose of your corpse."

She glared at Raziel, taking some of the onus off Michael. Now that she was here in Sheol, he had no choice but to accept the unpleasant circumstance that Martha's vision had saddled him with, and he had never been a man to waste time fighting the inevitable. There were more important battles in his future.

"I am ready," he said. "Though I believe the goddess must agree to this."

"What goddess?" the girl said.

"He's talking about you," Allie said soothingly. "Victoria Bellona, incarnation of the ancient Roman goddess of war."

Victoria Bellona was glaring at Allie now. "Not you too," she said in disgust. "What kind of Kool-Aid did you guys drink?"

Her question made no sense to Michael, though Allie laughed. "You'll see," she said. "It takes time, but sooner or later you'll realize this crazy world of ours is real."

"And you're an archangel?"

Allie grinned. "Hardly. In this sexist society, only men are angels, and most of them aren't archangels. You've got the last one who's single. The Archangel Michael, warrior of God."

The girl looked back at him. She didn't look like a Victoria Bellona, not with her slender frame and far-too-pretty face. Victoria Bellona should be a sturdy, almost masculine figure dressed in Roman armor.

What had she instructed him to call her? Tory? He would avoid it if he could, simply because it would annoy her. He planned to annoy her every chance he got.

Annoyance would keep her at a distance, and he needed that. He could say he was only human, but that wasn't true, and he could hardly blame his weaknesses on his fall from grace more than two hundred years ago, a snap of the fingers to these immortals. To him.

She was a liability, a temptation he didn't want to consider. He could already feel things that he didn't want to feel. If she'd been a whiner, he could have handed her over to someone capable like Allie or Rachel and ignored her. But there was something about the way she faced things, something about her bright green eyes, that called to him. And he couldn't afford to listen. He'd already wasted too much time on her.

"Make up your mind," he said. "Life with us and a formal marriage with me, or death with your mother. The contessa has never been disposed to be merciful and she was fond of Pedersen, at least as fond as she is capable of being. I do not expect your demise will be particularly pleasant."

She was looking at him with profound annoyance. Excellent. It would suit their marriage perfectly. "A formal marriage," she repeated thoughtfully. "I assume that means no . . . marital relations."

"I told you—I am celibate." Raziel started to say something, but Michael simply overrode him. "You won't even need to see me."

"Good."

"That's not precisely true," Allie broke in. "Granted, according to Martha this doesn't have to be a true marriage in our sense, but you'll still—"

"What my wife is saying is that you'll share quarters with Michael, but there will be plenty of room to keep your distance from each other if that is what you wish," Raziel cut in smoothly. "We can work out the other details later. In the meantime, we are ready for the ceremony."

Michael's unwilling bride was looking mutinous. "So soon? I'm still jet-lagged. Wing-lagged. Whatever."

"The sooner the better," Allie said with great sympathy after casting a glare Raziel's way. "Once it's over, you can settle in and rest."

The woman looked up at him, measuring. "I don't really have a choice in this, do I?"

"No." Michael did nothing to make it sound more palatable. She was better off knowing exactly what she was getting into.

"It's not as bad as you might think," Allie said. "I promise you."

Victoria Bellona might not be disposed to believe him, but he could tell she was beginning to trust Allie. "All right," she said. "Let's get it done."

Michael watched her disappear with Allie and the others. Raziel's wife wasn't the most docile of females, but if they brought Azazel's Rachel into the mix, it would help. Rachel could calm the most distraught of females, and even Allie must see the benefit of having Tory agreeable.

Raziel was looking at him, with Azazel, their former leader and now his second-in-command, standing behind him. "She is . . . not what I imagined," Michael said finally.

"No."

There was a long silence, and then Azazel stepped forward. "I'm surprised you were forced to kill Pedersen. He should have known his job."

"He had grown too attached to her. But in fact I didn't kill him. She did."

Another silence. "Interesting," Raziel said eventually. "Did he deserve it?"

"Ten times over. He trained her well—so well, she outsmarted him. She will serve." He said the words reluctantly. He had agreed to this—he'd had no choice—and in the end he'd seen the wisdom of it. But part of him was still fighting.

"You look tired," Azazel said. He was the closest friend Michael had among the Fallen. The former Alpha, he had returned a few years ago with his wife, Rachel, who had powers even she didn't know about. They would need her, as well as his own unwilling bride, in the upcoming fight. They would need everyone they could muster.

"I am tired," he admitted.

"Walk with me." It wasn't a request, but it was what Michael needed, and Azazel knew it. They started down the pebbled beach, slowly leaving

Raziel behind. The sound of the surf soothed him, the sough of the wind and the gulls that wheeled and cried overhead. The ocean, the place of healing, the place of origin. Humankind had first come from the water. He had no idea where his kind had come from, and there'd been no one to answer his questions. Uriel, guardian of heaven, would spin any lie that served his purpose, and the Supreme Being was gone. Once he'd given free will to the humans he'd simply stepped back, leaving his most trusted archangel in charge.

Unfortunately, that archangel had been Uriel, not Gabriel, Raphael, or even himself. That unwise choice had echoed through the millennia, bringing plague and disaster upon humankind. Uriel had to be stopped, before he destroyed the world completely.

Azazel broke their comfortable silence. "She's very pretty."

"Is she?"

"You know she is. Don't play the fool, Michael, it doesn't become you. This vision of Martha's came for a reason, and it was to help our cause, not hinder it. If I can feel the power of attraction between you two, then you certainly can't be unaware of it."

He didn't bother denying it. "It's an unpleasant fact of life, I admit it. She . . . calls to me. I have no intention of doing anything about it. This will be a marriage in name only. Anything else would only complicate matters."

Azazel shook his head. "I don't think that's what the vision meant."

"That's the thing about visions—you can interpret them any way you wish. I prefer to think her presence and her joining to me are all that is necessary. After that is done, she will simply be one of the soldiers."

"You need her blood."

"I'm not taking it. You know that—I won't take blood from a mate. The Supreme Being may have cursed us to be blood-eaters, but I can refuse to give in. I will make do with what Allie can provide."

Azazel frowned. "You know as well as I that her blood is weaker. The Source is for the Fallen who haven't mated. Even if you don't bed her, you will still have mated the goddess, and her blood will bring you back to full strength."

"No." It was his only weapon against the forces that had molded him into an instrument of justice and terror, wielder of the flaming sword, smiter of enemies who'd done so little to deserve their punishment. No, he refused to let them play with him any longer. He would take no blood but from the wrist of the Source, and all of them be damned.

They were already damned.

"You can't fight it forever," Azazel said. "Sooner or later you will have to accept that the Fallen are doomed to be blood-eaters. If it's a test of wills between you and the Supreme Power, do you really think you have a chance of winning?"

Michael looked out at the sea. "You fought your prophecy," he said. "You almost killed your wife, you were so determined to prove it wrong."

Azazel flushed. "Indeed. I don't recommend it. Women have long memories. In the end the prophecy was correct, even if we misunderstood the details. I've learned that visions don't lie, Michael."

"But they can be changed, and sometimes they're merely a warning of what to avoid."

Azazel shook his head. "You're a stubborn bastard, aren't you?"

"I have no idea whether I'm a bastard or not."

Azazel's laugh was short and humorless. "By the legal definition, I would think we definitely qualify. If you're talking about character, then there's no question."

Michael wasn't in the mood for Azazel's mind games, any more than he appreciated his unlikely good cheer. The Azazel he had known was sharp and cynical, even when he'd been joined with his beloved Sarah. Yet the appearance of a demon in his life had made him almost sanguine. It annoyed Michael.

"Just because your despised prophecy turned you into a revoltingly sentimental creature doesn't mean that mine will be similarly benign. And if it is, we will all be in trouble. If I start looking at the world with that sappy smile on my face, Uriel's army will surely destroy us. I'm our last, best hope to beat them, and the only reason I agreed to this ridiculous farce was because all of you were convinced we couldn't win if I didn't bring her back."

Azazel appeared unperturbed at his attack. "And you're not similarly convinced? Then why did you agree?"

"Simple. I understand warfare, and battle. If we believe we will prevail, we will. If Victoria Bellona's presence convinces us that we will win, then I'll happily put up with her, just to give us that edge."

Azazel surveyed him coolly. "I don't think there's anything happy about it. You can take her back if you really believe her presence here is useless."

"I can't. The contessa will kill her."

"And why do you care?"

"I don't," Michael snapped.

"Then . . ."

"Leave me be, Azazel. I have enough to deal with as it is."

Silence stretched between them, and then Azazel nodded. "We'd best go in. Presumably they're ready for us."

Michael took one last longing look at the sea. He couldn't rid himself of the feeling that he was about to take a step that would change the rest of his existence—a step he was being forced into.

But his entire existence was about duty and honor, fighting for what was right. Sacrifice meant nothing—there was no reason why this particular sacrifice should be anything but another annoyance. He would marry her. And then put her away in the farthest corner of the house and retreat to the training compound, and he would never have to see her.

"I'm ready," he said, turning his back on the ocean and looking up at the strange building that had housed the Fallen for eons. "It's time."

THEY HAD PUT me in flowing white clothes, stripping off my black turtleneck and pants, unplaiting my long black hair. The woman named Allie had chattered nonstop, her soft, soothing voice helping to ease some of my tension. The crown of wildflowers they put on me was ridiculous, but a glance in the mirror kept me from ripping it off. I was no Botticelli goddess rising from the sea, but with the black hair rippling down against my pale skin, I wasn't half-bad. I didn't want to consider why it mattered. Presumably nothing more than natural vanity. However, vanity had never mattered to me before, even when I thought Johann loved me. Before he'd delivered me to Pedersen and pocketed a healthy reward.

The women led me through the wide hallways to a garden where dozens of similarly garbed people were waiting for us, and I tried to ignore the clenching in my stomach.

Until I saw my husband-to-be.

He stood at one end, his face cool and impassive. Such an arresting face on the man. Angel. Whatever he was. Exquisitely beautiful. Exquisitely cold.

In the bright sunlight I could see him clearly for the first time. He was wearing white as all the others were, a loose open shirt, though he'd rolled up the sleeves, as if even a so-called wedding required hard work. I looked at his strong forearms, and for the first time I noticed tattoos snaking their way up beneath the white cloth. The shirt was loose at the neck as well, and there were more markings on his chest, his throat, twining around to the back of his head, markings I hadn't seen before. I halted, momentarily fascinated, and then Allie caught my arm and gently urged me forward.

Did they expect me to love, honor, and obey? I thought dizzily. And weren't they Old Testament angels—shouldn't there be a chuppah or something, a glass of wine to smash?

Allie took my hand and placed it in Michael's outstretched one, and his long fingers tightened around mine before I could pull it back. His skin was cold. There were tattoos on the back of his hand, and now that I was closer I could see them clearly. Symbols from every culture imaginable— Celtic knots, Native American glyphs, Asian kanji, Arabic calligraphy. They circled his hand and arm, disappearing into the sleeve like a serpent, and I had the sudden odd feeling that the line of markings could move, could slide along his skin onto mine, marking me as his.

There was no escape. Raziel moved in front of us and spoke in a language I had never heard, a beautiful, silvery sound that made my skin tingle. Allie had left me, and suddenly I felt abandoned, until the woman named Rachel took her place, clasping my other hand in her strong, calm one, soothing me.

My mind drifted in the bright sunlight. This was too strange, too bizarre to take in, and I let the words flow over me, dazed, until the sound of Michael's deep, rich voice startled me into paying attention again. He spoke in the same language Raziel had, and then Michael turned to me. If there was mercy in his dark eyes, I couldn't see it.

"You have a choice," he said. "You can stay with us, help us fight. We are at war with a force so evil that if we lose, the world will be destroyed. If that happens, you will die anyway. If you go back now, you may manage to survive the rage of the woman who raised you, but that is unlikely, as your twenty-fifth birthday approaches. But it is your choice. Do you choose to stay here, to become my bonded mate, or do you wish to return to your old life?"

It really was no choice. Even if death didn't await me there, the thought of being locked in that room for even an hour longer sent horror through me. Here was sunshine, and other women, and freedom such as I'd never known.

"I choose you," I said, meeting his cool, enigmatic gaze.

"Then let it be done," he murmured.

CHAPTER
SIX

THEN LET IT BE DONE," HE'D SAID. I'd spoken no vows other than my agreement, and there'd been no exchange of rings. Was that the equivalent of "I now pronounce you man and wife"?

Apparently not. Allie moved forward between us and pushed her flowing sleeve up past her elbow, exposing a pale arm and blue-veined wrist. Michael took her arm in both hands, then glanced up at me out of his dark, implacable eyes. "Should she not hold on to the Source as well?"

Rachel moved up beside me. "Put your hand on Allie's arm, Tory," she said, soft but determined.

What the hell was going on? I tried to back away, suddenly more uneasy than I had been since Michael had appeared in my life—and given the craziness of the last day, that was impressive.

"No." A woman I hadn't met spoke up from the

group of people surrounding us. I was vaguely aware of a young woman in her thirties, a troubled expression on her face. "That's not the way I saw it. I don't think—"

"Martha, let be," Michael said, his rich voice an incompatible mix of kindness and irritation. "If there is more we need to do, we can address that later."

"But—"

"Later, Martha." Raziel's voice finished the conversation, and the woman subsided reluctantly. *Martha*. I remembered the name from the chatter of the women. She was the seer who'd sent Michael on his ridiculous mission in the first place. Except this ridiculous mission was going to keep me alive, when Pedersen and my mother would have been certain to kill me.

Rachel took my cold hand and placed it on Allie's elbow, holding it there. Allie flashed me a reassuring smile. "Keep an open mind, Tory," she said quietly. "It will be all right."

I was getting a very bad feeling about this. Some of the men had begun an odd chanting, and the sound, so foreign and strange, gave me goose bumps. I wanted to get away, I wanted to run. I looked up. Michael's dark eyes impaled me and my feet were frozen to the ground.

"Let the bond be sealed by blood," Raziel said, not sounding particularly happy about the whole thing. I glanced back to Michael, and his eyes were half-closed, his mouth open, and it almost seemed as if his teeth had elongated. Impossible. He couldn't—

He struck like a snake, fastening his mouth to Allie's wrist. She didn't flinch, but I tried to pull away. Rachel's strong hand held me firm. What the hell was he doing to Allie? Giving her the mother of all hickeys? Why?

And then I saw the blood trickle down over her wrist. He lifted his head, and there was blood on his mouth, blood on his—his fangs, and he used his tongue to bring the last of it into his mouth.

"Oh, hell, no." I tried to yank free, but Rachel had anticipated my reaction, and her fingers tightened painfully.

"The union is sealed," Raziel said in an unhappy voice. "The Source has been blooded and the bond is accepted."

Michael released Allie's arm, only to take mine, and Rachel's tight grip had been a caress compared to his steely fingers. Everyone stepped back, leaving me to stare up in frozen horror into Michael's cold eyes. "It is done," he said.

He dragged me through the crowd of people murmuring disjointed congratulations. The woman named Martha was still offering some kind of protest, but Michael wasn't listening, seemingly intent on getting me out of there, which was a good idea, since I was on the verge of screaming.

We were moving so fast I could barely catch my breath, out of the garden and along the rocky beach.

Michael dragged me around the side of the building and headed toward a large, one-story structure that glowed in the sunlight. The halls were empty when he pushed me inside, towing me down white, unadorned corridors to a wide door at the far end. He pushed it open, shoved me in, and closed the door behind us.

"What . . ." I began, trying to catch my breath, "the hell . . . are you?"

He'd finally released me, and I rubbed my abused wrist. He moved to a wall of glass, staring out at the restless ocean, and took a deep breath before answering. "I told you. We are angels who have fallen from heaven, cursed to live out eternity on earth."

"Last I heard, angels weren't vampires," I snapped, trying to stay calm. And I'd thought I was in such good shape. I was nothing compared to the man I'd supposedly married.

He didn't bother looking at me. "They aren't. This is part of our curse. Just being kicked out of heaven wasn't enough of a punishment. We are cursed to drink blood as well. Blood-eaters are despised in our tradition. The Supreme Power thought it only fitting."

"So you go out and kill people and drink their blood?"

He made a disgusted noise. "Of course not. We can only drink the blood of our bonded mates."

I didn't like the sound of that at all. "What do you mean by that? If you think you're biting me, you're out of your mind. And I thought Allie was Raziel's . . . er . . . bonded mate."

"Allie is different. Allie is the Source. She provides nourishment for those of the Fallen who aren't bonded. If we eat the blood of anyone else, we could die. It is the Source or our own mates."

I still didn't like the sound of this. It was as if I'd fallen asleep and woken up in the middle of a Terry Gilliam movie. Much as I loved *Time Bandits*, I certainly didn't want to live in that world.

"And you chose the Source? I thought you kept telling me *I* was your bonded mate."

He turned to look at me, and there was no emotion on his face. It was as if I didn't exist. "I have no intention of touching you. We aren't even bonded by the rites of the Fallen. This is a legal union, sealed by blood. It didn't have to be your blood."

So much for Irish princesses or faux Botticellis, I thought, irrationally annoyed. I didn't want him touching me, did I? I certainly didn't want him coming anywhere near my veins. "Good thing," I said. "I'd put up a hell of a fight."

He was unimpressed. Good. I preferred having some tricks up my sleeve. I intended to get out of here the first chance I got, and I would need the element of surprise. Michael was far too observant.

I looked around. He'd dragged me into a small, utilitarian apartment with a comfortable-looking sofa, french doors overlooking the beckoning ocean, and an alcove off to the right with a smallish bed in it. I sighed in relief. Clearly not the bed to consummate a marriage. No television or computer, however. That was no problem. I'd had enough television and movies to last several lifetimes. They had taught me everything I knew. It was time to learn from the real world—as soon as I could get away from these people and start to live.

"What is this place?"

He'd been prowling the room, roaming into a kitchenette, peering into the refrigerator, opening the french doors. The warm sea breeze blew over me, and I closed my eyes for a moment, taking it in. "Your home," he said.

"Who else lives here?"

"Only you and I live in this place." It seemed as if he didn't even want to clump us together in words. "This building is the training center. The rest of the Fallen and their mates live in the main house."

Not good. No allies to come to my rescue if need be. I looked around me, uneasy. "We live here?"

"*You* live here. *My* quarters are in another section of the building."

"Oh," I said brightly. Things were looking up. I was alone in this part of the building with doors to the outside, to the hypnotizing ocean, and I suspected my new husband or mate or whatever was going to keep his distance. Getting out should be a piece of cake. "Well, if that's all, you can go."

His head jerked up and he surveyed me for a long moment. Were he anyone else, I might have seen the glimmer of a smile. "Yes, Your Majesty. If you want something to eat, check the refrigerator. Allie will come by later and explain how things work around here."

Allie, who'd held out her wrist and let him drink from it. I thought I hid my reflexive shudder, but his smile was unmistakable now, cynical, as he saw my reaction. "Why don't you take a nap? When you wake up, maybe you'll find this is only a dream."

"Is it?"

"No. But you can always hope."

I watched the door close behind him and felt some of the tension drain from my body. I wasn't sure what made me edgier—his hostility or his unearthly beauty.

I never would have thought beauty would be such a bothersome attribute in a husband, but it wasn't a comfortable thing. The sheer perfection of his skin, the intensity of his dark eyes, the grace of his lithe body, even the rope of tattoos that slithered around him, made me edgy. Johann had been a handsome young man—a youthful infatuation. Yet his impressive good looks had never disturbed me the way Michael's did. His high cheekbones, the sweep of his tawny lashes over those distant eyes, his surprisingly sensual mouth, made me feel . . . nervous. Which was silly, since he'd made it perfectly clear he wasn't coming any closer to me than was strictly necessary. Thank God. The gods. Though apparently I was one of the gods. Thank me?

No, that was ridiculous.

Or was it? Like the White Queen in *Through the Looking-Glass*, I had been raised to believe in six impossible things before breakfast. My life had never had any similarity to the lives on television or in the movies, nor anything in common with the lives of the other girls at the secluded school I attended or the nuns who watched over us. I had begun to believe there was no such thing as impossible.

I was the reincarnation of a Roman goddess. I had just married an angel who happened to be a vampire. After that, everything else was minor.

RAZIEL SAT IN his chair in the great hall, hands clutching the lion-headed arms tightly. Allie put her arms around him, drawing his head to her breasts. "Aren't you ever going to get used to it, my love?"

"No," he said against her in a sulky voice.

Her laugh was soft and sexy, and she knelt beside him, sliding a hand along his taut thighs. "Poor baby."

"Michael should have taken his mate's blood. He was just being stubborn, as usual. He's going to have to accept her sooner or later. Accept his curse. He's survived more than two hundred years on the blood of the Source, and I'm sick of it. Let him get his own."

"True enough." She pressed against him. "After all, she's a goddess. Even if she's not immortal, she should still live a long time."

The words hung between them, and finally Raziel

spoke. "We don't know how long you'll live, Allie. Is that what's been bothering you? Why you've sought out Martha? You haven't aged in the last ten years. I think my blood—"

"Hush," she said, moving her hand higher, brushing against his hardness. "We won't talk about that now. Instead, why don't you tell me what you felt when Michael took my wrist?"

"You know what I felt," he growled. "Fury. Jealousy."

"Yes, love." Her hand enclosed him. "And what else?"

He tried, not very hard, to push her hand away. "If you think I become aroused when I see you with another man, you are wrong. I'm not that perverse."

"You're wonderfully perverse, in all the best ways," she corrected him. "And no, I think you become aroused when you are reminded of what we share, and you want to get me alone and in private to act on it. To wipe out any trace of another man's touch."

A smile tugged at the corner of his mouth. "You think you know me so well."

"I do know you so well." She pushed her hair away from her neck, tilting her head for his full access. "I can feel what you feel. You can feel what I feel."

His rough laugh increased her arousal. "True enough, unless you shield your thoughts," he said, covering her hand with his, pushing it against his erection. "This isn't a good time."

"This is an excellent time," she murmured.

He reached for her, pulling her onto his lap very carefully, and slid his hand beneath her hair, tugging her closer. "You are a wise woman."

"I am," she agreed, closing her eyes, waiting for the first touch of his mouth against her neck, his teeth against her vein.

"We should be in bed for this."

"We should spend our lives in bed," she said. "Sometimes we just have to make do."

CHAPTER
SEVEN

I T WAS SHEER WEAKNESS, I ADMIT IT. I should have gotten the hell out of there the moment he left me. It was more than clear he wasn't coming back anytime soon, and it was a perfect time to leave. I hadn't established any routines where my presence might be missed; I could just go and no one would realize it until it was too late.

Go where? That was the question. According to the woman named Rachel, I was somewhere off the west coast of North America, which didn't narrow it down much. If Michael could leave and go out into the rest of the world, so could I. Of course, maybe flying was part of the escape route, and I didn't appear to be growing wings. Then again, no one in the crowd at the ceremony had appeared to have anything protruding under their clothes, including Michael. Which reminded me.

What I knew of angels came mainly from *Dogma*. In general I didn't watch fantasy movies—I had a voracious appetite for real life, normal people, everyday happenings. But I hadn't been able to resist *Dogma*. In that movie, the angels had no genitalia—maybe these didn't either. Maybe all this talk about celibacy was because they had no other choice.

I hadn't seen any children around, after all. Maybe I was worried about nothing. Though having someone drink my blood wasn't exactly nothing, but he'd made no move toward me.

I should go right now. But I was starving, exhausted, and thoroughly shaken. If I took off in this state, I wouldn't get far. I did as Michael had suggested, checking the refrigerator, and found cheese, fruit, yogurt—all my favorite things. In the door was bottled water from Norway and Scotland, and cans of Diet Coke.

I'd never tasted it. I'd seen it in movies all the time—product placement, they called it. But soda wasn't allowed at the convent school, and nothing like that had ever appeared at the *castello*.

It only took me a moment to figure out how the top opened. There was a hiss as brown liquid bubbled out of the small hole I'd created. I took a tiny sip.

And spat it out in horror. People actually liked this crap?

But this was my new world. Not just Sheol, but beyond, where I firmly intended to be, and everybody seemed to drink this instead of water. I took another sip, letting the bubbles sting my tongue before swallowing. Not much better.

I pulled out cheese and crackers, hoping to disguise the taste, and sat down on the white sofa in front of the sliding glass doors that overlooked the sea. The food didn't quite kill the taste but made it palatable, and I worked my way through the can, then forced myself to take another.

It was already getting darker. What time was it in Italy? Did the contessa know Pedersen was dead, and that I had killed him? Did it even matter?

The sea breeze was blowing in, and I could taste the salt on my lips. Part of me longed for it, to feel the water on my feet, my skin. But I was exhausted by all I had been through.

I looked at the bed longingly. There was no reason why I had to escape immediately. It would be better if I acclimated myself to this strange place first. Besides, I had never been so weary in my life.

I took a third can of soda and walked over to the bed. It was bigger than my narrow one in Italy, but smaller than the beds in the movies. It was more than big enough for me, and I stretched out on it, setting the open can of soda on the side table.

It was sinfully, divinely comfortable. Could something be both? Then again, that would describe a fallen angel perfectly. Sinful and divine. A fascinating contradiction, and if things were different, I'd be more than happy to stay here and explore it. It wasn't as if Michael was any threat to me—this marriage was a formality, nothing more. He kept insisting he was celibate, and he had no interest in either my body or my blood. There was no real reason to be in such a hurry.

Except I was finding the celibacy thing a little hard to believe, assuming he had all his equipment. There was something about him, the tightly coiled intensity, the way he moved, the way he looked at things, at me, that felt . . . sexual. Not that I had a great deal of experience in the matter, but I knew the difference between creatures who displayed a sexless presence and those who exuded sexuality. Michael, for all his protestations, was definitely the latter.

And whether I liked it or not, when I looked at him I felt something. I couldn't identify it, didn't want to, but it made me uneasy, irritable, unsettled. As if I wanted something from him and I wasn't sure what.

Not my type at all. I liked sweet, gentle men who didn't try to tell me what to do. I'd had enough of that with the contessa and Pedersen. The last thing I wanted was a stern, cold man bossing me around.

But right now our plans coincided. He had told me to stay put and go to sleep, and I was exhausted, with a comfortable bed beneath me. I stretched out, kicking off the sandals Allie had given me and wiggling my toes. I'd need to find out what they'd done with my clothes and the euros I had stashed in an inner pocket of my jeans. I'd have to find a bank where I could trade them in, but that shouldn't be difficult once I reached civilization. Depending on how far civilization was.

I could hear the rough cries of the seabirds above the rush of the surf. The sound of the ocean had to be the most soothing noise in the world.

I closed my eyes and slept.

"SHE'S GOING TO WHAT?" Michael demanded, furious.

"She's going to die," Martha said in a tight voice, clearly distressed. "On her twenty-fifth birthday. One month from now."

"And why the fuck did you wait till now to tell me?" Michael snarled.

"Behave yourself, Michael," Allie said, sitting next to Martha at the table. "It doesn't do to badger people." The six of them were alone in the vast meeting hall: the two ruling couples, Raziel and Allie, Azazel and his wife, Rachel, otherwise known as the demon Lilith, plus Michael and the seer.

"I don't badger people. Am I badgering you, Martha?"

The seer looked up at him out of troubled gray eyes. "You're trying," she said quietly. "You know I can't control these things. Visions have been coming to me in bits and pieces, and sometimes they are simply shadows at first. The last one was clearer. She's going to die on her birthday, in battle. You will bed her, blood her, train her, and she will then die for us."

"No," he snapped. He wasn't sure why. She was an albatross, an unwanted complication in his life when he desperately needed it to be simple. They were telling him it was finite, yet he refused to accept what was plainly a reprieve from a life sentence.

"I don't see why it bothers you so much," Raziel said from his seat at the head of the table. "You fought this from the very beginning. You don't want her in your life. This should make it all very convenient—in a few weeks' time, you get to be the grieving widower. And this gives us one very crucial piece of information. The key words are *she dies in battle*. We've had no idea when Uriel is planning to strike. Now we know."

"Now we know," he echoed tonelessly. "Is there anything else you'd like to share?"

"Nothing I haven't already told you," Martha said, bearing up under his intimidating glare. He could usually scare the pants off most of the inhabitants of Sheol. Unfortunately, the five people in the room were impervious to his fierce temper. "You must consummate the marriage for the prophecy to come true. If you don't bed and blood her, everything changes, and I can't see what changes those are. They are so full of blood and darkness that I might as well be blind. You have to take her, Archangel."

"You mean if I *don't* take her, she won't die?" he demanded.

"I don't know. It's possible we may all be destroyed

by Uriel's armies if you don't fulfill the prophecy. The only way we know we'll be safe is if you complete the bond."

He felt cold inside. "No," he said. "It was one thing bringing her here to help us. I was willing to make that sacrifice. But I'm not going to sign her death warrant by completing this ridiculous marriage, one I never wanted in the first place."

"She'll almost certainly die anyway," Raziel said, his voice even. "And she would have died if you hadn't brought her here. We simply changed the place and manner of her death. And we've given her four more weeks."

Michael whirled on Martha. "Is that true?" he demanded. "Can you guarantee she's going to die no matter what I do?"

"No," Martha said, and he felt a measure of relief. Martha was incapable of lying. "I believe her to be doomed no matter what, but my vision hasn't shown me what would happen to her if you refused to complete the bond."

"I do refuse. For one thing, I'm celibate. For another, I won't take blood from anyone but the Source. And I'm not going to sentence her to death when there may be alternatives."

Martha, practical as always, sighed. "I tried to say something at the ceremony, but no one listened, and the girl looked shell-shocked as it was. If you weren't supposed to bond with her and mate with her, then why did you bring her all this way?"

"Because you told me to, goddamn it!" Michael snarled. "You didn't tell me it would kill her."

"I told you my vision said the only way we would vanquish Uriel was with the help of the Roman goddess of war, and that you needed to bond with her. Which means *bond* with her, Michael," she said, a trace of annoyance in her usually soft voice. "It means have sex with her and take her blood."

"We fuck and then she dies. No."

"Her destiny will follow her. Perhaps that's why I didn't see her death before. It was only after she was brought here that the prophecy became clear. I firmly believe she will die on her twenty-fifth birthday no matter where she is, Michael, and there isn't a thing you can do about it."

"That's where you're wrong. She won't die if the prophecy isn't fulfilled, and I'm not touching her and bringing about her death. Tell me what your visions tell you."

"It's not that simple—"

"Tell me." He didn't raise his voice—he didn't have to. When he used that tone, everyone obeyed.

"I see you bedding her and taking her blood, making the union complete. I see you training her with the others in the big room. I see you . . . cherishing her." Martha's voice shook a little bit at the words, as if she remembered her own grief. "And I see her falling beneath the sword on the blood-soaked beach. On her twenty-fifth birthday, twenty-six days from now. So it is foretold."

There was an unhappy silence in the room. Finally Rachel spoke. "It's unfortunate, Michael, but it must be done. It's not like it's a huge sacrifice on your part. You may have given up sex for who knows how long, but you must remember how to do it. And like everyone else here, you're ridiculously gorgeous. All you have to do is be a little bit more charming—"

Azazel's derisive laugh stopped her. "We're talking about Michael here. He's a warrior, love. He doesn't understand charm."

"He can learn it."

"Not in one month's time, trust me."

"I'm not raping her," Michael said flatly.

"Of course not," Raziel said.

But Martha was still looking troubled. "You can't afford to wait, my lord. You need to explain things to her."

"And of course she'll flop on her back and spread her legs." He was brimming with fury. He had brought her here to watch her die. If he touched her. "It doesn't matter. I refuse to take her blood."

Allie looked at him without pity. "Look at it this way—she'll be dead in no time and you won't have to be inconvenienced by her."

He pushed away from the table, pacing the room. "Go to hell, Allie. I told you I'm not doing it."

Raziel froze in swift anger, then began to rise, but Allie simply tugged him back down. "Don't pay any attention to him. He's just having a temper tantrum."

Michael stopped short. He had always prided

himself on his self-control, and right at that moment he wanted to hit something. He quickly centered himself, taking a calming breath. "No," he said again. "I brought her here, I married her. I'll train her and look after her, but I'm not fucking her and I'm not taking her blood and bringing about her death. We aren't death-takers anymore—Raziel broke that command. Besides, her blood would probably kill me."

"She's your mate," Martha said. "It would make you stronger."

"She's a temporary inconvenience, for you all as well as me," he shot back. There was a shocked silence at his callous words. In truth, his deliberate cruelty shocked even him, but he wasn't about to show it. "There isn't time for this," he went on, trying to sound reasonable. "If the Armies of Heaven are going to attack in one month, we need to spend every spare moment training."

"I don't know why you're arguing," Raziel said. "There was a time when you shagged anything female."

"They didn't die afterward," he snapped.

His words were cold. As cold as the ice he could feel forming inside him. He didn't even know her. He was a warrior, used to death. She'd lived almost twenty-five pampered years, which was better than many people got.

Azazel rose, taking his wife's hand. "If there's no changing your mind, I guess we're done here."

"We're done," Raziel said. He glanced at Martha. "Unless there's anything else?"

"Nothing," she said. "Not now."

Michael wanted to throttle her, but it wasn't her fault, and in fact he'd always liked Martha. Thomas, her husband, had been one of his best warriors, and she'd taken his death with dignified grief.

None of this was anyone's fault, and he needed to take a step back and look at it rationally, as one more battle to be fought in the war against Uriel and the Armies of Heaven. Battles were his life—one more was nothing.

He wasn't going to do it. But there was a quiet little voice inside, a wicked, insidious one: *You know this is what you want. You have the perfect excuse, and this way there won't be any long-term repercussions. You can have her, and then she'll go away. And you know you want her. You've wanted her since you first set eyes on her. Wanted her, when you've been impervious to every other woman you've seen for eons.*

And her blood. He could smell it dancing through her veins, and for the first time he understood the obsession that drove the bonded couples. He'd refused to bond, refused to take blood from anyone but the Source. He could deny Uriel that triumph.

The girl—no, she was a woman, despite the untried aura about her. She called to him.

He would not listen to that voice. He knew women, and she was afraid of him and desperate not to show it. If he took her, then her death was assured. If he left her alone, there was room for hope.

But the fate of the world hung on this. Could he afford to ignore his duty?

It wouldn't come to that. He'd figure out some way. In the meantime, he was going to do what he did best—push his body to a state of exhaustion in training, and not think about anything else.

CHAPTER
EIGHT

WHEN I AWOKE, THE SUN WAS sending wide shafts of light across the floor of my bedroom, and I sat up, panicked, disoriented. It took me only a moment to remember where I was. I'd traded one prison for another, and looking out the glass doors to the glinting ocean beyond, I didn't regret my choice.

I pushed out of the comfortable bed, amazed that I'd apparently slept through the night, and quickly made it in military fashion as Pedersen had always insisted. Pedersen. He was dead, by my hands, and I should feel something, anything. All my life he'd been my tormentor and enemy, yet I felt no satisfaction at his death. No sorrow either. I just felt . . . odd. It was as if he were an enemy soldier and I was in the midst of a war. I'd had no choice. I wasn't going to waste time lamenting that necessity.

I showered quickly and dressed in the loose white clothes in the closet. To my astonishment, there were bras in my size, as well as lacy underwear. The clothes were utilitarian, a variation on a martial arts gi, but the underwear was pretty, feminine, almost decadent. There was even a delicate negligee, clearly made for a more romantic bride than I was.

I actually liked the wicked underwear. It was my secret, a part of me that I didn't have to share with anyone else. Particularly the beautiful man who now seemed to be my husband.

I went out into the living area. There were flowers, a bright profusion of color, that had to have come from Allie. The woman who'd offered her wrist to Michael. I shivered, then lifted my head. I could smell coffee. The delicious scent was unmistakable, even though I hadn't smelled it in years, not since Johann and I had made our escape. Either the contessa didn't believe in coffee or she simply didn't think her offspring deserved it.

There was a carafe sitting on the smooth-top surface of the stove, and it was hot. I looked around me—I'd locked the doors, and I knew for certain no one had been here recently. How could the coffee be hot? For that matter, when had the flowers arrived?

Those were the least of my worries. I poured myself a mug, added lots of cream and real sugar, and took a sip. Ambrosia. Maybe this new life wasn't so bad.

I took the mug and pushed open the french doors leading out to the small flagstone terrace and the steps descending to the sea. The air was crisp and cool, and I took a deep breath, loving it. The smell of freedom.

I walked barefoot down to the edge of the shore, letting the water lap at my toes. It was cold, breathtakingly so, and I looked out past the gentle swell into eternity. I glanced around, but there was no one in sight—the beach outside my door felt secluded, but people could easily walk by. I drained the coffee, set the mug down in the sand, and walked out, fully clothed, into the surf for the first time in my life.

I didn't dare take my time—the cold would send me running back. I walked until the water reached my waist, held my nose, and ducked under, letting the salt sea wash over me.

The current pushed me gently, and I wasn't afraid. I shook my wet hair from my face, letting the cool, blessed waters flow around me, and I remembered stories I'd read of baptism. That's what it felt like, I thought. A benediction.

But it was too cold to stay in for long. I made my way out of the water, my wet clothes clinging to me, and I suddenly realized I was hungry—starving, in fact. I couldn't remember if there was anything left in the fridge, and I'd never cooked a day in my life, even though I'd watched enough cooking shows on cable TV to qualify me as an expert. I'd have to see if Allie or Rachel could point me in the direction of the kitchens and something decent to eat. I was feeling carnivorous—I wanted scrambled eggs with cheese and fat sausages and brioche with raspberry confit.

I headed straight for a hot shower, dumping my sodden clothes in the sink and luxuriating beneath the steamy water. Then I dressed, finger-combed my hair, and walked out to see a covered tray on the table in front of the sofa. I didn't care what it was. At this point I would have eaten beets and olives covered in maple syrup, three things I disliked intensely. I took off the lid and looked down in a combination of delight and dismay.

Scrambled eggs, fat sausages, fresh brioche with a red syrup that I knew, without question, was raspberry. Not only had something been able to read my mind and provide exactly what I wanted, it had also anticipated me. There was a fresh carafe of coffee and a glass of orange juice I just knew was fresh-squeezed.

I shook my head, sitting down to my feast. It wasn't any stranger than being carried off by an angel who drank blood and battled God. Actually, it wasn't any stranger than spending my life imprisoned by a mother who hated me and being told I was the Roman goddess of war.

Six impossible things before breakfast, I reminded myself. Which apparently included breakfast itself.

This world was beginning to look more and more appealing. As long as beautiful, disturbing Michael kept his distance, I'd be just fine.

"Hurry up," came a rich, unexpected voice from behind me. "It's time to train."

I turned to glare at my supposed husband. "I locked the door. How did you get in?"

"Don't be ridiculous. Locked doors won't keep me out."

"Then what will?" I asked pointedly.

"Nothing."

He was wearing all white, something similar to the clothes I had found in my closet, and I realized their resemblance to a martial arts uniform was intentional. "What makes you think I'm interested in training?"

"There's a war coming. You're the goddess of war."

I speared the last sausage on my fork and leaned back on the sofa. "So you say. I doubt it. I have yet to notice that I have any supernatural powers, and a god deserves to have some. And what the hell makes you think I'm on your side? You practically kidnapped me—"

"Bullshit. You've had a choice all along. You have one now. You can stay in this room and read romance novels, or you can come and train with the others. I'll put Metatron in charge of you—you won't even have to see me."

How the hell did he know about the romance novels? I wasn't about to ask. Instead I said, "Who's Metatron?"

"Former leader of the Armies of Heaven, and the most recent angel to fall. You'll like him. He's a surly son of a bitch."

"So are you and I don't like you."

I don't know if I expected a reaction to that, but I didn't get one. "As it should be," he said. "Are you going to eat that sausage or fellate it?"

Fellate it? For a moment I couldn't place the word, and then I remembered. My education had been unlimited, and I had run across some extremely interesting books.

I looked at the sausage critically, met his gaze, and took a sharp bite out of it, hoping to make him flinch. He didn't.

Tossing the fork down on the plate, I rose. "I'm ready."

"I doubt it," he said. "But you will be."

THE ARCHANGEL MICHAEL was going to send word down to the kitchens. No matter how much she wanted sausages, she wasn't going to get them. This situation was absurd enough—he didn't need her taunting him with her food.

There were more than two score men and women in the main room going through their moves, and more outside in the private courtyard. He could hear the clash of metal, the knock of stick against stick, the kick against the bag, the grunt as something hit hard flesh. The smell of clean sweat and discipline. And then everything stopped as they all turned to look at the goddess of war.

She met them look for look, not the slightest bit intimidated. He liked that about her. She didn't seem to have an ounce of fear in her body—except, perhaps, when it came to him.

"This is Victoria Bellona, Goddess of War. Victoria Bellona, these are the cream of the fighters among the Fallen. You'll have to be very good to belong with these soldiers."

She looked at them with a measuring gaze, probably underestimating them. The weakest of them could take her in under a minute; the strongest could kill her in seconds. He could only hope Metatron could teach her enough tools to keep her alive.

Assuming there was any possibility she might live. He suspected she'd die whether he touched her or not, but he wasn't going to take the chance. She had less than a month, and she had no idea. He didn't want to watch her die. Though as far as he knew, he could die before her. Martha hadn't shared that particular information.

She probably didn't have it. Her gift was completely inconvenient, knowledge coming too late to help, some of it useless, some of it of earth-shattering importance. That was why Azazel and Raziel—and, yes, he had to count himself—treated her prediction about the Roman goddess so seriously. That was why he'd agreed to go. If this was one of the times she was right, they couldn't afford to let it slip past.

"Metatron," he called out. "I want you to take over her training. See what she knows and what you can teach her in the next month."

"Why the next month?" the man grunted.

"Because we're running out of time." He had no intention of elaborating. Even after five years, he didn't entirely trust Metatron. There was something not quite right about him.

"I'll do it," Asbel offered, and Michael froze. Not that he had anything against Asbel, but the angel was unmated, and Michael wasn't in the mood to trust anyone around Victoria Bellona. Though Metatron was unmated as well. It was Asbel's tendency to appear out of nowhere that got on his last nerve.

"Metatron," he said in a flat voice, and the big man nodded.

At least this way he could keep an eye on him. The last to fall had done so reluctantly, after being brought to the brink of death in battle with Azazel. Putting him together with the girl would keep two problems contained.

Metatron shrugged, indifferent. He was a good soldier. He followed orders without question, was lethal with lance and sword, and didn't give a shit whether he lived or died, which made him willing to take chances. "Your Honor," he addressed his new charge in a deep, ironic voice.

"Just Tory," she said to Metatron, moving off with

him without a backward glance. Which Michael found annoying, though he wasn't sure why. He turned his back as well, concentrating on loosening up, then checking in with each member of his small, dedicated force before he allowed himself to glance back at her.

She moved well, he thought critically, watching as she ducked and parried Metatron's carefully restrained blows. She had an innate grace, an understanding of combat that couldn't be taught, which was something. He shouldn't be surprised by that—she was, after all, the goddess of war. She also made stupid mistakes, which annoyed him. Annoyed him enough that finally he could stand no more, and he crossed the room in a few long strides, taking the practice sword from Metatron.

"No, no," he said impatiently. "You're reacting too quickly. Your form is good, relaxed, but you keep jumping in a moment too soon. Hold yourself like this. . . ." He put his hands on her shoulders, adjusting her position, then used his foot to nudge hers into a wider stance. And then froze, with his leg between hers, his hands clasping her shoulders.

He released her abruptly, backing away, mentally shaking himself. What was wrong with him? "Practice waiting a moment longer rather than rushing. It gives you more control. Wait for your opponent to come to you."

"And what if he doesn't?" she said quietly. "What if he keeps retreating?"

With any other woman, he might think she was talking about something else entirely. But Victoria Bellona had no carnal interest in him, no carnal interest in anybody. Which was a relief, since he was suddenly having a difficult time controlling his wayward urges.

"Then you find someone else willing to battle." He turned his back on her and her far-too-perceptive green eyes.

"Or go back to your rooms and let the warriors do their job," Metatron said in his deep, disapproving voice. He was a sexist to the core and had very little use for women.

The girl was looking pretty, weak, and helpless, and Michael knew a moment's doubt. He was trying to keep his distance from her, but he was fairly certain she was neither weak nor helpless.

She looked up at the giant warrior. "Metatron," she said meditatively. "You guys are very strange. We've got a Ninja Turtle and a Transformer. What's next, Wolverine and the Power Rangers?"

Metatron looked at her with profound dislike. "She is too flippant," he said. "This is a waste of my time."

"Let me try once more," she begged in a deceptively sweet voice.

Metatron nodded, the fool. He was an excellent soldier, but he had a tendency to underestimate his opponents. And Victoria Bellona was most definitely an opponent.

A few seconds later the ground shuddered as Metatron went down in as neat a move as Michael could remember seeing. So she had some skills—her defeat of Pedersen hadn't been a fluke. This was going to prove even more interesting.

Dangerously so.

CHAPTER
NINE

ARROGANT ASSHOLE. I LOOKED down at the giant lying at my feet. He'd fallen hard, harder than a warrior ought to, but that came from thinking his opponent was nothing but a useless girl. He was blinking, dazed, and I waited for his eyes to clear before holding out a hand to him.

A moment later he was up with a roar, knocking aside my hand and heading straight toward me with a murderous glare in his eyes. I had the wooden sword they used for training, and I timed it perfectly, smashing it across his throat at the precise moment it would do the most damage. Down he went again, on his stomach, and this time he stayed down.

My husband was watching me out of those unreadable dark eyes, and I wondered if I'd betrayed too much. "Lucky hit," I said with a shrug.

"Indeed." His voice was noncommittal. He turned

to Metatron. "Get up. If you can't handle being hit by a little girl, you're useless to me."

"Little girl?" I echoed, drawing up to my full five feet nine in bare feet.

Metatron didn't look any too happy with his comment either. He rolled over and scrambled to his feet, glaring at both of us. "She's better than she'd have you think."

I ground my teeth. "Not really. You weren't paying attention."

"Try me again," he growled.

Not likely. He'd pummel the shit out of me, and this time I didn't dare defend myself with any amount of skill. Fortunately Michael turned to me. "Go and work with Rachel. She can teach you some defensive moves in case you run into anyone more dangerous than Uriel's most powerful angel. She has some skills you might find interesting, if she feels like divulging them."

"Cheating bitch," Metatron muttered beneath his breath, and I wasn't sure if he meant me or Rachel.

"I heard that." Rachel's cool voice floated across the busy room with surprising clarity, and Metatron flushed. It was an interesting sight. The man was huge, more robot than human, and he was blushing. Though that brought up an interesting question.

I turned to Michael. "Are you human?"

Michael had turned to leave, but he paused. "I'm not anything. Neither angel nor human, living nor dead, saved nor doomed. At least, when you die, you won't be sentenced to eternal torment as the Fallen are. Though if you end up in a heaven with Uriel in charge, I'm not sure there will be much of a difference."

"But—"

"I don't have time to discuss philosophy with you. Rachel's waiting for you." He strode away. I watched him go—he gave the impression of incredible strength without bulkiness. No bulging muscles, just sleek, indomitable power. His skin was a perfect shade of sun-kissed gold, his dark eyes enigmatic as they swept over me, revealing nothing. He moved with an almost catlike grace, silent. He would be a mesmerizing, dangerous predator, and he should have frightened me. Instead I was fascinated. Drawn.

I tore my eyes away and met Rachel's gaze. I didn't like what I saw. She looked far too knowing, and I didn't want her jumping to any conclusions about me. I could feel the curious eyes of the Fallen on my back. I shouldn't have lost my temper with Metatron. I was going to have to work hard to regain the image of marginal skills.

I managed a casual, ambling kind of walk as I joined Rachel by a set of open doors. She was smiling, and I wasn't sure I trusted it, but I smiled back, all innocence. "Can you imagine the luck?" I said lightly. "Knocking a mountain down on the first day here."

"Twice." She cocked her head, surveying me. "Come. Let's go someplace where we can talk."

"I thought we were supposed to train."

"We will. I have my own way of working, and Michael knows better than to intercede."

"You mean he doesn't bully you like he does everyone else?"

"He tries. He doesn't get very far with me." She took my arm, leading me out through the courtyard and toward the main building. "We don't need any curious busybodies overhearing us."

I gave her a questioning look. "What are you going to talk about that we don't want witnesses?"

"Power. Gifts. How to fight back when you need to."

"As far as I can tell, I don't have any powers. I think the goddess thing is simply a courtesy title."

"You simply haven't discovered your powers yet. I've been where you are. I can help."

I looked at her doubtfully, then chose to misunderstand her. "You're right. I can't count on luck if I end up in this war Michael's talking about. I need to know how to defend myself."

She gave me an impatient scowl. "You're more than capable of defending yourself against anyone Uriel can send against us. I'm talking about defending yourself against Michael."

I started to protest, then shut it. I was just going to have to do a better job of convincing these people that I was incompetent. Rachel had picked up on the one thing that would snare me. Whether I wanted to admit it or not, I instinctively knew Michael was the greatest threat to me, and I was having a hard time consigning him to an unimportant section of my consciousness.

"You like it here," she said, not a question.

I wanted to immediately deny it, but there was something about Rachel that made lying hard. I glanced around, following her at an easy pace through the spacious hallways of the compound. "It's an improvement over the last place I lived. Considering that was a prison, it doesn't take much to improve things."

She didn't respond to that. "And you like Michael."

I hooted with laughter. "All right, I'll admit that getting out of my first prison has its merits, but the Archangel Michael is a royal pain in the butt who doesn't like me any better than I like him."

A small smile curled the corner of her mouth. "I won't disagree with that," she said, and I felt a hint of disappointment. "You're married to him, mated to him. What are you going to do next?"

I didn't even hesitate. "Get away from here. I'm not really worried about him—I'm not his type. Someone, maybe you, has him convinced that the only way he'll win his war against the Armies of God is to have me there as well for cannon fodder. Too bad—it's not my fight."

"I'm not the one who told him. My visions are few and far between—Martha is the one who saw it. And they aren't the Armies of God. God gave humans free will and then left the whole mess in

Uriel's charge, and there's a human saying: 'Absolute power corrupts absolutely.' The Armies of Heaven are under his control, and they're the ones we need to defeat."

"Good luck with that," I muttered.

We'd reached Rachel's rooms, and she pushed open the doors, drawing me in. It was a far cry from my spartan quarters. The living room was sparsely finished, but the ubiquitous white had vanished. One wall was a deep Chinese red, and there were jewel-toned pillows scattered on the black lacquer sofa. Beyond I could see a huge bed covered in silk.

"This is better than the operating room I'm sleeping in."

"You should see where Michael sleeps."

I tensed. "How do you know I haven't? And why do you know what it looks like?"

Her laugh was low and surprisingly charming. "I know you haven't because Michael is insisting this is a marriage of protocol and nothing else. And I've seen his room because I visited him with Azazel after he was wounded during a skirmish with the Nephilim."

"Nephilim? What's that?"

Rachel shuddered. "I don't think you want to know. There aren't any left on this continent, so they're nothing to worry about."

"Who says I'm staying on this continent?"

She looked at me, momentarily silenced. "They're

monsters," she said finally. "Come on." She took my arm and pulled me through the rooms, out into a private courtyard, gesturing toward a comfortable-looking chaise. "Have a seat and I'll get us something to drink. Do you like Diet Coke?"

"God, no." I shuddered. "Is that all you people drink? Besides blood, that is."

She shook her head, presumably at my flippant remark. "Iced tea, then?"

"You can bring me Diet Coke. I suppose I should get used to it," I said in a resigned tone.

A moment later she was back, a cold, sweating silver can in her hand. I took a tentative sip of the fuzzy stuff, and it tasted marginally better than it had last night. Rachel stretched out in the other chaise, her own can in her hand, and looked at me with those penetrating eyes. "Actually, I need to talk to you about something other than your latent powers."

"So Michael set me up," I grumbled. "You're not talking me into anything."

She shook her head. "He has nothing to do with this. In fact, he'd be furious if he found out."

"Well, I'm all in favor of anything that annoys him." The thought made me cheerful. "So what do you want?"

"We need Michael to have sex with you and drink your blood, and he's refusing."

MICHAEL GAVE METATRON a long, assessing look. His new bride—God, he hated to think of her that way—looked soft and fragile and confused, yet she'd just managed to kick the butt of arguably Sheol's strongest warrior. Metatron was huge—a foot taller and a hundred pounds heavier than she was—but she'd flattened him, twice, with deceptive ease.

"What's wrong with you?" he demanded.

Metatron glowered. In the few years he'd lived in Sheol, he had yet to integrate completely with the other Fallen, doubtless because he'd spent countless centuries fighting them. "She's a witch. Thou shalt not suffer a witch to live."

He also had an annoying habit of quoting the ancient texts, whichever suited his purpose. Metatron knew the Old Testament and the Apocrypha backward and forward, and he had answers for everything, even when they were totally contradictory.

"She's not a witch, she's the Roman goddess of war."

"I see no difference."

Michael bit back his annoyance. He'd never liked Metatron, but the giant was too useful a soldier to ignore. "Are you well enough to spar?"

Metatron's response was a derisive sniff, and almost before Michael realized it, he attacked.

Almost. No one took Michael off guard, and he parried Metatron's sudden lunge, but just barely, the huge weight of him knocking Michael sideways a bit before he recovered with a hard kick to the solar plexus. Metatron grunted but didn't go down.

Five minutes of brutal action, and neither of them

had won. Metatron was winded—it was hard for a big man to move fast enough to counter Michael's swift deadliness. But he made up for it with brute strength. Michael could feel the blood dripping down his face from a cut near his eye, and his entire body felt as if it had been put through a meat grinder. He was still standing, and so was Metatron, but even if the man wasn't bleeding, he looked just about done in.

Michael could have finished him quickly, but he was too smart for that. You challenged your men just enough, and then you let them be. He needed Metatron to believe himself invincible in battle. He needed all his men and women to believe that.

Blood was splattering his white shirt. "I'll go clean up," he said.

Metatron nodded, trying to pretend he wasn't out of breath, and Michael turned away. The giant had been as strong as ever—there was no reasonable way a smaller opponent like Victoria Bellona could have bested him. He'd felt no use of supernatural power, and he was always aware when that came into play, as it had with Rachel. Maybe Tory was right, maybe it was simply a fluke, but he was gathering more and more proof that his wife was stronger than she pretended to be.

He shut the door of the training room behind him, knowing his people wouldn't dare slack off, and headed down the hall toward his rooms. Rachel would make sure that Tory wasn't hurt. Some warriors were good at hiding an injury until they were out of sight; some injuries didn't appear until later, and those could be fatal. He couldn't afford to lose Tory any sooner than was predestined. She was necessary if they were to have any chance of triumphing over Uriel.

No, he'd better check on her first, then clean up. Like it or not, she was his responsibility, and if there was any question about her safety, he needed answers.

His head still rang a bit from the force of Metatron's blows. If he could feel it, then he shuddered to think what Tory was feeling. He quickened his pace.

She wasn't in her rooms. There could be a reasonable explanation for that, but fear suddenly shot through him. She might be in the infirmary, lapsing into a coma. She might have collapsed—

He stopped, made himself breathe deeply. She was with Rachel. He trusted Rachel more than anyone, even Allie. She would take excellent care of Tory.

But he wasn't going anywhere until he was sure.

CHAPTER
TEN

I SET MY CAN OF DIET COKE DOWN ON the flagstone terrace and started to rise.

"Just hear me out," Rachel said. "We're in a battle not just for our existence but for the future of mankind."

I didn't bother to hide my skepticism. "Why would you care about mankind? Apparently I don't qualify and you haven't lived among them for years." Not that I believed that for one moment. I had yet to see proof, and until then I was determined to see myself as simply a healthy young woman.

"This world was created for mankind. Angels and gods exist because of human belief. Even if we survived, our lives would be worthless without humans."

"So who's the great threat to mankind? Satan? Lucifer?" I tossed the names off casually. I had done my reading. Lucifer was supposedly a fallen angel, just like these others.

If I'd hoped to offend Rachel, I'd failed. She smiled wryly. "The polar opposite."

"God? You're telling me God's going to destroy the world?"

"I thought Michael explained this to you. For all intents and purposes, there is no God. He gave humans free will and then turned everything over to the archangel Uriel."

"I take it that was a mistake?"

"Big mistake. Where do you think the Old Testament came from, with all the smiting and the pillars of salt? Uriel has always thought mankind was a mistake, and he's been trying to control them ever since. Now he simply wants to get rid of them completely."

"And God is going to let him?"

"He's not involved anymore. The only beings who can stop Uriel and the Armies of Heaven are the Fallen. It's that simple. And you're key to that victory."

"How?" I demanded. "Why?"

Rachel shook her head. "Martha's visions aren't that precise, but so far they've usually been correct. She's the one who saw that you were needed in order for us to prevail. Without you, the world is doomed."

"Great. So once I save the world, do I get to be God?" I said cheerfully. "Oh, no, I forgot, I already *am* a god. So tell me, exactly what makes you think I'm a goddess? Apparently I'm not immortal—the contessa and Pedersen were planning to kill me. And I don't seem to have any superpowers, apart from a certain facility with martial arts. So why can't I hurl thunderbolts and walk on water and live forever?"

"Because no one believes in you anymore," Rachel said flatly. "We need the faith of the people to ensure our immortality, and people have forgotten you ever existed. If it weren't for mankind's unfortunate affection for war, you probably wouldn't exist at all. All the other pagan gods have disappeared entirely."

I couldn't hide a grin. The idea of being a pagan goddess was so absurd, it held an odd sort of appeal. "Okay, I'll buy that. Where are my superpowers?"

"You'll find them. When you need them."

"And for some reason you think my having sex with Michael is going to save the world?" I said skeptically. "I doubt it. And he's not drinking my blood. I'm not that kinky."

"We assumed that Michael simply bringing you here, marrying you, would be enough to ensure that he would prevail. Martha says no. It must be a true marriage."

"If she thinks I'm going to fall in love with him, she's out of her mind," I said. "You can't order that sort of thing."

"Who says marriages have anything to do with love?" Rachel said. "Mutual respect can be as good a foundation as lust."

I opened my mouth to object, then shut it again. I kept forgetting that movies weren't real life. In movies it was all about love and passion. I wasn't conversant enough with real life, or the Sheol variant of it, to know what went on there.

I had no idea whether there was mutual respect in our twisted marriage. Did I respect him? I respected his strength, his pigheadedness, his stubbornness. Apart from that, there was, damn it all, an occasional stirring of lust, at least on my side, which I found completely disheartening.

Then again, if the world was going to end, what was the harm in indulging it? "So we're supposed to fuck like rabbits and he gets to drink my blood? Why isn't he the one asking me?"

"He's refused."

I was an expert at hiding my reactions, my emotions. My mother would have eaten me alive if she'd ever known what I was thinking. The thought that my unwanted husband desired neither my body nor my blood was actually ridiculously hurtful. I felt rejected on the most elemental of levels.

"That makes two of us," I said. "At least he's shown sense for once."

"His pride will kill us all."

"You think it's pride?"

"I know Michael. He's prey to human desires just like the rest of the Fallen, and his appetites are strong, even though he's managed to sublimate them. He wants you. He wants your body and he needs your blood, and he's going to do everything he can to keep away from you so he won't be tempted."

This made no sense. "Why? He had no qualms about forcing me into a marriage. Why stop there?"

There was just the hint of a shadow in Rachel's eyes, and then it was gone before I could call her on it. "It's complicated."

I glanced around me at the perfect little court-yard, the privacy, the filtered sunlight overhead warming me. "Are we in any hurry? It's going to take more than that to make me jump into bed."

Rachel sighed. "Michael is a warrior. You know that. Stories and legends of his past show up in almost every culture, and throughout his existence he has been dedicated to the art of war, the art of battle. He has focused everything on that one end, including his celibacy."

"So you're telling me he's never had sex?"

She shook her head. "When he was driven from heaven, he fell hard. For a while he became obsessed with sensual pleasures. He is the most legendary, inventive warrior in all of the universe, in all of his-tory. He put that same dedication into sex."

I shivered. I didn't want to consider why. Sex with Johann had been affectionate and pleasant after I got used to the initial discomfort and mess. I really couldn't imagine that particular act performed with the fierce intensity I had already seen in Michael.

"So?" I managed to sound breezy. "He's a—what do you call it?—a sex machine. For everyone but me, apparently."

"He stopped. He bonded once, but she was killed

almost immediately by one of the Nephilim. And he only bedded women, never took their blood. He refuses to drink from anyone but the Source, yet he still manages to maintain his strength. If he bonded, if he took your blood, his power would be unstoppable."

"Clearly he's not interested."

"Clearly he's too interested," Rachel corrected me. "He refuses to bond, insisting it would weaken him. He's wrong, of course. He refuses to drink, to let Uriel win. What he gives away in focus by bonding, he'll regain in strength."

"This is moot. He doesn't want me and I don't want him touching me."

Impatience flared in Rachel's eyes. "Don't be disingenuous. If there's one thing I understand, it's how women feel."

"What makes you such an expert?" I shot back.

She made a dismissive noise. "Most of the women here are human. I am not. I told you, I've been where you are. I've been alive almost as long as the Fallen. I am Lilith, the first woman, the patron of women everywhere. I comfort the broken, I help the barren, I—"

"Not doing so good a job helping the barren around here, are you?" I said. "I haven't seen any children since I arrived."

She ignored me. "I *understand*," she said again. "You're fascinated by him—who wouldn't be? You feel the same draw that he does, and both of you are fighting it. All you have to do is go to his room and strip off your clothes. I promise you that he'll take care of the rest."

"All I have to do?" I echoed, appalled. "I don't think so. If the future of the world requires me to give my body to someone I dislike, then I guess civilization is going to come to an end."

"It won't." Michael's deep voice came from directly behind us, and I scrambled off the chaise, my face warm, my heart pounding.

Rachel moved more slowly, and I wondered if she'd known he was listening. And just how long he had been there. "Eavesdropping is an unpleasant habit, Michael," she said smoothly.

"You knew I was there." He verified my suspicion. "You were supposed to be helping her discover her powers, not turning her into a whore. What the hell do you think you're doing? You know what I said."

Rachel looked oddly guilty. "I know what you said, Michael. And I know we're fighting for our lives."

"You think I don't know that?" he said. I started to sidle out, not wanting to listen while they argued over whether I was going to have sex with him or not, for God's sake, but he caught my wrist in one strong hand, staying me.

I considered seeing whether I could flip him. I knew I could break his hold, because he underestimated me, but I wasn't ready to let him realize the extent of my abilities. I stood there, gaze averted, willing the heat away from my face.

"You're being a stubborn idiot. If Raziel ordered you—"

"He won't. I've made my decision—she remains untouched."

Uh, already touched, I wanted to say, but wisely kept my mouth shut. The very thought of lying beneath his strong, hard body, all that hot, golden skin against mine, was deeply disturbing. I hadn't much experience to go by, but sex with Michael would be a far cry from what I'd shared with Johann. And the idea frightened me. Fascinated me.

Rachel threw up her hands in disgust. "As you wish. We'll simply have to hope that Martha is wrong this time. If you refuse to listen . . . "

But he was already dragging me back into the house, away from Rachel with her intense eyes and her unexpected kindness. Rachel, the first woman. I'd forgotten to ask her what had happened to Eve.

Michael wasn't hurting me, but after a gentle tug I knew he wasn't letting me go without a major move on my part. I let him pull me along the corridors of the house, out into the hazy sunshine, and back to the annex that held my room and the training quarters. His room as well, but I wasn't going to be seeing it.

He pushed open the door to my rooms and finally released my wrist, presumably expecting me to go inside meekly. Underestimating me yet again.

I slipped my hand around and caught his wrist, tugging him after me. "We need to talk."

For a moment he didn't move, and it was a stand-off. I probably could have hauled him into my room, but I wasn't ready to go that far. Finally he nodded, detached my grip, and followed me inside.

RACHEL HAD BEEN maddening enough, Michael thought, looking at Tory through hooded eyes. Now he had to deal with his wife asking questions he wasn't prepared to answer. But he already knew her well enough to realize she wasn't simply going to let go.

He headed straight for the kitchen, helping himself to the chilled pitcher of water, then sank down on the sofa, deliberately not asking her if she wanted anything. His skin felt too tight, as it always did when he was around her. He'd chosen celibacy, and it had been no trouble at all until she'd appeared in the contessa's airless salon and blown everything all to hell.

He could smell her, smell her blood, and he stared at her neck for a long moment, allowing himself the brief, forbidden, totally erotic fantasy of drinking from her, sucking the rich tang of her blood.

Once more Uriel was manipulating him into acts that would create nothing but death and despair, and he had sworn never to blindly follow orders again. The guilt that stained his soul was already too heavy a burden. He refused to compound it.

He could have her. That was no surprise—he had always been able to have any woman he wanted. All he had to do was focus on her and she would be in his bed, on her back, her knees, any way he wanted her. He did nothing by half measures. He could kill anyone he wanted, fuck anyone he wanted, and he'd learned to keep that power under tight control.

It was straining at the leash now, his desire for her, and the bondage image only made him hotter. He wanted her so badly that he had run himself into a state of exhaustion last night after dumping her here, rather than risk the temptation to come back and take what everyone wanted him to take. Everyone but her.

"They want us to sleep together," she said.

Did she have to have such a soft, delectable mouth? He wanted that mouth on his body, her small tongue tracing his wards and tattoos. He didn't blink. "No, they don't. They want us to fuck."

She didn't flinch at the crude word—he had to give her that. "For some reason, they think I can change your mind," she said. "That I'd *want* to change your mind. You need to make it clear to them that you have absolutely no interest in me sexually, and then maybe they'll leave us alone."

"I never lie."

It took her a moment to realize what he'd said. "What would the lie be?" she asked warily.

He wasn't interested in playing games. "You know the answer to that as well as I do. If you were an anonymous body, I could do what I had to do with no difficulty. You're a little harder to dismiss."

She actually looked amused. "I think you'll manage. If you've been celibate for so long, I hardly think I'm likely to change your mind."

He said nothing.

She took the chair opposite him, and he watched the way her strong, lean body flowed, graceful and compact, every move in perfect control. Metatron should have known better than to underestimate her. *He* should have known better. He wouldn't make that mistake again.

"Why are you celibate? Do you think having sex will ruin your focus?" she persisted.

"No."

"Then I don't see why you've chosen a life of celibacy."

"And I don't see why you're obsessed with whom I do or do not fuck," he countered.

He was beginning to piss her off. Good. It was better that way. "That's an ugly word," she said.

"Is it? I suppose it depends on your context. And what you think of the act itself."

"Clearly you don't like it, if you've gone without sex for hundreds of years." He could hear the triumph in her voice, as if she'd made a decisive hit.

He let his eyelids droop lazily over his eyes. "I got bored. There are only so many interesting variations you can try without causing permanent damage." He saw her flinch, and controlled his amusement.

"You like to hurt people?"

"Sometimes. When it increases their pleasure." In fact, pain and bondage were only a small part of the whole mesmerizing world of sexuality, and he hadn't grown bored. He'd become obsessed, trying to fill some emptiness inside himself. He'd never succeeded, and he'd finally given up trying, turning his back on the world of soulless pleasure. He could read the worry in her eyes, despite the effort she put into appearing unfazed. "I wouldn't hurt you."

Where the hell had that come from? He wasn't going to have sex with her—why was he even discussing it?

Her eyes widened, but for a moment she said nothing. Finally she said, "Your job is to inflict pain. You're a killer."

"I'm a warrior," he said. "As are you."

"I've never killed . . ." The words trailed off as she remembered.

He watched her carefully, curious. She would have to kill again, without hesitation, if she was to be of any help to them. "It was a necessary death," he said finally.

"Is any death necessary?"

"You don't need my answer to such an elemental question. Only your own."

She was still considering. And then, like the click of a switch, she nodded. Accepted. She pushed her rich, dark hair away from her pale face, and once again he acknowledged how beautiful she was. Not the perfect beauty of the Fallen, but the attraction of something else, something more complex and troublesome. "Rachel wanted me to seduce you."

"I'm not surprised." He kept his voice, his expression, neutral.

"I told her no."

"Of course you did," he said softly. "Sex is the last thing on your mind." He shouldn't have said it when he knew it was patently untrue, but he wanted to see if he could get to her.

Once more she surprised him. Her smile was slow, sensual, and he wanted to curse as his body leapt in response. "Oh, I don't know about that," she said. "I imagine I think about sex just as often as you do."

He kept his face expressionless, even as he felt his skin grow hot. She would probably die anyway. Why not? "You're playing with fire, little girl," he said in a steady voice.

"Am I?" She shrugged, and even that mundane gesture held a wealth of sensual grace. "Apparently you're immune to my dubious charms."

A smile came before he could stop it, and she blinked, momentarily nonplussed, as if she couldn't believe what she was seeing. Her startled eyes met his, and he let his omnipresent guard drop, just for a moment. It was like an electric shock jolting his body, the sudden knowledge that all of them were right, she was his. And he couldn't, wouldn't, have her.

He moved closer, without realizing how it

happened—so close, all he had to do was reach out and she would be in his arms, wrapped against his hungry body. He lifted his hand, surprised to see it didn't shake, and cupped her face, his thumb gently brushing her soft lips.

He almost told her. Told her that his kiss would lead to her death. That even if he felt his centuries of determination crumble in the face of his need, he wouldn't give in.

"We're not doing this," she whispered.

"Of course not." He could stop. His self-control was legendary. It was a small enough test, simply to prove it to himself, to lean forward and replace his thumb with his lips, brushing her mouth softly. He pulled away, almost too quickly, as desire rushed over him.

She looked at him, her green eyes startled but uncomfortably knowing. "Of course not."

CHAPTER
ELEVEN

I STOOD ALONE IN THE MIDDLE OF MY room after he left. What were the lines I'd heard so often in the movies? *Time to get the hell out of Dodge. Let's blow this Popsicle stand.* I had no idea why people seemed to hate Dodge so much, and in all the movies I'd watched I'd never seen a Popsicle stand, but I understood the concept. I needed to get the hell out of there, and I'd waited too long, seduced by the ocean and the friendship. Seduced by my husband's beautiful face and body, I was caving. Charmed by him despite myself, despite his best efforts. Charmed by that sudden, unbidden smile.

What would it be like to see that smile without all the baggage? To see him really smile at me?

Why not do what Rachel asked? I fought to ignore the little voice that niggled in my head. He was deliciously gorgeous, but it wasn't merely his physical beauty that had such an odd effect on me. All the men here were beautiful, angelically so. And none of the others caused me even the slightest twinge.

There was something about the Archangel Michael that pulled me on a deep, irrational level. His slow, sexy smile had almost brought me to my knees. And if I gave in, I'd never leave. Never taste the richness of life that had always been out of reach. I wanted to be loved, I wanted children, I wanted to see and experience everything. If I stayed here, Michael would be my world, that rare, devastating smile would be my reward, and I wasn't going to let that happen.

I looked out the french doors to the sea shimmering in the misty sunlight. There were people on the beach, some running, some going through martial arts exercises with impressively good form. *I wouldn't mind sparring with some of them*, I thought. *If I were going to stay*. No escape that way. The house backed up against a steep cliff, and while I could attempt the climb, I could hardly do so in broad daylight. I had to stay put, at least for the moment.

Rachel wanted me to sleep with him. They all wanted me to sleep with him, everyone except Michael himself, which, if you thought about it, was insulting. There was nothing wrong with me. My body was lithe and strong, my face pretty enough even though it fell far short of movie-star perfection. Why didn't he want me?

But he does, the little voice whispered in my head.

He did, and I knew it, in the unconscious, elemental female way that had existed throughout history, all the way back to the first man and first woman. Beneath the cool gaze he used to try to intimidate me there lurked a blaze, so strong it made me uneasy. I refused to let anything frighten me. But if anything did, it would be the heat in the icy fallen archangel.

I pushed open the doors, letting the soft sea air into my room, and went out to join the army on the beach.

IN THE END, slipping away was easier than I had expected. In the workout room I sparred a bit with a couple of the men—the angels—including a particularly kind one named Asbel. He had the same perfect beauty, but on him it somehow looked more human, more approachable. By the time we finished, we were both exhausted and laughing.

"We're glad you're here, Victoria Bellona," he said as we were catching our breath.

I'd grown tired of telling people to call me Tory. I glanced around. Michael was across the huge room, ignoring me, and I wished I were as good at dismissing him from my mind as he appeared to be at disregarding me. I pulled my attention back to Asbel. "It's certainly better than the last place I lived," I said. "Though not where I was expecting to go." I let my eyes go back to Michael. "And not what I expected to marry."

Asbel touched my arm with surprising sympathy. He smelled like cinnamon, always a comforting scent. Michael smelled of the night sky.

"I'm sorry to hear that," Asbel said quietly. "If there's any way I can help, all you have to do is ask."

"Can you help me get away from here?" I said flippantly, then turned, distracted, as Martha approached. If I had a bone to pick with anyone in this place, it was with Martha.

"Michael suggested we might spar," she said in her soft voice.

"Really?" I glanced over at him. I seemed to be spending all my spare time looking at him, which was really pathetic. "Why?"

"He said you'd relish a chance to kick my ass, considering I was the reason they brought you here."

That managed to get my attention. I grinned reluctantly. "It's tempting. I don't suppose your visions are your fault. It was the Greeks who killed the messenger who arrived with bad news, and I'm Roman, apparently. I'm sure you didn't mean me any harm."

Martha smiled back at me. She was a few years older than I was, but one look in her calm gray eyes told me she'd lived through more than I ever had— survived more—and the last of my resentment vanished. "I have a better idea," I said. "Why don't the two of us beat up on Michael?"

That coaxed a smile from her. "Now, that's tempting, but I think he could manage both of us with one hand tied behind his back. I could use a little help with my kicks. I have a tendency to telegraph what I'm going to do next, at least when I spar here. Maybe in the heat of battle the enemy will be too wound up to notice."

"You can't count on anything. Let's get away from here and I'll show you some moves."

We joined the others on the beach, away from Michael's distracting presence. Martha surprised me. She was strong, resilient, and smart, and if she could just get past her habit of looking exactly where she was going to attack next, she'd be in good shape for the coming battle everyone kept talking about. I resisted every temptation to floor her until the very last, and when I had her on her back I laughed. "Sorry, I just couldn't help it." I released her and held out a hand, pulling her to her feet again. "Do me a favor, Martha. If you ever have another premonition concerning me, please, *please*, do not tell anyone. Particularly not me."

Something flickered in her eyes. "I promise," she said, her voice slightly hollow.

Everyone was out during the day at regular intervals, everyone except the first woman I'd met, Allie. The one Michael had fed from. Odd, how easily I could think of that without being shocked. *Fed* from her. I'd accepted it, for some reason.

The women were strong, and what they lacked in power they made up for in speed and inventiveness. They had been well schooled, and they knew they would be fighting for their lives and the lives of their husbands. I had no idea how many might survive if such a battle ever came to pass, but I knew their enemy would be wise not to underestimate them.

The Armies of Heaven were the enemy, Rachel had said. Surely that was wrong. Heaven was where good people went when they died, a happy place full of old friends and smiling faces. How could heaven have an army?

I showed more of my power with the women than with the stronger men. I had every intention of fooling the fallen angels into believing I was essentially worthless as a fellow warrior, a woman with a few clever moves but not much else. With the women I pushed harder, driving them, forcing them to use their wits and every last bit of their skill, just as a good teacher would do. I didn't want these women to die, and I wanted to do what little I could to expand their abilities. The angels could fend for themselves.

At one point I felt Michael's eyes on me, and I knew he stood just inside the open doors to the workout room, in the shadows, so he couldn't be seen. I didn't need to look. I already knew what his gaze felt like, a cool wash over my heated skin as I remembered the feel of his mouth against mine. I licked my lips, searching for his taste, but the salt of the ocean superseded it. I'd missed my chance—he was never going to kiss me again.

I immediately stumbled, deliberately, and went

down in the sand beneath Martha's triumphant cry. By the time I bounded back to my feet, he was gone.

It was simple enough to move farther and farther away from them as I went through my own moves. I had a well-worn series of exercises I went through, and though I toned them down for anyone who seemed to be watching, I was able to move down the beach, away from the others.

I warmed up, stretched, and ran in place for a little to get my muscles ready for the change. And then I took off in a casual sprint, just another runner working on endurance.

By the time I had gone about two miles up the beach, I was feeling less optimistic. There was no sign of civilization, no houses, no border separating Sheol from the rest of the world. I wondered whether we were on an island.

The coastline stayed the same, a mix of grass and stone, the high cliffs to my right, the ocean to my left; otherwise I might have thought I was running in circles. I was beginning to tire a bit, and I fell back into a walk. I was far enough away by now, at least ten miles by my estimation. It would take them too long to catch up with me.

I was hungry. I hadn't had the sense to grab something to eat from the eternally stocked kitchen, but then, I'd taken off without a firm plan. Not the wisest idea, but I was so desperate to leave I'd taken the first chance I got.

It was getting late now, the shadows growing long as I continued along the beach. At this time of year, in late March, the sun here seemed to set early, around six o'clock. I would have hours to keep moving, to ensure my safety. I couldn't afford to let them find me.

The shadow brushed by my consciousness, and I looked up, squinting against the sunlight, as the outline of a huge bird soared by. But it wasn't a bird, and I was an idiot. Because there was no sign beneath their clothes, I had forgotten that the angels were still equipped with one more weapon.

Their wings.

I began to run.

HE SWOOPED DOWN like a bird of prey and caught her midstride, yanking her flailing body against his before he took off, soaring upward, high, higher, until the air grew thin and cold and her struggles slowed, until frost sparkled on the nose he wanted to kiss, the skin he wanted to lick and suck and bite. He shifted her in his arms, cradling her, staring at her pale, soft mouth, and he had the sudden overwhelming urge to breathe warmth into her. His head moved closer, and her eyes opened, looking up at him, as if she knew what he wanted. He jerked back, keeping his gaze focused on the sky rather than her face, until he descended toward Sheol with his annoying, errant wife cradled in his arms.

In truth, he had no idea why he he'd gone after

her. She could have walked for days, weeks, and found nothing, no escape from the future she'd been born to, and it would have taken the decision away from him. She'd taken nothing with her, and he knew she was much smarter than that. Her desperation to get away from him was so strong it had clouded her better judgment.

Good. That would keep her at a distance. That was all he wanted, for her to be out of sight and out of mind. But he didn't want her dying on the beach, alone, in pain. She had so little time left, shorter than the usual frail human existence, and he didn't want any of it to be stolen from her.

By the time he reached the compound she'd begun to stir, and the feel of her warm, strong body in his arms did what he knew it would do. There was nothing wrong with his cock, nothing missing in his desires. He just chose to ignore them. Which was becoming harder as time went on.

He landed lightly outside the french doors and kicked them open, striding into the room and dumping her on her bed. She immediately tried to scramble up, but he simply pushed her back down.

"I'm not going to touch you," he said. "Ever. You don't need to risk your life by running away into nowhere, and trust me, the beach leads absolutely nowhere. The only way out of Sheol is through the gates, and they're guarded, warded, protected. You can't open them. So stop trying to escape, and I promise to leave you alone."

She said nothing. She lay in the middle of the bed. Her dark hair had come loose from its plait, and her face was even paler than usual, her green eyes blazing up at him. It was getting more and more difficult to keep his gaze away from the delicious swell of her breasts, the temptation of her mouth. *No,* he reminded himself sharply. *No.*

"Do I have your word you won't try to escape?"

"No."

"Fine." He spun on his heel and stalked from the room, slamming the door as he went. The locks and wards clicked into place, sealing the room. She would be able to open the windows, to let the sea breeze in, but she wouldn't be able to escape. Let her try the pleasures of house arrest again and see how she liked it.

It suited him perfectly. He needed time to regain his equilibrium. He'd almost kissed her again. He had to be out of his mind. Because if he did, he knew what would follow, as surely as the night followed the day, and he didn't want that. Couldn't want that.

Why not? the voice in his head demanded. *Who would it hurt? Martha says you must. She'll die anyway. Why not?*

One hundred years of celibacy, two hundred years of taking nourishment only from the Source—and it had made him strong, invincible. He had watched history unfold from his place with Uriel, had seen the disasters wrought by lust. It had brought the Fallen to their knees, destroyed cities and worlds.

There was too much at stake to risk losing even one bit of his power.

His skin felt tight, his heart was pounding, and he was still hard, his damned, betraying body telling him what he wouldn't admit. It was a waste of time denying it. He wanted her. Needed her.

He wouldn't take her.

CHAPTER

TWELVE

I DIDN'T MOVE FOR A LONG TIME. AT least this time I didn't have the roiling nausea that had accompanied the first time he'd flown with me, but I didn't want to move. I had too much to think about. About opening my eyes during that short, breathless flight to see him staring down at me. I'd wanted him to kiss me, really kiss me. I'd looked up into his eyes, and if I truly had been a goddess, I would have willed him to put that hard, beautiful mouth against mine, to breathe life and warmth back into me. The longing was so powerful it was like a tangible thing, so strong that I was certain he felt it too; but then he soared upward, into the icy cold night, and everything went black, and I went unkissed. And I wondered if he felt the same longing, the same regret for missed chances.

Finally I rose, walking over to the open window. The moon was high in the sky and a wind had come up, whipping the trees at the base of the cliff, and that strange, aching feeling built, filling my chest, churning my stomach, washing through me with a wave of what I knew was desire. Real, honest, adult desire, something I'd never felt before. I didn't like it.

I needed to eat. I had to stay strong if I was going to have any chance of escape. There was a huge salad with cheese and meat and chickpeas in the fridge, so I wolfed down the entire thing, followed by the ubiquitous Diet Coke, which was improving on further acquaintance. Rather like the Archangel Michael— and that way lay danger. I took a quick shower, changed my clothes, and headed for the door as the moon shone bright overhead.

I needed the sea wind on my upturned face, the moon shining down on me. I felt restless, sexual, at odds with my body and my life, and I needed to move, to run, to work off all this strange, disturbing energy.

The door was locked. I stared at it balefully, but it was impervious to my annoyance. I checked the other door, just to be certain, but of course it was locked as well. People opened locked doors with credit cards, according to the movies. I didn't own one, but there were other forms of plastic in the kitchen that would serve the purpose.

I found a thin, hard spatula and headed back to the front door, prepared to slide it through the crack between door and frame. And then stared in astonishment.

There was no crack. The door and frame were solid, as if carved out of one piece of wood. It was sealed—there was no place to slide the spatula.

The french doors were the same, the joinery gone, smooth wood in its place. But they still had mullioned windowpanes, and in a moment of blind fury I picked up a chair and flung it at the doors.

It bounced back, almost hitting me. With a curse I threw myself at it, with the same results, except I landed sideways on the couch.

I knew a lot of curses. Watch enough movies and you can get very fluent in bad language, and I let it all fly. The rat-fucking bastard had locked me in. Not only that, but he'd put some sort of voodoo whammy on the doors and windows so I couldn't break out.

I was going to kill him.

I pulled myself upright from my ungainly sprawl and glared at the front door. Rachel had insisted that I was a goddess. If that was so, where the fuck were my powers? If I was an ancient Roman goddess of war, surely I could demolish something as simple as a lock?

I knew Latin. I knew eleven languages, and had been in the process of learning new ones when I'd been called to my mother's salon. People used Latin for spells, didn't they? And for unearthly power. And it was certainly the right language for the mythical Victoria Bellona.

I eyed the door, and I made a little deal with

myself. If I could open that door without an axe or a key, then I would accept that I was who they said I was—the goddess of war, here to fight the Armies of Heaven.

It would have to be Latin. I couldn't call on the Prince of Darkness like they did in witchcraft movies, since I had a strong suspicion that the Prince of Darkness would be on the side of the Fallen. As for appealing to the gods, supposedly I was one of them. I'd just go for straightforward Latin. Not a commonly used word such as *aperire*, to open. I needed something more forceful. *Erumpere* was to break open. The imperative form of that would be *erumpite*, wouldn't it? I eyed the door with a baleful glare.

"*Erumpite!*" I said in a ringing voice.

Nothing happened.

"*Effringito!*" I tried again.

Nothing. "*Aperito!*"

I was ready to give up, when something prickled along my arms. It was impossible, of course. Even so, I rose and started toward the door, just on the off chance . . .

It opened. I didn't even have to touch the door-knob. At my approach the door simply popped open, standing ajar, and I stared at it in disbelief.

Well, this was entirely cool. Apparently all I had to do was make a demand in Latin and it would come true. And I was very, very good at Latin.

I checked the doors to the beach, but they were still locked, and I decided not to waste my time with them. One avenue of escape was better than none, and it was getting late. I stepped out into the corridor, moving silently, and headed down the hall. I was seriously annoyed. How dare he try to lock me in?

I had just reached the building's main door when I noticed the faint light coming from the workout room. Shadows flickered, as if someone was moving around in there, and I knew who would be down there in the middle of the night. He hadn't gone straight to his room after locking me in. He'd gone to work off the frustration that roiled within him, frustration that was also threading through my body.

If I had any brains I'd get the hell out of there. Then again, sometimes being a fool was absolutely irresistible. Particularly when I'd get to savor the look on his face when I strolled in.

The doors were open to the night air, that seductive breeze blowing across the dimly lit room. There were several mats strewn around on the floor, but only one man was in the room. He was a blur of grace and speed, spinning, leaping, dancing through the air like a god. He wore no shirt, only the loose white pants he'd had on earlier in the day, and for the first time I got a good look at the tattoos that snaked and swirled around his body. I watched them slide up his lean, muscled torso, around his biceps, encircling his neck, dancing with him as he moved. If I hadn't realized he was a supernatural being before,

I knew it now. No human could leap that high, move that fluidly, dangerously.

He stopped suddenly, and I was afraid he knew I was watching, but he simply walked over and picked up a bucket of water. He poured it over his body, and I watched it sluice down over his chest, his arms, dampening the loose pants so that they clung to him. I gulped for air.

He lifted his head, suddenly intent, though he didn't look in my direction. "How did you get out?"

"Magic. I'm a goddess, remember?" I strolled into the room, determined to prove just how unmoved I was by all that wet, gorgeous male flesh.

"I remember. I didn't think you did."

"I thought I'd give it a try. Harry Potter movies are good for something."

"Harry Potter?" he echoed, clearly confused.

"Don't you watch movies here?"

"No."

I shrugged. "Your loss." Though in fact I'd seen enough movies to last me this lifetime and the next. "A little Latin goes a long way."

He said nothing, watching me. He was faster, deadlier, more graceful, than anyone I'd ever seen in my life, better than the best of the truly impressive warriors I'd watched and sparred with today. Better than Metatron, who'd been suckered so easily; far better than Pedersen. Could I take him?

I moved into the moonlight. "I don't want to be here."

"Tell me something new."

"You don't want me here."

He said nothing, waiting.

"I have a proposal. I'll fight you."

He laughed. I wasn't sure if I'd heard him laugh before, and I could have done without it this time, since it was at my expense. "Don't waste my time," he said.

I bit back my instinctive response. "If I lose, I'll stop trying to escape. I'll be the nice, docile wife and you won't even need to think about me."

"I don't think about you now."

That was a lie, but I didn't call him on it. "What have you got to lose?" I could do it, I was sure of it. I had opened those doors; I had bested their most powerful soldier with barely any effort. I gave him a silky smile. "Are you afraid of being shown up? I could have you on your back in a matter of seconds."

"No," he said, taking a step closer. "I could have you on yours."

My temper flared. "Don't do that!"

"Do what?"

"Pretend that you have even the faintest interest in me sexually. You've made it clear you're willing to risk the fate of the world rather than sleep with me."

I'd shocked him. And then that same slow smile curved his beautiful mouth, and I was lost. The water still glistened on his chest, and something tightened inside me.

"That rankles, does it?" he murmured. "You know as well as I do that it isn't your charms that are lacking."

"I know all about those kinds of excuses. 'It's not you, it's me,'" I said with a trace of bitterness.

He rolled his eyes. "Look, I've been celibate for more than a hundred years. I'm not about to change my mind for no reason."

"The fate of the world is no reason?" I shot back.

Now he seemed genuinely amused, and he took another step toward me. "Are you trying to talk me into it?"

"No! I just want to get the hell out of here, and I'll do anything I can to make that happen."

"Including fucking me?"

The word shocked me. Not that I hadn't heard it before, not that he hadn't used it before. But in this dark, heated atmosphere, it suddenly felt real, visceral. Possible.

I could call his bluff. My palms were sweating, but I wasn't going to let him win. "Anything."

I couldn't read the expression in his eyes. It looked almost feral, and for a moment a very real fear sliced through me. Not that he would win. But that my victory might defeat me in ways I couldn't even imagine.

"Yes," he said.

For a moment I didn't understand him. "Yes, what?"

"Yes, I'll fight you for your right to leave. If you

win, you get to walk away, leave this place, and you won't even remember you were here."

"I've got a very good memory." Was I feeling triumph? Or an odd sense of disappointment?

"We have ways of making you forget."

I blanched at that, but shook it off. "Deal."

"You haven't asked me what happens if I win." His voice matched his body, beautiful, dangerous, seductive.

I tried to sound bored. "I told you. I stay put and leave you alone."

He shook his head. "No. I fuck you, *then* you stay put and leave me alone."

I froze. His words shook me, the cool, insinuating tone that seemed to slip under my skin. I tried to pull myself together. "So you've decided the fate of the world deserves that kind of sacrifice? Who talked you into it?"

"Not a sacrifice," he said softly. "And I'm not taking your blood, only your—no, I'll spare you that particular word. You don't like *fuck*—you're hardly ready for the mother of all swearwords. I'll take your body. I've decided to call your bluff. I don't think you're likely to pay up, and the sooner you face that, the sooner I won't even have to think about you. We'll get it done and get it over with."

Fury swept through me. For a moment I had considered what it might be like to lie beneath him, and my body had reacted with fierce, hot longing. Had he known what even I hadn't been completely aware of? That beneath my determination to get the hell away from him—from here—was a dark, secret need for him?

"You're a cold-blooded bastard, aren't you?" I said. "Pissing me off isn't the best way to win."

"On the contrary. When people are angry, they tend to make mistakes, react emotionally. In battle you need to be cool, removed."

"No one would ever accuse you of reacting emotionally," I snapped.

"No, they wouldn't." He took a step back, dismissing me. "Go back to your room, Victoria Bellona, if you're not ready to play."

The last remaining hold on my temper broke. "My name is Tory," I snarled. "And I'm going to wipe the floor with you."

He laughed again, and this time he sounded almost happy. Of course he was—he lived for fighting, for warfare, for battle. "We have a bargain, *Tory*?" The emphasis on my name was derisive.

I kicked off my shoes. "We have a bargain."

MICHAEL DIDN'T STOP to think about it. He knew what he was doing, knew it was stupid and rash, knew he'd wanted any excuse to put his hands on her, and now he finally had it. As long as he didn't take her blood, the prophecy would remain unfulfilled.

He knew she was good—she'd tried hard to hide her fighting skills, but the moment Metatron had gone down for the first time, he'd known. By the time she'd flattened Metatron again, he was surprised everyone else in the place hadn't recognized just how dangerous his wife was. But she was as good at dissimulating as she was at combat, and he'd watched her as she moved, luring her opponents, pushing them just enough until she faked her defeat. She'd done more good for the women than he'd been able to do in weeks. There was no way she was going to stay in her rooms after this—he would put her in charge of the wives, secure in the knowledge that she would bring out the best in them while he concentrated on the Fallen.

He gave her a smile calculated to drive her temper higher still. He'd given her a boon, warning her that rage would only weaken her, but she'd been too angry to listen. Combat was more than blocking, more than attack and defense. It was strategy, diagnosing your opponent's style to see three moves ahead. When you were filled with anger, you couldn't see things as clearly.

He stretched out a hand and beckoned her mockingly. "I'll give you the first hit."

A second later he was flat on his back, her knees on his shoulders, pinning him down. She held him for a brief moment longer than she should have, simply because he'd been so shocked, but a moment later she was off him, flying through the air to land on her feet on the mat halfway across the room.

The move should have slammed her against the

wall. He flexed his shoulders, watching her. "I'm impressed. You surprised me."

"It's never wise to underestimate your opponent," she said smugly, dancing closer.

He smiled at her pleasantly, then moved, sweeping her legs out from under her in one swift stroke. She didn't fall, but caught herself and flipped back up, a maneuver she shouldn't have been able to do. He must have given away some of his surprise, because she looked even more smug. "Goddess, remember?"

A moment later she was flat on her back and he was on top of her, straddling her the same way she'd straddled him, his knees digging into her shoulders. "Angel, remember?"

She flipped him off effortlessly, and they were both on their feet again, staring at each other. She wasn't breathing heavily. Neither was he.

He could sense her pulse, full and strong, and a sudden raging hunger swept through him, so shocking that for a moment he froze. He'd never felt anything like it, that powerful surge of need that could have brought him to his knees more easily than all her moves.

She slammed into him, flattening him, straddling him, and for a moment he didn't move, staring up at her, at the sweat-damp skin and the blood throbbing in her neck, inhaling the sweetness of her scent. He wrapped his fingers around her hips, his thumbs pressing against her slowly, rhythmically.

She froze as well, looking down at him. Her pupils were huge in the dimly lit room, and she was beginning to breathe more rapidly. Her small breasts beneath the tank top were perfect, and he wanted his mouth on them. Needed to taste them, more than he needed her blood, and he needed her blood to survive.

"Tory." He called her, and slowly, slowly she leaned down, as if pulled by some invisible thread, her mouth coming closer, moving toward his, and he lifted his hand to slide beneath her heavy fall of hair, to pull her closer. Then the spell broke and she tore herself away, with such violence that she went spinning across the room, knocking over the small lamp he kept lit while he did his nightly workout.

The room was plunged into darkness, and he wondered whether she would run. He could sense it almost as if he were feeling it himself, her powerful need to escape, to get away from him, from what was between them. But something—pride?—stopped her, and he knew she wouldn't leave until she bested him.

And he knew she couldn't best him. They could pound each other into the floor, but she would never win. The question remained: could he?

He leapt to his feet effortlessly. His eyes were already accustomed to the faint moonlight streaming through the windows overhead. She stood there, her skin dusted with silver, her nipples hard. It was possible that the fighting aroused her.

But it wasn't the fight. *He* aroused her. It was what lay between them; he knew it as well as she did. Maybe better. Martha had been right all along. Tory wasn't just a means to an end, she was his bonded mate; and whether she lived a month or lived a century, nothing would change. She was his.

For better or worse.

CHAPTER
THIRTEEN

H E WAS STRONG. STRONGER THAN anyone I'd ever fought before, stronger than I would have thought possible. Fast, graceful, wicked, he blocked my every move. He threw me as if I weighed nothing, and for every slight gain I made he countered it with a stronger one. He learned fast, and he was merciless, slamming me into the floor, even though I managed to get up each time; he couldn't have known I'd be so resilient. With any other human, the battle would be long over, the loser a heap of broken bones and blood in the middle of the floor.

With any *other* human? With any human. The more he pushed me, the more I was forced to admit the inevitable. I wasn't human. No ordinary person could withstand the punishment he was inflicting on me and keep fighting back, bloody but unbowed. He knew it too—I sensed he was looking for any chance to stop this. He hit me at the back of the legs, and I went down, rolled over, and sprang back up, kicking him in the kidneys. He grunted, the only recognition of what should have been a debilitating blow, and caught my ankle as I kicked again, flipping me.

I slammed down this time, my ribs aching, my breath coming in deep rasps, my heart pounding. He was breathing heavily as well, though not as much as I was, and had a cut over one eye. He came to stand over me like a conquering hero. "You accept defeat?"

I managed a convincing snuffle. "I . . . I . . ." I began, trying to sound tearful. And then I spun upward, higher than I would have thought I could, kicking him in the jaw before landing back in a crouch.

His head snapped back, and I wondered if I'd broken his neck. I didn't wait to see. I kicked again, hard in the middle of his flat, muscled stomach, and he went down, spread-eagle on one of the mats, clawing for breath.

I had him. I leapt on him, my sharp knees aiming for his solar plexus, ready to deliver the blow that would render him either unconscious or dead, and I was in full battle mode, not caring.

A moment later I was underneath him, his legs wrapped around mine, his hands on my wrists like manacles, his hips pinning me, his chest crushing me.

I tried to slam my head into his, but he reared up

out of my reach. I put all my strength into it, trying to throw him off me, but he was inexorable, and I was trapped, staked out on the mat like a butterfly, all my weapons spent.

I considered spitting at him, but it would do no good. I let my head fall back against the thick mat, closing my eyes, panting, trying to get my breathing under control.

"I hate you," I muttered, refusing to look at him.

"Where's your grace in defeat?" he taunted me, and I hated him even more. "We wagered, we fought, you lost."

I opened my eyes so that he could see the complete disgust and fury in my gaze. I still couldn't breathe properly, and I didn't like him on top of me. He was too heavy, and I wanted him off me, away from me, not gazing down at me with that speculative expression on his beautiful face.

"Great. Congratulations. Now let me up," I snapped.

He was looking at me with a cool, detached air. "You got too cocky," he said. "You thought you had me, and you didn't watch closely enough."

"You can instruct me later. In the meantime, I'm tired and I want to go to bed."

"So do I."

It wasn't until that moment that I remembered our conversation. What he would do if he won. My heart, which had just begun to slow after the exertion, suddenly began slamming in my chest once more. "You weren't serious." My voice wasn't quite as strong as I'd hoped.

"We wagered. You lost."

"We didn't wager *that*."

"We did," he said.

I lay beneath him, quiet, seemingly defeated. "I don't want to."

"I don't care."

He had no way to anticipate the sudden jerk of my body, my last attempt to flip him and escape. I centered the energy, drawing it to me, and released it in one powerful surge.

And remained motionless, trapped beneath him.

A shaft of moonlight lit his face, and he looked oddly tender as he bowed his head toward mine.

In my entire life I'd only kissed one boy, Johann, and he had been almost as innocent as I was back then. I'd never been kissed by someone who knew how to do it. Michael did.

I'd expected his mouth to be punishing. Instead, his lips brushed against mine, merely a touch, and I knew I could keep fighting. Could slam my head against him, could bite him.

But I wasn't going to. I wanted his mouth, his kiss. I was hungry, hungry for life, hungry for him, all thought of escape disappearing as his lips touched mine again, soft, lingering. I closed my eyes, savoring the feel of him, the taste of him, ready for this.

He pressed my mouth open with his, and the touch of his tongue was a shock. It was disturbingly intimate, his tongue pushing into my mouth, as his body would push into mine.

His tongue caught mine, and he was licking me, biting me, and the aches and pains in my body disappeared, until the only sensations were centered on my mouth and the sudden, clenching need between my legs.

He was there, pressing against me, a solid ridge of desire, and I gave myself up to the dark, insidious pleasure of his tongue in my mouth. It was dangerous, this hot, dark place that called to me, drew me in. His mouth, his hard body, his golden skin, his scent—everything was intoxicating. It was the solid expression of what had called to me when I was locked in my room, called to me with the night breeze and the smell of the sea. I stopped fighting what I had always known. I longed for him, ached for him, the feeling visceral and overwhelming.

He'd lifted his weight off me, only his hips pinioning me, and he released my wrists, moving one hand down between us, touching my breast. More heat suffused me, and I moaned.

He took his mouth away, and I wanted to cry out in protest as he sat back on his heels, taking all his weight from me. "Take off your shirt," he said roughly.

I was so disoriented that I looked up at him, uncomprehending, so he simply took the hem of my tank top and stripped it off. I lay half-naked beneath him, my small breasts exposed to his critical gaze. I didn't move, didn't try to cover myself—that would have been a coward's way. I simply let him look, judge.

A faint smile crossed his austere face. "If I have to fall once more from grace, at least you're going to make it worthwhile." His hands encircled my waist, then slid up my ribs to cover my breasts, cupping them, his thumbs brushing against the hard nipples, and I made a soft sound of need that thoroughly shamed me.

He leaned down and kissed me again, a soft, lingering kiss, before his mouth moved down, and I could feel him at my neck, sucking at the vein he was supposed to pierce, and I steeled myself, wondering why the ache between my legs was intensifying at the thought.

His teeth grazed my skin, but he moved lower, and I choked at the first touch of his tongue against one breast. The sensation was almost painful, and I put my hands on his shoulders, not sure what I wanted him to do.

It was the first time I'd touched him without wanting to hurt him. His skin was so warm beneath my hands, warm and alive, and his tattoos danced beneath my touch, moving across his skin with sensuous grace. I couldn't read the markings, didn't want to, but I felt their power, and I felt their need. I was clutching him, holding tightly, as his hand reached for the drawstring of my loose pants.

Yes, I thought. *This is what I've wanted, what I've*

needed, for so long. I want sex, I want life, I want love. Don't stop, please, don't stop.

His mouth covered my breast, sucking it, and I arched up, my hips reflexively searching for him. He made a low growl in his throat, one of need, one of dominance, but I didn't care. He could take me any way he wanted, as long as he took me.

He moved to the other breast. The cool night air hit my wet skin, another absurd arousal, and I could feel myself slipping into some thick cocoon of desire where no thought of the future, no worries about repercussions, nothing existed but the moment and the feel of his skin against mine.

He blew on my breast, and my fingers dug deeper into his shoulders. "Don't stop," I whispered, half-terrified he'd pull away. "Please, don't stop."

He froze. And then he began to curse, low and foul.

I didn't move as the cold washed over me, the knowledge that he was going to stop. I'd known it instinctively, and I wondered if I could conquer him in *this* battle, push him over and move on him, take him in my mouth, wipe out any reservations, any doubts.

I couldn't. I pulled myself together as he drew back, anger on his face, and I didn't know if the anger was for him or for me.

"No," he said flatly. He rose in one fluid motion, then tossed my discarded tank top at me before turning away. "Get dressed."

I was furious. I wanted to hurt him, rip him apart, but I already knew he was stronger than I. "No."

He said nothing, his strong, beautiful back to me, and the elaborate markings curled around his shoulder blades where his wings should be. I had fooled myself, forgetting who and what he was. An angel, for God's sake. And I'd been about to give myself to him. Hell, about to force myself on him.

His face was hidden, the shape of his close-cropped head giving no hint of what he was feeling. Without another word, he walked away, out the open door, to the ocean.

I jumped to my feet and ran after him, determined to catch him and haul him back, determined to make him face what he didn't want to face; but on the doorstep I stopped, staring up in wonder.

He'd taken flight. Wings spread out from his back, dark, graceful, arched, as he soared upward, and I watched him disappear into the night sky, a gorgeous creature of myth and story.

I would have given anything to follow him, up into the sky, carried by the wind. I was a goddess, but all the longing in the world couldn't make me sprout wings and follow him into the night, no matter how much I wanted to.

I looked at the tank top in my hands, then back up at the night-dark sky. I wasn't going back to my room to wallow in misery. I wasn't going to run away, not while everything I valued lay trashed. I wasn't ready to accept defeat.

His room was easy enough to find, and there was no mistaking it. It was a monk's cell, a stone floor with no rugs to soften it, unadorned walls, a narrow cot against the wall. I stripped off the rest of my clothes, folding them neatly and placing them on the cold floor, then climbed, naked, into the hard bed and pulled the rough-textured sheet over me.

And I waited.

MICHAEL FLEW HIGH, higher still, until the air was thin and ice crystallized on his wings, before he spun, circling, spearing through the night, then spiraling down into the sea. The icy water surrounded him, the familiar peace moving through his body. Healing, calm, the water cradled him, and he floated, his mind a blank.

He didn't want to think, didn't want to feel. He wanted oblivion for a few short hours. But the healing waters of the ocean couldn't give him what he needed, couldn't take away the taste of her mouth, the feel of her breasts, the sounds she made. It couldn't wash away the heated desire that still danced just beneath his skin.

He lost track of time. When he finally emerged from the water, the night was nearing its end, faint tendrils of light appearing over the mountain behind the compound. He still had a couple of hours before training started. He could fall into his bed and sleep.

He rinsed the seawater off in the outdoor shower, stripped off his sodden pants, and walked through the quiet building. She could have run away again, but right now he couldn't gather the energy to go in search of her. She hadn't gone far. He could feel her presence; he'd know in his bones if she'd left. She was probably barricaded in her bedroom, ready to kill him if he came near her.

Which was the way he wanted it. He needed her green eyes cold with fury, her mouth set in anger. He couldn't fight this on his own. He needed her to fight it too.

He pushed open the door to his tiny room and shut it behind him, not bothering to turn on the light. The small window set high in the wall let in more than enough light to see the outlines of the few pieces of furniture he allowed himself. He could see his bed in the corner.

And then he could see the figure lying in it, huddled between his sheets, her long black hair spread out on the pillow. Flight had availed him nothing. The cold sea hadn't cooled his blood; the night air hadn't banked the heat that surged through him.

She must have heard him come in. She rose on one elbow, looking at him, and the sheet fell away, exposing one small, perfect breast. And he needed to suck at it, to slide his hand between her legs and feel the wetness of her desire. He'd tried everything he could to fight this.

For the first time in his limitless existence, he had lost a battle.

Her eyes ran over his nude body, and he saw

her reaction to the jutting push of his cock before she hid it. "I always pay my debts." Her voice was deceptively calm, but he could hear the faint tremor beneath it.

He kept his expression unreadable, helped by the shadows in the room. "When did you last have sex?"

The question startled her, and she had to think for a moment. "Seven years ago."

"And how many times have you had sex? How many partners?"

"None of your—"

"How many?"

Her mouth tightened, when he wanted it soft and giving. "One partner. Three times."

"Fuck."

"Yeah," she said.

"I could lock you in your room again. I'm stronger than you are."

"You could. But I'd escape again."

"I could let you go."

"You're that desperate not to have sex with me?" she said. Her eyes lowered to the middle of his body. "It doesn't look like it."

He walked over to the bed and pulled the sheet all the way down. She was naked, of course, and her pale skin was perfect in the early-morning light, the small patch of curls between her legs sweet and enticing. The room was too warm, yet her nipples were erect.

"You're not paying a debt," he said. "Are you?"

She hesitated. "No," she said, and leaned back against the pillow. "And you aren't doing your duty, are you?"

"No." He knelt on the bed, straddling her carefully. There was barely enough room for the two of them. It didn't matter. They were going to be so close they wouldn't need extra space. "No," he said again, moving between her legs, lifting them. He took her mouth, her sweet, inexperienced mouth, with his, and then simply pushed inside her, hard, knowing she'd be wet and ready for him.

He slid deep, her body clutching at him, and he groaned at the sheer, celestial pleasure of it. This was perfection, this was creation, this was everything he needed, everything worth living for. He pushed deeper still, and her legs wrapped around his hips, and he savored the shivers of response from inside her.

He broke the kiss, looking down at her. Her eyes were closed, but she opened them then, looking into his with a connection as deep, as intimate, as his cock inside her. Her hands cupped his face, her thumbs brushing against his mouth. "I told you not to stop," she whispered.

"My mistake," he said as he began to move.

He knew women's bodies so well, and he'd forgotten nothing. He was acutely aware of her response as his own fiery need fought for control. She was resisting it, he realized, trying to clamp down on each burgeoning peak, struggling to stop her climax, and through his blind haze of lust he wondered if she was holding off to maximize her pleasure. Or was she regretting her choice?

He pushed in deep, holding still. He couldn't keep driving toward completion while she fought it. She was frightened, he realized suddenly.

He straightened his arms, looking down at her. "What are you doing?"

His wife, his fierce warrior, looked almost tearful. "Something's wrong. Something's wrong with my body."

"Am I hurting you?" If he was, he would have to stop. But it wasn't pain lashing through her, he was sure of it. It was frustrated desire, fighting to get out.

She shook her head. "It just feels . . . upsetting."

He didn't smile. She wouldn't thank him for his amusement. He moved down over her, relishing the stab of her hard nipples against his chest, and kissed her. Their bodies were slick with sweat, and he could feel the shivers racking her body.

He pulled out almost completely, and she let out a cry of loss. He slid his hand down her stomach to her clitoris, touching her as he suddenly slammed into her, and she shattered, her body clamping around him. She shrieked against his shoulder, in shock, in pleasure, her fingers digging into him so tightly he would have thought she'd draw blood. That was another arousal, and he thrust, again and again, hard, riding her orgasm, prolonging it, and when she finally fell back, limp, he let himself go, releasing his seed into her, filling her, his head dropping to the pillow beside her as his wings unfurled to lock around them, cradling them in softness. Her neck was before him, soft and vulnerable, and he was overcome with the need for her. He nipped it just lightly enough to draw blood, which he licked from her sweat-damp skin, the taste of it better than the ambrosia he'd once known. He felt his fangs elongate, just as he felt his cock harden again, and he knew it would take nothing to sink through her skin to the vein pumping beneath the flesh. But he didn't.

He kissed her neck, savoring it. And then he rolled off her, pulling her with him on the narrow cot, keeping her tight against his body, his cock hard inside her. He liked that. He could sleep like that, safe in her body, her blood in his mouth, his arms around her, the sweet scent of her all around him. He could sleep like that, when he seldom allowed himself to sleep. He could be at peace for the first time in his memory.

And he slept.

CHAPTER
FOURTEEN

I LAY IN HIS ARMS, UNMOVING, AS THE pounding of my heart slowly returned to normal. The room felt cool, but he was warm, so warm, and I wanted to burrow closer. I wanted to lick the sweat from his shoulder, to rub my skin against his. The explosions that had rocked my body were still simmering beneath the surface, and I was ready to explode again.

I hadn't realized it could feel like that. It wasn't as if I hadn't pleasured myself, locked up in my prison, but something had always stopped me after that first little peak of pleasure. I'd turned over and gone to sleep, edgy and unsatisfied, figuring I wasn't doing it right.

I'd needed a man. And not just any man—I'd thought I loved Johann, but what I'd done with him had no connection to what had just happened with Michael. My breasts were acutely sensitive, my womb ached, and I still wanted more.

The very thought horrified me so much that I slid out of bed without thinking. By the time I backed up I realized he was still asleep. He hadn't even noticed I'd pulled away.

I stood there in the dawning light, watching him. He was beautiful as he slept, the fresh stubble on his chin a golden-brown color, matching the close-cropped hair. With his cool, distant eyes closed he looked like a different man. One capable of kindness, tenderness. Not the warrior I knew him to be, but someone almost human.

But I shouldn't fool myself. He wasn't human, and neither was I. I touched my neck, then looked at my hand. Just the faintest trace of blood. I thought he hadn't drunk from me, but clearly he'd done the bare minimum. So the world wouldn't end and the Fallen would be happy. See me jumping for joy.

I moved back to the bed silently, reaching for my neatly folded clothes. He slept like the dead, and as I stared at him I noticed for the first time the dark circles under his eyes. He was a man—an angel—who didn't sleep well.

I could see him clearly in the growing light, his smooth back, the line of elegant tattoos snaking around his shoulder blades. No wings. Where did they come from? Did they just magically appear when he needed them? Apparently so.

Holding my clothes to my chest, I slipped out into the hallway, half-afraid I'd run into some early riser. Still, I figured running into a stranger when I was stark naked was better than risking waking Michael. I closed the door silently, then yanked on my clothes. I went from mistake to mistake, and if I stayed any longer I'd be screwed.

I stifled a snort of laughter. Or not. As if things weren't complicated enough, now Michael and I would be doing a little dance of would we or wouldn't we, and I couldn't stand the thought of it. He said there was only one way out, through the main gate. Okay, I'd find that main gate, or climb up the cliff face using sheer willpower. Whatever I was going to do, I wasn't going to look him in the face again. Not after what we'd done, the way he'd touched me, the way I'd lost myself so completely in his arms. He now held too dangerous a weapon over me. A wise warrior knew when to retreat and regroup. And when to run like hell.

As I stepped outside, streaks of early sunlight crept over the cliffs behind the house, spangling the water with jewel-bright drops, and for a moment I wondered if I had time to strip off my clothes and jump in. The cool salt air called to me.

I ignored it. Once I escaped from here, there would be any number of oceans to find. Once I escaped, I would be free.

I'd forgotten my shoes. They were in the workout room—I'd need them if I was going to travel any distance. I turned back toward the door, when a faint prickling stirred the hair at the back of my neck.

I blamed Michael. If I hadn't been so bleary from

the hours I'd spent in his bed, I would have been more alert. A lifetime of training, and all it took was a moment of inattention, as a shadow passed behind me, pain exploded in my head, and the slate pathway rushed up to meet me.

MICHAEL'S EYES FLEW open. For a moment he didn't move, trying to orient himself. He was in his own bed, naked, the way he usually slept. But something felt different. *He* felt different, and it took him only a moment to remember. The feel of her was still imprinted on his skin, as if holding her had made a permanent change to his flesh. The scent of her, flowers and sex, spiked his morning arousal. She'd left, thank God. Because otherwise he'd be inside her right now, he'd be taking her blood, and what they'd done under cover of darkness would be a very different thing in the saner light of day.

He sat up, shaking his head to clear the errant thoughts. He'd slept. He'd actually slept, for the first time in recent memory. Not that he needed much sleep—he was built to survive on very little, and as long as he trained he was fine. But it had been too long since he'd slept even a few minutes, and his body was filled with an intense satisfaction.

Or maybe it was something other than sleep that had filled his body with intense satisfaction.

It had been a mistake. He knew that, and he couldn't afford to let it happen again. He had enough willpower to topple cities, and had done so under

Uriel's savage direction. One lone female would be simple enough to control compared to the other creatures he'd battled and bested for millennia.

Except that she wasn't one lone female. She was Victoria Bellona, Goddess of War. She was Tory, soft and vulnerable, shattering in his arms, beneath his touch. Tory, the taste of her blood lingering in his mouth, teasing him with what he could have, should have. Would never have. It had been too damned close to a complete surrender. Once he pierced her vein and drank deeply, she'd be doomed.

And he'd slaughtered too many innocents.

He rose, heading out into the hallway, past the workout room where last night had started, walking straight into the ocean. The ocean would heal him, clear away the confusion. It would bring him peace, wash her memory, her touch, her scent, from his body, and he would emerge renewed, invulnerable, never to touch her again. The healing waters would free him of this obsession.

The sea was frigid, and he sliced through it, swimming steadily, working his muscles, letting the blessed relief of hard work thrum through him. When he was out so far that the house was merely a speck in the distance, he dove, deep into the very heart of the ocean, so deep he could feel the pressure of the water all around him. And then he let go, floating, his eyes closed as he drew the power of the water into him, washing away uncertainty and doubt, washing away weakness and confusion.

He didn't want it. Didn't want the answer he was getting. Humans were always complaining. "Lord, show me a sign," they said. And then, "Not that sign."

This wasn't what he wanted. He opened his eyes, as if that might change what he knew to be true. Opened his eyes to see a shark slide by, then turn gracefully, heading back for another look.

Michael remained still, meeting the creature's black, merciless eyes. A predator, a warrior, just as he was. They recognized each other, but there was no need to test their skills. The shark brushed against him, a strange sort of greeting, and disappeared into the sea, in search of easier prey. Or in search of its mate.

Did sharks mate for life? Presumably not; they were solitary creatures. As was he. But the ocean was telling him otherwise. The ocean was saying what his body had told him, what his heart had told him, what his stubborn brain had told him, and he'd ignored it.

Tory was his mate. For less than a month, and then she would die. And running away from it wouldn't change that truth.

He kicked, moving upward toward the light, feeling the pressure of the water ease away, until he spun upward, released into the warm morning air, feeling the sun wash over him as he unfurled his wings. He could talk to her, he supposed. He could control the raging need inside him, the beast that should never have been released in the first place. He could—

It hit him like a bolt of lightning, and he began to fall, tumbling toward the rocky cliffs. Righting himself, he landed on the ledge above the compound as he realized what had been troubling him all along, the nagging emptiness that he'd ignored as part of his unsuitable desire for her.

She was gone. It was that absence that had woken him from the first sound sleep he'd had in what felt like decades. That emptiness had driven him into the sea. Tory was no longer in Sheol, and she was in trouble.

IT WAS COLD, dark, and terrible. I couldn't see, couldn't breathe, wrapped in some kind of enveloping shroud as we moved higher and higher. I was in the arms of an angel, and there was no safety or comfort.

I tried to struggle out of the covering, but the arms that were holding me loosened, and for one breathless, terrifying moment I thought he was going to let go of me, let me plummet to my death, either into the merciless depth of the ocean or to smash against the unforgiving earth.

Who held me? Had Michael decided to get rid of me for good? He'd sworn he wouldn't touch me, and within forty-eight hours we'd been in his bed.

It was getting colder, and I knew my kidnapper was moving higher, higher still, where the atmosphere was so thin I couldn't catch my breath, smothered as I was by the cloth.

I was blacking out, losing consciousness, and I wondered if he was simply going to kill me this way, by cold and lack of oxygen. Everything was fading, and even though I had no idea whom I could trust, I couldn't help it. The last sound I made before I lost consciousness was a pitiful cry for help.

"Michael."

MICHAEL HEARD HER. Calling his name, desperate, afraid. His warrior bride was afraid, and he needed to find her.

He had to fight the unnerving panic. He closed his eyes, trying to sense her, picture the places she might be. She was nowhere on the beach—he would feel her life force if she were. Unless she was dead.

But that was impossible—Sheol was safety personified. The gates were still barred, and she had to be hidden somewhere. Unless someone had flown her away. Unless, once more, a traitor lurked in their midst.

She was no longer in Sheol. He knew it with a feeling of dread. She was gone, and therefore someone—some angel—had taken her. He landed hard, moving through the annex purposefully. It took him a moment to pull on clothes, and he caught the scent of her, of them, on his sheets. She smelled like jasmine, and he cursed, heading for her rooms.

Of course she was gone. But nothing had been taken. No change of clothes, no food had been eaten, she hadn't even taken a shower. In fact, she hadn't been back here since she'd left him—he would know it, sense it, if she had. Would smell the lingering, erotic trace of jasmine and sex as she moved through the room. He resisted the impulse to slam the door behind him, stalking down the corridor in a mix of fury and panic. She hadn't run this time. He knew it. She had cried out for him. She was in danger.

"What's wrong?" The voice startled him enough that he jumped, irrational hope warring with despair. He turned to see Asbel standing there, watching him with a concerned expression.

"Have you seen Tory?" he demanded, shocked that his voice was so raw.

"Tory? Oh, you mean the goddess. Why don't you ask Rachel?" Asbel suggested, nodding toward the shore, and Michael cursed. Azazel and his wife were walking by the edge of the water, holding hands. He wanted to snarl.

Rachel was the very last person he wanted to talk to. She was a far cry from the usually docile Fallen wives, possibly because she had once been a demon— *the* demon, the Lilith—and he still wasn't convinced she hadn't found a way to tap into her ancient powers. Besides, he'd gotten the clear impression that Rachel considered herself Tory's champion, against *him*.

"What's wrong?" Azazel demanded when Michael reached them.

"Tory's gone." He glared at Rachel. "Did you help her? Do something to take her away from me?"

"Take her away from *you*?" she said. "I thought you didn't want any part of her. Or is it only a particular part you were interested in?"

His already shaky temper flared. "She's in trouble," he snapped. "Someone's taken her. Did you have anything to do with it?"

"Of course we didn't," Azazel said calmly. "We need her. We need you to cooperate. We were coming here to talk to you both, to try to convince you—"

The last thing he wanted to hear was Azazel telling him he had to have sex. Not now.

"It's been taken care of." His voice was still raw. "Bedded and blooded. So where the fuck is she?"

Rachel looked even more surprised. "I don't believe I've ever seen the stoic Archangel Michael so wound up."

He wanted to snarl, but he kept himself under control. Azazel was very protective of his wife, and any disrespect would result in a confrontation. Right now he didn't have the time for politics. "This isn't about me, Rachel," he said in a tightly controlled voice. "This is about her."

"About Tory." Rachel used the name deliberately, like a prod. Of course she would notice that he'd avoided calling her by name.

"About Tory," he agreed. "She's not in Sheol."

Rachel's amusement vanished. "She has to be."

"She's not. I heard her call me. In fact, I think that's what woke me up. Someone took her, and I felt her struggle."

Azazel looked grave. "We'd best tell Raziel right away. He'll send someone to check the gate, but if that's still intact, then there's no way anyone could get in here."

"What if he was already in?"

The expression on Azazel's face matched his own foreboding. "You can't think we have another traitor!"

Michael hadn't even realized Asbel was still with them until he spoke up. "There could be. If it comes to it, my money's on Metatron. She humiliated him in the workout room, and he's never made friends with any of the Fallen. I think he'd do anything he could to get back to Uriel."

"How could someone want to get back to Uriel? He's a soul-killing bastard," Rachel protested.

"He could destroy more than her soul," Michael said. "You're right, Asbel. Metatron was his chief angel for millennia, and he's the logical suspect. If he brought the goddess to the Dark City, I expect the archangel would allow him to stay."

The blood drained from Rachel's face, leaving her ghostly pale, a look Michael hadn't seen on her since they'd brought her broken body here—broken by the Dark City. No wonder she was frozen, saying nothing. She'd managed to escape, but not before they'd had a chance to torture her.

Asbel broke in. "Why assume Tory was taken to the Dark City? Maybe someone just took pity on her and flew her out of here."

Michael controlled his start of irritation. Asbel had always been quiet and unassuming; suddenly he was a voice of reason when Michael least wanted to hear it. "We all know that's not true. Uriel must have her."

Rachel closed her eyes for a moment. The slight shudder that ripped through her lean body told him everything, and a blind fury closed in around him.

It was gone the moment it hit, and he focused on Rachel. "I'm going to bring her back."

"You can't!" Asbel protested. "You're needed here. There's no guarantee that that's where she's gone, or even if anyone's taken her. And if they have . . . you know what Beloch is like. She's probably already dead. If she's lucky."

The look Michael gave him would have frozen a hardier soul. "Are you telling me what I should do, Asbel?"

He shook his head. "Of course not, Michael."

"I'll tell you what I'm wondering," Rachel said in a shaky voice. "I'm wondering why you suddenly care so damned much."

"None of your damned business," he snapped.

"The training . . ." Asbel began, his voice trailing away beneath Michael's glare.

For a moment Michael couldn't move, torn between duty and the overwhelming, crushing need to get to Tory. And for the first time in the eons of his existence, duty lost. "Go. Tell Raziel what has happened. He will know what to do."

"This is a bad idea," Asbel said.

But he couldn't be worried about bad ideas. Without another word he spread his wings in the misty morning light and soared up, up into the milky thickness of clouds.

The Dark City awaited him, the world of pain and punishment, the home of murderous Beloch and the vicious Truth Breakers and the guilt that ran through Michael like blood. It was past time he faced it. They'd taken Tory.

He was ready to kill again.

CHAPTER
FIFTEEN

EVERYTHING HURT. SO BADLY THAT I didn't want to move, didn't even want to open my eyes. First things first—I definitely didn't want to throw up. If I stayed very still and took calm, even breaths, the nausea would pass. As long as I didn't move, I was okay.

My stomach roiled, then slowly, slowly settled, at least enough for me to consider opening my eyes, though I had no intention of moving any other part of my body. Wherever I was smelled like mold and death, and I briefly considered whether I even wanted to look.

Curiosity got the better of me. I opened my eyes to blackness.

Okay, fine. Screw it, I needed more sleep anyway. My stomach still hadn't decided whether it was going to continue doing the dance from hell or go back to behaving itself, and pain moved through my muscles like a machine intent on destruction.

I fought back the only way I could. I surrendered to the darkness and slept.

WHEN I WOKE for the second time. the darkness had faded. I tilted my head, very carefully, and saw a small, narrow window up high in one wall, letting in a gray, fitful light, so gray that everything around me seemed colorless. I looked down at my own body. Still faintly pink flesh, and I could see fading bruises from my sparring match with Michael. But I didn't want to think about that—or what had followed.

I sat up, very slowly, determined not to make a sound even though I felt stiff and sore. The only way past the pain was through it, I knew that. I looked around, taking in my surroundings.

A cell. There was no other word for it, and not a monastic cell like the room I didn't want to think about, Michael's room. This was a prison cell. The narrow iron bed was covered with gray-toned bedding, the walls made out of gray stone. There was a bucket in the corner, and I had the uneasy suspicion that that was to be my plumbing. Fortunately I had the bladder of a camel, because I was not—I repeat, *not*—using a bucket.

I glanced up at the ceiling. No security cameras in sight. So why was I so certain that someone was watching me? Because someone most definitely was—malevolent eyes followed my every move as I slowly got to my feet.

There was a narrow wooden door in the wall opposite the tiny window. It was locked, though I couldn't see how. I muttered the Latin I had used when Michael had locked me in, but nothing happened. I tested the wood to see whether I was capable of splintering it, but I knew immediately that it wouldn't give underneath my strongest kicks. I was stuck here until someone wanted to let me out.

I shook my body, trying to work out the kinks. The stiffness was fading, and in a little while I could ignore it completely. I looked at the window set high in the wall. Too small for me to climb through, but at least I could get an idea of where I was. Did Michael have some kind of prison cell for people who managed to break through his powerful self-control? Some kind of oubliette where he could toss me and forget about me? Was it even Michael who'd brought me here? I didn't think so, my latent instincts kicking in. Whoever had brought me here needed to know I wasn't about to go gentle into that good night. I went back to the narrow, tumbled bed, noticing with apprehension that there were shackles attached to the frame. At least they hadn't used those. Yet.

So far my track record when it came to escaping imprisonment wasn't good. One escape in the almost twenty-five years I'd lived at the *castello*; one escape from Sheol that had only brought me to an endless beach. I'd gotten out of my locked room, only to end up in a cell where my so-called goddess powers didn't seem to work.

I dragged the bed across the stone floor, wincing at the screech it made, and then climbed up on it. It still wasn't tall enough, but by balancing on the iron headboard I could grab hold of the window ledge, so I hauled myself up to peer outside.

And then fell back on the bed, the shock of it physical.

I was in no place I had ever seen, or even imagined. It looked as if I were in the midst of a movie from the 1930s or 1940s—all black-and-white and sepia-toned. People were moving outside, gray people with no color to their hair or faces; an antique car drove by, and in the distance I could see a cadre of what looked like the military. Gray, cold, merciless, marching in formation.

I lifted my arm to look at it. Still warm, creamy flesh, pale as always, but with the flush of life in it. The jeans I had tugged on before going to Michael's room were a clear, faded blue, the tank top a deep maroon. I was in color in a world that wasn't. And I knew, instinctively, that this was a Very Bad Place.

It wasn't such a great leap. A world without color was bound to be wrong. Despite the fact that I had distrusted Sheol, it was heavenly compared to this dark, dismal place.

The question was, who had brought me here? And why?

I had flown—the nausea and muscle pain told me that, even if I couldn't remember a thing. Last I knew, I had been at the door to the training annex, and a shadow had come over me. Had I been knocked unconscious? Drugged? I had no idea. Just that blackness had followed.

Who had done this to me? Michael? He was the most obvious choice. Everyone else had wanted me in his bed. I had broken through his armor, his defenses. I had caused his latest fall from grace, as surely as the first angels had fallen for love of human women.

Of course, there were a number of differences. For one thing, he didn't love me. It had been sex, pure and simple—well, maybe not so pure. But sex, not love. For another, I wasn't human, even if I was distressingly mortal.

No, it hadn't been Michael. But the question remained—who had brought me here?

There was an even more overpowering concern: I was freaking starving. I tried to envision a rich meal appearing at my doorstep, with rare steak and garlic mashed potatoes, but nothing arrived, and thinking about it was making me even hungrier, so I stopped, concentrating again on the window. Could I possibly fit through its narrow confines? Even if I broke out the mullions, I doubted I could make it without chewing off my own arm.

Not a feasible idea, though at that point I was hungry enough to consider it.

I looked around me for weapons. The room was empty—nothing in it but the bed frame and bucket. I rose and looked at the frame more carefully. There were flat pieces of metal between the springs and the frame, and I twisted one loose. It wasn't huge, maybe five inches long, but the metal was sharp, and it was better than nothing.

In the meantime, I had no choice but to sit and wait.

IT DIDN'T TAKE long. The door opened, revealing two women who looked like something out of a bad World War II movie. "Ve have vays of making you talk," I muttered to myself as the two Vikings marched into the room and hauled me to my feet.

I let them. In the best of times I was fairly sure I could have taken the two of them—their beefy muscle bordered on fat, and I was very, very good.

But I was also weak and hungry, and had no idea where to go. At least these women were letting me out of here. I would be patient and see where they took me.

It wasn't promising. We were in some kind of underground warren—windowless hallways led to more windowless hallways, and the two women marched at my sides like armed guards. I was barefoot—my shoes were still lying in the workout room in Sheol.

But this wasn't Sheol. These weren't the wives of the Fallen, and this was no haven. This was a Bad

Place, and when they pushed open a heavy door and gestured me inside, I wasn't particularly eager to go.

A shove in the middle of my back took care of my reluctance, and I found myself in a vast, empty stone room, the door closing and locking behind us as they followed me in.

"Stand against that wall," one of the women ordered, and I was almost surprised that she didn't have a stereotypical villainess's accent. She sounded soft, almost sweet.

I glanced at the bare wall. Probably not a firing squad—there was no sign of blood on the wall or the floor. Still, I wasn't about to obey meekly without a reason.

"Why?"

"Do as you're told," the first woman said. The second was busy fiddling with something attached to a long tube, and I was beginning to feel very uneasy about the whole thing.

"I don't do anything unless I have a good reason for it," I said sweetly. "What the hell is that—"

The water hit me full force, slamming me back against the wall. The second woman was wielding what looked like a fireman's hose, and I fell to my knees beneath the painful onslaught, unable to fight back. It was bitterly cold, soaking me to the bone, and I had hideous visions of Holocaust movies. Didn't the Nazis herd victims into a room and turn a hose on them? Had I somehow slipped through a time warp? If I could believe in angels and vampires and ancient Roman goddesses, was time travel far behind?

I curled into a ball, protecting my body from the worst of the assault, and then I rolled across the floor, under the blast of water, before the women could react. I caught one woman across the knees and she went down hard; then I grabbed the hose from the second one and proceeded to use it on them. The two bodies skidded across the floor in front of the gushing water, slamming up against the wall, and if I'd been kind I would have shut off the nozzle. I wasn't feeling kind.

"Enough!" a voice thundered from the previously locked door, now standing open, revealing a tall, cloaked figure; and with no move on my part the water suddenly slowed to a trickle. I dropped the hose in disgust, prepared to take on the two women, who'd scrambled to their feet and were slowly advancing on me, when the new voice came again.

"Enough, I said."

I turned and snarled, "Mind your own business. I can take them."

There were twin gasps of horror from my two tormenters, and they looked at me as if they expected lightning to strike. "Yes, my lord," one of them murmured, sounding totally cowed. She grabbed the other woman's meaty paw and dragged her from the room, both of them looking as sodden and bedraggled as I felt.

I finally turned my attention on the newcomer,

surveying him with interest. He looked like something out of a Harry Potter movie—tall and wizardly, with flowing gray hair, kindly eyes, and the soft mouth of a sybarite. He looked genial, harmless, but I wasn't in the mood to play nice. He was also as gray and colorless as everyone else.

"Who are you?" I demanded, shoving my sopping hair away from my face.

"I believe, my dear, that I am your host."

"Welcome to the fun house," I muttered, looking around me. "Do you always put guests in a prison cell and then use a fire hose to wash them down? I assure you, I don't have lice."

"Of course you don't, my dear. And I'm afraid Gerda and Hilda were a bit too enthusiastic. But you're not exactly my guest. More my prisoner, in fact. Hence the cell."

Part of me was absolutely fascinated that anyone would actually use the word *hence* in conversation. The rest of me was looking at him with less than my initial approval.

"And would you like to explain why, Mr. . . . ?" I waited for him to fill in the name.

"Oh, excuse me, I've been terribly remiss. I am Beloch, ruler of the Dark City. And you are Victoria Bellona, are you not?"

I nodded cautiously.

"Well, then," he said briskly, "why don't you change your clothes and I'll have someone bring you to my study where we can talk."

"Is there any food around here?" I demanded, unable to bear my rumbling stomach any longer.

"Gluttony is one of the seven deadly sins, my dear."

"Is it? I've never been particularly big on the Bible."

He looked as if he'd bitten into the sourest pickle on the face of this earth. "Indeed," he said, and the temperature in the room dropped ten degrees.

No, that isn't a figure of speech. Everything in the already chilly room got worse, and I could see my breath in front of me.

I needed to dig up the circumspection I'd used around my mother and Pedersen if I was going to get out of this alive. "But I am always interested in learning more," I said brightly.

I had no idea whether I'd managed to fool the old man or not. He simply nodded. "I would be more than happy to instruct you. In the meantime, I suggest you return to your 'prison cell' and get out of those wet clothes."

"There weren't any dry ones to change into."

He looked irritated. "There are now. Allow me to escort you."

As if I had a choice. He held out his arm, very old-school, and I took it. He felt strangely insubstantial beneath the plain fabric of the robe, and I was tempted to push up the sleeve to see just how bony he was. I resisted—this was a creature of immense power, no matter how frail and colorless his body seemed to be. I let him lead me along the deserted hallways till we returned to the now-familiar rectangle. The bed was freshly made, and there was a dull gray dress spread across the covers.

I looked up at the faux Dumbledore. "I do hope you don't have any illusions that I'll go to bed with you. I don't care how you dress me up, I've had enough sex to last me for a decade."

For a moment that avuncular smile faded, replaced by profound irritation. And then he was smiling again, the sweet expression that made me nervous. "I assure you, my child, that is the last thing I want from you."

I believed him. I'd taken one look at the supposedly celibate Michael and seen the heat and desire seething beneath his controlled surface. There was nothing beneath this old man's façade but ice.

He pushed me into my room gently enough. "Someone will bring you to me in half an hour, and we can talk over dinner. Will that suit you?"

He could have said we'd torture gerbils over dinner and I'd have agreed, I was so damned hungry, but I managed to gather my scattered dignity. I nodded.

"Good," he murmured. "And when you come, you can tell me all about Michael."

"What about Michael?" I said warily.

"Why, how to kill him, of course."

MICHAEL DESCENDED SLOWLY through the ink-dark sky. He didn't need to see where he was going—he knew the Dark City far too well. He'd hoped, foolishly, that he had turned his back on it forever. Then again, he had thought he'd turned his back on sentimental caring for foolish women who got themselves kidnapped.

He'd felt the net close over him as he slipped down, down, into the miasma that enveloped the cursed place. He knew without testing his theory that he wouldn't be able to fly out. He was trapped, and there would be only one way out. And for the first time in his endless existence, he wondered if he could face it.

CHAPTER
SIXTEEN

I DO WISH TO ASSURE YOU THAT I'M FAR more interested in Michael than in your charming self," the man calling himself Beloch said affably over his cup of tea. "As far as I'm concerned, you're simply collateral damage, something I can let go of quite easily. Once I dispense with Michael, you may feel free to go wherever you wish. You have my word on it."

I sat in an elegant carved chair in the middle of what looked like a library, the formal dress draped around me. Once I'd put it on, it had become suffused with a rich garnet color, well suited to my pale skin and dark hair. Not that there was anyone around to notice. I'd tucked my makeshift knife into the deep pocket of the hem, though it was too small to be much more than an annoyance. Still, it made me feel better. I held a cup of tea in my hand, untouched. I despised tea—it reminded me of the few forced gatherings with my mother, where I was put through my social paces. A nice sweet cup of black coffee would be lovely, but clear tea, stinking of bergamot, with a slice of lemon floating in it like a corpse, was my idea of hell. Particularly when I was this hungry.

I kept my knees together, doing my best to look demure, and listened attentively. I didn't believe him for one minute, but I certainly wasn't about to tell him that. He struck me as one of those old men who assumed people treated their word as golden, and I wasn't going to enlighten him. I didn't trust anybody. After the debacle of last night, spent melting and shattering beneath Michael's tattooed body, I didn't even trust myself.

"He kidnapped you, didn't he?" Beloch continued. "Dragged you to that wretched little gathering in the mist when you yearned to be free. I've known Michael a long, long time—you must hate him very much."

I said nothing, bringing my tea to my lips and pretending to sip.

"Unless, of course, I am wrong?" Beloch said shrewdly. "Perhaps Michael has more charm than I realized."

"I wouldn't put *charm* and *Michael* in the same sentence," I said dryly. In my mind I could see Michael, feel him poised above me, his endless dark eyes staring down into mine as he filled me, thrust into me slowly, steadily, and a little shiver of delayed reaction swept over me. How could I possibly have an orgasm twelve hours after I'd last touched him? Apparently anything was possible.

I could only hope the old man's sharp eyes hadn't noticed. "So I can assume it wasn't Michael who sent me here. I'd wondered whether he was trying to get rid of me."

Beloch smiled at me, but I could see the wheels turning in his head. He hadn't considering spinning that particular lie, and lie it was, thank God. "You were presented to me by one of the Fallen. But you may trust me when I tell you that Michael would hand you over to me in a minute if it suited his purpose. He is dangerous, ruthless, and he means you nothing but ill."

Just as Johann had handed me back to Pedersen. I shook away the memory.

"So you have a spy in Sheol? Who is it?" I didn't particularly expect an answer, but I was curious.

He clearly didn't like the question. "I don't think we need to discuss that, do you?"

Yes, I did, but I politely mirrored his phony smile. "I was just curious."

"Curiosity is a sin of idleness. It is of no concern to you. You have no wish to return to Sheol, do you?"

Of course I didn't. I wanted away from fallen angels and strange places with no color and no life. I suspected he wasn't going to give me any choice in the matter.

I was getting tired of this polite fencing. I set the wretched tea down on the small table beside me. "I don't like being kidnapped, and as far as I can tell, your spy did the same thing Michael did." Well, not quite the same thing, I thought, feeling a flash of heat wash through me. "So why don't you tell me exactly what you want from me, and what I have to do to get out of here?"

He frowned. "Why, nothing at all, my child. It is Michael I want. He will come for you, and when he does, you may go."

I laughed, and Beloch didn't like that either. "I don't think so," I said. "He was ordered to bring me to Sheol, to bond with me, and he did. Then he was told to take me to bed and drink my blood. He did that. I think his responsibilities are at an end, and if I know Michael, he'll be happy never to see me again."

A flurry of emotions crossed Beloch's seamed face: disgust, excitement, craftiness, triumph. "He took your blood? I am surprised."

Not exactly, I thought, remembering the tiny pinprick. I had no idea whether that was enough to count, but I suspected it wasn't. I shrugged. "I figured once that was taken care of, no one would care what happened to me. Michael could forget about me, the Fallen could ignore me, and I could leave."

"Alas, I'm afraid that is not the case. By giving your body and your blood to Michael, you bound yourself to him irrevocably. It changes things."

"It was just a drop of blood," I said with belated honesty. "Barely a scratch."

"It is enough. He will come for you. And when he does, he will be mine."

I surveyed Beloch for a long moment and smirked. "I don't think he swings that way."

Beloch's face turned dark with anger, though in this world that just meant a darker gray. I wondered if he would turn color if I touched him. I had no interest in getting close enough to try.

"You are unworthy," he said stiffly.

"Look at it this way—you aren't about to set me free and we both know it. This way you don't have to feel guilty about it."

"Guilt is a human emotion. I am not human."

Oh, God, not another one, I thought wearily, though I'd already guessed as much. "Then what are you?"

Nope, no answer this time either. "We can torture you," he said softly, "but I tire of that. And it would be so much more effective if I have him here to watch."

He wasn't human, but neither was I. I was strong, and sneaky, and desperation did wonders for one's fighting ability. "He won't care," I said in a bored voice. "How many times must I tell you? He's done what he had to do, and now you've done him a great service by getting rid of me. He won't come after me."

He leaned forward to set his empty teacup on

the chair beside him, and I made my move. I'd already surreptitiously gathered my voluminous skirts in my hands, and it was a simple enough matter to leap up, aiming a kick directly at his jaw. If I was really lucky, it would snap his head back and break his neck. At the very least it would stun him.

He went down like a stone.

I was almost to the door when the shock hit me like a powerful electric current, slamming me against the wall and pinning me there, three feet off the floor. I couldn't move, couldn't kick or struggle or even turn my head—I was stuck like a butterfly pinned to some sadistic collector's board. Pain coursed through my body in never-ending waves, and I couldn't even cry out. All I could do was hang there as the old man made his way over to me, slowly, taking his time.

When he reached me I could just see him from the corner of my eye. I'd felt my foot connect with his face, yet there wasn't a mark on him. It should have split his lip, caused a nosebleed—or at least a look of intense irritation. But he appeared untouched.

"Foolish child," he murmured, and his dry, papery hand stroked my face, sending shivers down my spine. "You have no idea with whom you're dealing. There is absolutely nothing you can do."

I tried to say something scathing, but I was mute. I glared at him, and he smiled benevolently. "Ah, my dear. You will be an entertaining guest for the short time I have you. I only wish it could be longer, but these things are written in stone. Literally. I could show you the tablets."

What things? Why short time? But I couldn't ask and he wasn't about to offer, so I put the approximation of a snarl into my eyes. He smiled. "Don't worry, my dear. The moment Michael sets foot in the Dark City, he'll be dead. You won't have to deal with him ever again." His hand ran down my arm, then administered a vicious little pinch. "I'm afraid you'll have to put up with me."

He moved away, his long robes flowing behind him. "I believe I'll leave you here for the time being while we come up with the perfect prison for you. Someplace not so hard to break into that he'll give up, but not so easy that he recognizes the trap. This will require some careful planning, but I'm certain the Truth Breakers will be more than up to the task. They'll come for you soon. In the meantime you'll be fine here. There's more tea, though I'm afraid it's rather cold by now, and I did leave a few of the biscuits for you to nibble on. You must keep up your strength, after all." He chucked me under the chin, and I would have given anything to be able to move my mouth and bite his fingers off.

But I was still frozen as he left the room, humming beneath his breath, closing the door behind him.

The hold released, and I collapsed on the floor in

a welter of skirts and pain, hugging myself, moaning. Everything hurt so badly, and I had learned early on to be impervious to pain. It took a lot to disable me—Pedersen had even used a Taser on me once, and I had managed just fine.

This felt like a Taser on steroids. Everything in my body was jangled and confused, my throat felt as if a hand had crushed it, and my heart slammed against my chest. I had underestimated Beloch. Clearly a big mistake.

He could kill me quite easily. So why was he fretting about my being here only a short time? Where would he send me next, and why?

At least I was sure of one thing, and it was a soothing thought. Michael would never come here. If Beloch had that much power over me, then Michael would be in extreme danger; and if anything happened to him, the entire community of the Fallen would be in deep shit. As would the world.

I didn't want that to happen. I liked the people I'd met in Sheol—Allie and Rachel, Asbel and the other men I'd trained with, even Martha, for all that her damned prophecy had landed me in this mess. I liked the place, for all it was just another prison. If I had to live in prison, I could be happy in the one by the ocean I'd fallen in love with.

They needed Michael to win the battle against the Armies of Heaven. Exactly where were those armies? Here in what he called the Dark City?

He wouldn't come for me. He'd done what he

had to do, and he was probably happy to get rid of me. He wouldn't risk everything with a misguided rescue attempt.

I was nothing to him.

Beloch was doomed to disappointment.

CHAPTER
SEVENTEEN

I MUST HAVE SLEPT. THE ORIENTAL RUG beneath me was thick and beautiful, even if there were no rich colors to appreciate, and I really didn't have the strength to pull myself up to one of the uncomfortable chairs. I still felt shaken— as if my entire body had short-circuited—and I needed to rest.

I was starving. I knew he'd left food behind, but even for the sake of cookies I couldn't bring myself to stand up. Besides, he'd probably poisoned them. I was dying of thirst, my empty stomach was in a knot, and I felt as if I'd been electrocuted. All in all, not a good day so far.

Then again, I was never one to grovel. Cursing beneath my breath, I managed to haul myself up, collapsing into one of the chairs. The cold tea still smelled like bergamot, and sepia-colored cookies weren't that tempting. I leaned back in the chair and closed my eyes, working on drawing my energy back together.

It was something I'd learned from Pedersen. No, scratch that. It was part of the martial arts training that Pedersen had dismissed as unimportant. Since the one thing he and the contessa had not done was to restrict my reading and video watching, it had been easy enough to continue with the spiritual aspects of martial arts on my own. In the end, I suspected it was one of the reasons I'd grown stronger than Pedersen. There was only so much the human body was capable of, so much physical training could accomplish. When that failed, you needed to count on inner resources.

Then again, if I was a goddess and Pedersen a mere mortal, he'd been outgunned from the beginning. I hated the thought that I'd had an unfair advantage over that bastard.

I heard footsteps in the hallway, but the fight had gone out of me. Even if I managed to escape, where the hell could I go in this strange, colorless world? The lock clicked and two black-robed figures stood there, looking like something out of the Spanish Inquisition. The black of their garments was so intense it was almost blinding in the toned-down room, and the hoods covered their heads and faces like the robes of penitents. They put their black-gloved hands on me and I went without struggling. What had Beloch called them? Truth Breakers? Now, there was a name to strike terror into a mortal soul.

But I wasn't mortal. And I would be hard to break.

"Easy, boys," I said, channeling every insouciant heroine I'd ever seen on-screen. "I'll go quietly."

No response. My wrists were shackled, and I hadn't even noticed when they'd done that. I let them lead me down, deeper and deeper into the bowels of this colorless world, until we came to a place that looked ominously like an operating room, complete with surgical instruments and a viewing window for either medical students or apprentice torturers to watch. I had no intention of going quietly.

One of them released his vicious grip on my arm and moved forward to unlock the door. The other black-robed creature's grip on me was much lighter; if I could just count on a moment's inattention, I could break free from him quite easily.

I waited for my chance, seemingly cowed and docile, watching the stronger man's every move. I could catch him as he turned, kicking him as I wrenched my wrists free from the second man and looped my manacled hands around his neck, while—

No, that wouldn't work. Maybe take out the man holding me first? But the first one was stronger, judging by the pain in my arm, and it made sense to disable him first while his back was turned, an unfair advantage I had no hesitation using. I tensed, ready to yank my arm free and spring—when the man beside me jumped, in a fast, graceful blur of movement my eyes couldn't follow. The first Truth Breaker was down, and the second one was stripping the black robe from the body with ruthless speed, exposing a burly man in striped boxers and a wife-beater. I stared down at the seemingly ordinary creature in astonishment, and then the robe was flung at me. I caught it reflexively in my bound hands, staring at the second man.

"Put the fucking thing on," Michael's voice snarled from beneath the enveloping hood as he dragged the man's body into the torture room.

Panic and joy swamped me. I wasn't going to let either show. "What the hell are you doing here?"

"Saving your ass." He turned back to me, shoving the hood off his head. His face in color was a shock, when my eyes had grown used to the black and white that surrounded me. "Are you putting that robe on so we have a chance in hell of getting out of here?"

"Are you going to unfasten these handcuffs so I can?" I responded, uncowed.

He gave a long-suffering sigh, as if I were the one who'd screwed up, and a second later the cuffs fell on the floor. He kicked them into the room and shut the door.

"How did you do that?" I demanded, impressed, as I pulled the enveloping robe around me.

He didn't answer my question. "Pull the hood low, and keep your hands tucked into the sleeves so no one will see they're different."

"And for that matter, why are they different? What is this place? And why did you bother to come after me? I would have thought you'd be well rid of me." And then I stopped asking questions. I could feel them coming closer.

He felt them too. He reached over and yanked the hood down so low over my head that I couldn't see, replacing his own at the same time. "Be prepared to run for it," he muttered as he began hauling me down the dark corridor.

"Can't we fly?" I demanded, stumbling after him.

"Not here," he said grimly.

True enough. The halls were too narrow. I had never seen him clearly enough to guess at the wingspan, but I doubted these narrow corridors could contain him. So I ran.

In the best of times I could run for miles without tiring. In the best of times I hadn't been zapped by the mother of all Tasers and I wasn't running for my life. There was no way to set a reasonable pace with Michael hauling me—all I could do was run, trying to ignore my pounding heart and rapidly diminishing breathing.

The halls were growing more and more narrow. The light was growing dimmer. And our pursuers, if they'd even been after us, were farther away, until we could no longer sense them.

The corridors were tunnels now, with grim brownish lights set high into the stone walls. The paths forked, over and over, but Michael never hesitated, taking one turn after another.

"In here," he said roughly, taking my arm and shoving me through a small doorway.

I went willingly, into a cocoon of darkness so intense that panic swamped me. I heard the *thunk* of a door closing, and it was all too much. I had never been claustrophobic in my life, but suddenly I was overwhelmed. I felt the walls closing down around me; my breathing was strangled in my throat, and I thought I was going to die—

Hard arms encircled me and tugged me against Michael's strong body, his hand on the back of my neck, pressing my cowled face to his shoulder. I shivered, trying to regain my calm. *Stupid, stupid, stupid,* I ranted at myself as I gasped for breath. *You can't afford to give in to any sign of weakness. Fight it, fight it—*

"Stop fighting," Michael growled in my ear. "You're making it worse. Let go. I've got you."

I've got you. Why did those words make me want to cry? I shut my eyes, though in the darkness I didn't need to, and concentrated on the slow, steady beat of Michael's heart against my racing, fluttering one. Concentrated on the hand at my neck, soothing me with slow, calming strokes. Concentrated on his solid body against mine, holding me close, his breath against my forehead, calm and certain. "I've got you," he said again.

And I let go.

MICHAEL FELT THE fight leave her body, felt her slowly go limp. He picked her up, cradling her against him, and moved deeper into the storeroom.

He knew this place, knew it better than anyone. For the time being they were safe, until he decided on their next move.

He moved to the far wall, not needing his eyes to know where he was going, and sank down, Tory still in his arms. For a change she wasn't fighting him. He'd been afraid, so afraid that he was too late. That he would come to Beloch's room and find her one of them. Leached of color, leached of life.

He should have known Beloch couldn't take her so easily. She was a fighter, a warrior like he was. It would take more than Beloch to defeat her.

She curled up against him, oddly trusting. The time in his bed was still disturbing, and it must be doubly troubling for her, given her limited experience. Then again, perhaps she didn't know just how powerful their joining had been. As if worlds had collided and blended. This must be what bonding really was, whether he liked it or not. This must be what finding your true mate meant.

He shouldn't have done it. He hadn't taken enough blood, but he'd still come dangerously close to fulfilling the prophecy that would kill her.

He fought the urge to pull her closer. She was either asleep or resting, and she didn't need anything disturbing her. She needed as much time as he dared give her.

He dropped his face into her hair, breathing in the jasmine scent of her. No wonder he'd been unable to resist her. It must be chemical, hormonal.

Something that was out of his control. A cruel trick of fate.

He'd been both voracious and celibate at various times in his existence, and he hadn't felt much difference. Celibacy was simpler. He'd only had one mate, and he'd never taken her blood. She'd died before he had a chance to know her, and he couldn't even remember the sex. Tory was different, damnably so, and Martha and the others must have known it.

Man up. Wasn't that the term humans used nowadays? *Don't complain about what fate has handed you—deal with it and move on.*

He'd fought Tory, and he'd lost the first battle. Taking her to bed had definitely been a defeat, no matter how good it had felt. He didn't need to tell her that. They had to learn to fight together, to get out of the Dark City and out of this world of endless night. In time to face the final battle that would take her life.

Gods should be immortal, as angels were. Not that angels couldn't die—the Nephilim and Uriel had seen to that. But Tory's life seemed so much more fragile, for all her astonishing strength. It would be snuffed out in too little time. Life would be a great deal simpler if he didn't give a damn.

He should set her down, but the floor was solid rock, and she'd be more comfortable in his arms. Over the years he'd held many women, both before and after his fall, effortlessly. But no one had ever felt as right as Tory did, fit as perfectly against the mercilessly hard contours of his flesh. It was as if he couldn't tell where he ended and she began. More of fate's cruel tricks. Though maybe fate had nothing to do with it.

If he didn't know better, he might have thought this was some sadistic game of Uriel's. To send him someone who burrowed into his soul and then rip her away again.

But even Uriel with his almost limitless power couldn't control emotions, passion, the unbreakable bond that was being forged between them. And when it *was* broken by her death, it would feel as if part of him were being ripped away. And it would hurt forever.

He felt her stir, and he prepared to tighten his grip if she started to panic again. He could feel the sudden tension in her body, and then she relaxed it, deliberately.

"I'm sorry," she said in a soft voice. "I'm not usually that weak."

"You aren't weak." He kept his tone matter-of-fact. "Beloch is a master of manipulation."

"He didn't manipulate me. I saw through the son of a bitch immediately."

The room was very dark, but his eyes were fine-tuned to it. She was looking both stubborn and shaken. "You'd be the first," he said.

She snorted. "How long have I been here? A day? He came swanning in when two Nazi hags were using a fire hose on me. Even though he stopped them, I figured anyone who was in charge of a place like this had to be a royal ugly dude."

"Royal ugly dude?" he echoed, bemused.

"*Bill and Ted's Excellent Adventure*," she said cryptically. And then, "A movie."

"I don't watch movies."

"I know."

She hadn't made any effort to climb out of his arms, and he didn't make any effort to move her. They would separate when he got her back to Sheol, but for now he could let her rest against him.

"I suppose you have a plan for getting out of here?" she said. "Do you even know where we are?"

"Yes, and yes. I spent . . . a long time in the Dark City. I know its ins and outs by memory."

"You were a prisoner here as well?"

He didn't want to answer her. He couldn't lie to her, but how could he tell her the truth? That he'd carried out Uriel's orders. That he'd played the game, determined to follow his ordained course. And might still have been here, had not Uriel cast him out when things had finally become too much for him to stomach.

He leaned his head back against the wall, half-afraid his move would send her scrambling off his lap, but she stayed put. "Cryptic Guy again," she said. "Okay, I can handle that. You want to tell me what the plan is?"

"We get out of here. The tunnels are a maze, and one of Beloch's favorite pastimes is to send prisoners down here to wander until he gets tired of the sport. Sometimes they starve to death. One killed himself by banging his head against the rock. The only other person who knows his way through these tunnels is Metatron, and he's back in Sheol."

"Only other? I take it that means you know how to get out of here."

"Yes. You want to tell me who brought you here? Was it Metatron?"

"I have no idea. I left your— I was heading toward my room when someone knocked me unconscious. I don't remember clearly, but when I woke up I was here, dealing with female prison guards and an evil Dumbledore—"

"A Dumbledore?" he interrupted. "What's that?"

She sighed. "Never mind. I'll explain later. I asked Beloch who brought me here but he wouldn't tell me. Is Metatron missing? Do you think he took me?"

"He's in Sheol. No one else was missing, only you. I have no idea who took you, but I mean to find out when we get back."

"And if I don't want to go?" Her voice was very quiet, but she hadn't moved from his lap, and he sensed only a frisson of tension in her body.

"You want to stay here?"

"Of course not. But . . . can't I go somewhere else? You fulfilled the prophecy, you did your duty. Surely they wouldn't insist I stay on?"

"I don't know," he said carefully.

Her heart was speeding up, he could sense it. "You have no reason to want me there, do you?"

There it was, laid out in front of him, and for the

life of him he couldn't think of an excuse to keep her with him. He could only come up with the truth.

"Yes," he said. "I do."

Silence in the all-encompassing darkness. Her heart was pounding faster now, and he was afraid she was going to pull out of his arms. "Why?"

He didn't think about it. He just did it. He slid his hand behind her neck, tilted her head up, and kissed her.

CHAPTER
EIGHTEEN

DARKNESS. THICK, ENVELOPING darkness, with his strong body surrounding me, his hot, wet mouth on mine. All arguments fled. I wanted this. Needed this. Ever since I'd left his bed, a part of me had been missing, and now it was found again. He had come for me. And I was his.

His tongue slid into my mouth, and I felt unaccountably shy even after last night, but it didn't seem to matter. When I tentatively moved my tongue against his, he let out a low growl of unmistakable approval, and I wanted to get closer. I wanted him inside me again, I wanted to take his cock into my mouth the way they did in the books I'd read. I wanted everything.

Common sense deserted me as I sank into a sensual dream, with his long, deft fingers cradling my face, holding it at just the right angle for his deep, possessing kiss. Nothing mattered but Michael, his mouth, his body, the way he touched me. My breasts felt tight, almost painful, and I shifted, rubbing them against his hard, muscled chest, trying to find some kind of ease. He lifted his head, moving his mouth down the side of my face to my jaw, and I could feel the damp heat of his breath against me. He slipped one hand between our bodies, covering my breast, teasing, pulling at my tight nipple, and a spark of reaction spiked through me.

There was too much fabric between us. I needed his skin against mine, his callused fingers rough against my softness. I wanted his mouth on my breasts, sucking them, pulling at them, and I squirmed again, needing more, so much more.

I was holding on to his shoulders, clinging to him as the only shelter in a storm of sensuality, but I let go, reaching for the shirt that covered his strong, muscled chest, needing to pull it away and feel the heated flesh beneath it, to let my fingers glide over him.

But his hand captured mine, and he lifted me off him, setting me on the hard ground beside him. I felt bereft. "Don't," he said in a ragged voice.

"Why not?" I didn't care how desperate I sounded. I wanted so many things from him I couldn't put them into words. I was vibrating with need and I no longer cared about hiding it.

"This is too dangerous."

"For whom?" I demanded.

"For both of us. If I'm going to get you out of here safely, I need to have my brain working, and it doesn't when I touch you."

That was little consolation for the feeling of absolute emptiness that washed over me. The ground was hard beneath my butt, and I was cold without his arms around me. Cold and frightened, when it took a lot to frighten me. I tried to fight off the insidious effect of his touch, his kiss, but at that particular moment, I didn't give a rat's ass about getting out of there. All I cared about was getting his hands on me again.

"Okay," I managed to say. At least the darkness provided a bit of protection—he wouldn't know how complete my capitulation was. How desperately I wanted him. It should help me as well—I couldn't see his astonishingly provocative beauty. I told myself he could be anyone in the darkness.

It didn't work.

Silence pressed down on me, filling the inky blackness, and I wanted to draw in on myself, wrap my arms around my knees, give myself what comfort I could.

He cursed beneath his breath. "Fuck it," he said, and I felt him surge to his feet beside me. I pulled my knees up, resting my head against them as he moved around the room.

I couldn't imagine how he could. It was too dark to see anything, yet he wasn't bumping into things and cursing. I heard the scrape of something against the floor and jumped nervously.

"You feel strong enough to move?" His voice was cool, impersonal, as if he hadn't just kissed me into a limp pool of desire.

Pride overrode the lingering aftermath of Beloch's special effects and my even more powerful reaction to Michael's mouth, and I scrambled to my feet. I swayed for a moment, but he couldn't see the hand I used to steady myself. "Of course," I said, sounding positively perky. "Don't even think I can't keep up with you."

Even if I couldn't see him, I could sense his amusement. "What did Beloch do to you?"

"He didn't touch me," I said quickly. Even the thought of that old man's hands on me made me shudder.

"Of course he didn't. Beloch is asexual. He doesn't understand human drives and human weaknesses. But he hurt you. How?"

I shrugged, then realized he couldn't see it. "I kicked him in the head and tried to escape. Next thing I knew, I was pinned halfway up the wall feeling like I'd been electrocuted. I didn't drop until he left the room, and I—I may have fallen asleep." I'd passed out, but I wasn't going to tell him that.

"You passed out," he said, and I wanted to punch him.

"Maybe." I was grudging. "Whatever it was, it was nasty. I can still feel it." I was weaker than usual, but sheer pride would keep me going. "Don't think I can't keep up with you, Your Saintliness. It'll be a cold day in hell that I can't do anything you can do and do it ten times better."

He was suddenly very close, standing right in front of me, and I hadn't even realized he'd moved. "I doubt it," he said. "And stop calling me names."

He was so close that his heavy robe brushed against my own, and the rough fabric caught, mingled, moving against me. "When you start calling me Tory."

There was an audible sigh as his hands grasped my robe, pushing it back on my shoulders. At some point he must have opened his own robe, because when he took the edges of mine and pulled me against him he was wearing only a thin shirt and what felt like jeans. My head went against his shoulder, naturally, as his arms encircled me, as the robes encircled us, and he just held me, his heart against mine, slow and steady, a reassurance. It was going to be okay.

We stood there for a long while. Long enough for our body heat to mingle in the damp, chilly air, passing back and forth, warming us. Long enough for my skin to tingle, long enough for that damned aching feeling between my legs. Long enough for me to feel the hard ridge below the waistband of his jeans.

"We have to get out of here," he said, pushing me away gently.

I wanted to howl like a baby who'd had her toy ripped away from her. That, or her mother's breast. "Okay," I said calmly. "What are we waiting for?"

He took my hand, and I could have followed him anywhere, even into this pitch-dark world. "Can you see where you're going?" I asked.

"Yes."

"Angel X-ray vision?"

"There are more ways to see than simply using your eyes."

"'Use the Force, Luke,'" I muttered under my breath.

"What?"

"Never mind."

We didn't leave the way we'd come in, though I wasn't sure if that was a good thing or a bad one. I had assumed we were in a simple storeroom, but Michael pushed boxes out of his way—effortlessly, of course—and we moved deeper into the blackness. I could feel the walls closing in around me, and realized we were in some sort of tunnel. I said nothing, putting all my energy into regulating my breath so he wouldn't realize I was fighting panic. *You're not claustrophobic,* I told myself firmly. *You never have been. Stop it.*

A cold sweat covered my face and my heart was hammering, the blood racing in my veins, but there was no way I was going to admit to this sudden, unreasonable fear, not to him, not to anyone. I could handle it. I could handle anything. As long as he led me, I could follow.

I lost track of time. I was famished, I had to pee, every bone in my body ached, but I kept moving. If

I said something he'd probably swoop me up and carry me, and I didn't want to be any more of a burden.

I was so intent on staying on my feet that I didn't pay attention, and when he stopped I barreled into him. A mistake. Those feelings flared to life once more, and I stepped back before he realized that I wanted to move closer still.

"Stay put," he whispered. Unnecessary—where was I going to go?

Apparently we'd reached the end of the tunnel. He released my hand, and I stood still as he fiddled with the door. He opened it slowly, but the blinding daylight I'd been expecting failed to materialize—there were only shadows. He pulled me through, closing the door behind him, and I looked around with interest.

We seemed to be under some kind of portico. Beyond I could see those strange, vintage-looking cars going by in their shades of gray, and while I assumed it was evening, for all I knew this could be broad daylight. It was called the Dark City for a reason.

"Exactly what is this place?" I said, keeping my voice down, though there didn't seem to be anyone to hear us. "And who or what is Beloch?"

You'd think I would have gotten used to him ignoring me. At that moment, if I could have had one wish in the world, it would have been to tie Michael to a stake and torture him until he answered my questions. I had so many I was forgetting the easier ones. I guess there was a limit to how much uncertainty I could handle—when I reached my fill, some of the older questions simply disappeared.

"Stay here," he said. "I'm going to get us a car."

"Can't I come with you?"

He glanced back at me. "I'm going to steal a car. It works better if I'm alone. I'll come back for you, I promise."

Well, if he didn't, then he was damned stupid to have come here in the first place, I told myself. "Okay," I said. "Beloch was expecting you. How did you get past his guards?"

"I'm very good at what I do," he said in a silken voice. "Can I go get the car now, or do you have other silly questions?"

I didn't consider my questions silly, but I was tired of arguing. "Go ahead," I said with an airy wave of my hand.

He still hadn't answered the key question—why had he come? Had Martha come up with a new fillip to the prophecy? Did I need to be on-site for the Fallen to prevail? And if Uriel was the Big Bad, then who exactly was Beloch?

I tried to stay put, I really did. But as minutes ticked by like hours, I grew more and more restless, and I couldn't resist stepping out into the street to see if I could catch sight of him, first pulling the enveloping hood back over my head and tucking my betraying hands into the wide black sleeves. There were people around, watching me, couples strolling by the sluggish river nearby, a cadre of men in paramilitary uniforms approaching from a distance. I quickly ducked back into the shadows, but it was too late—they'd seen me.

I glanced behind me. Whatever door we'd come through had disappeared, leaving me trapped. I could do nothing but stand my ground and try to bluff. Truth Breakers, hadn't Michael said that's what we were? Did they have women Truth Breakers, or would I have to lower my voice and walk with a swagger? The man whose robe I was wearing had looked shockingly average, with his boxers and undershirt and burly chest.

The men were marching in matched step, and I wished I'd listened to Michael and stayed put. It was too late now. I drew myself up to my full height and waited. I could feel my arms, my hands, tingling, growing hot, and I wondered why. I was preparing for battle, not certain whether I could overpower half a dozen trained soldiers, no matter how confident I was in my skills. But my hands twitched and burned as I watched them.

"Truth Breaker," the leader addressed me when they came to a stop in front of me. "May we assist you?"

Truth Breakers were scary dudes, generally silent

from what I'd observed. I bowed gracefully in greeting and then shook my head. A hand wave of dismissal would have been more effective, but my Technicolor flesh would betray me.

The leader wasn't inclined to let it go that easily. "I can have my men escort Your Excellency back to Beloch. It's not safe for you to be alone in the streets."

"He's not alone." It was Michael, suddenly beside me like, well, an avenging angel. And the burning feeling vanished; my hands felt normal again. How very strange.

"You have no interest in him," he continued in a voice that seemed to have built-in echoes.

"We have no interest in him," the leader parroted. "Move on, men."

"'These are not the droids you're looking for,'" I muttered, watching them go. I didn't need to see Michael's face to know he was greatly displeased with me. Our détente was over in record time.

"I told you to stay put." His voice was little more than a growl.

"You do that a lot," I said, trying to sound breezily unconcerned. "The definition of insanity is to repeat the same action over and over again and expect different results. In case you haven't figured it out yet, I'm not particularly biddable."

"You're not particularly smart," he shot back. "I didn't go to all this trouble to get us out of there only to have you blunder back in."

If my hood had been back, he would have seen my feral smile. Then again, it would have left him unmoved.

"And exactly why did you go to all that trouble? You still haven't told me. I would have thought you were well rid of me." The last time I'd asked that question, he'd kissed me rather than answer, effectively turning my brain to mush. I wanted him to kiss me again.

He hesitated, and for one brief moment I thought I was going to get a straight answer. "Orders," he said after a moment, his voice flat. "I'm just following orders."

I was suddenly deflated. It was reasonable. More likely than any other possibility. Why would he put his head in a noose without a damned good excuse?

But I didn't believe him. Swathed in impenetrable black, his voice cool and clipped, he had another reason for coming after me, I just knew it.

Or maybe I'd seen too many movies. Scratch that—of course I'd seen too many movies. Michael was no romantic hero fighting a desperate attraction. He was a soldier, a general, a warrior, and he needed me for cannon fodder.

I shook off the depressing thought. "So did you have time to steal us the car before you came galloping to the rescue?"

"Of course. Keep your head down and for once in your life try to behave."

"How do you know it's once in my life? You've only known me—what is it? Three days?"

"It feels like a lifetime," he said sourly. "Just please shut the fuck up."

"Well, since you asked so nicely."

I followed him out into the gloomy half-light, in search of his stolen car.

CHAPTER
NINETEEN

MICHAEL WAS FURIOUS. SHE'D deliberately disobeyed him, putting them both in danger by leaving her hiding place. He'd been a fool to come after her, he thought morosely as he led her toward the alleyway where he'd stashed the car. Even reticent Asbel had told him not to go. He'd ignored all the voices, ignored his own better judgment, and raced after her like a moonstruck loon.

He should be back in Sheol training his army. She was probably going to die anyway—what did it matter where or how? The date would stay the same.

But she would have died in agony after weeks of torture if he'd left her in this miserable place. Or maybe she would have managed to charm Beloch enough to be kept as a pet.

Second-guessing was a waste of time. He was bringing her back to Sheol and he was going to find the son of a bitch who'd taken her. Who'd betrayed them. The upcoming battle was uneven enough without a traitor in their midst.

She climbed into the old car without a word, her cowled head surveying the vintage interior.

"No seat belts," she observed.

"No one dies here, except at the hands of the Nightmen and the Truth Breakers. Or Beloch."

"The Nightmen. Is that who those men were?"

"Yes." He put the car in gear and slowly drove forward out of the narrow alley. He knew the layout of the Dark City—it was engraved in his brain. It was an advantage he had over any of Beloch's men, and it was that knowledge that would keep them safe.

"When can I take off this damned hood?" Her voice was muffled.

"Not until we're well away from here. We look different, remember? If you're suffocating you can slide down out of sight and pull it off, but I wouldn't recommend it."

"Why are we different? Are they all really this color, or is something messing with our perceptions?"

"They're dead."

That shut her up—for all of thirty seconds. "And this is hell?"

"No, Victoria Bellona. This is heaven."

IF HE WASN'T going to give me a straight answer, then I wasn't going to bother asking any more questions. I knew what heaven was like. It was a beautiful place with clouds and happy smiling people and angels. . . .

Well, they got the angel part wrong. Unless there were still traditional heavenly angels who wore the white robes and golden halos and spent their time playing harps instead of training for war.

I glanced over at my hooded companion. His wings seemed to be invisible unless he was flying. Though there had been that almost mystical moment when I'd felt the unbelievable softness of feathers wrapped around us in his narrow bed.

Did a golden halo appear at the same time, and I'd just been too busy to notice?

"What?" he demanded suddenly. We were driving slowly and cautiously down narrow lanes, the gray houses crowding close around us.

"Where's your halo?"

His response was a string of words no self-respecting angel should use. "What were you expecting, a gold ring balanced over my head like the sword of Damocles?"

"Did you know Damocles?" I asked, momentarily diverted.

"No."

"Are you old enough to have known Damocles?"

"I was already old when Damocles was a child," he snapped. "Just how gullible are you?"

"Pretty damned gullible. I believe in fallen angels and vampires and men who can fly and places without color and, apparently, heaven."

He seemed to be grinding his teeth. I was tempted to point out that that wasn't good for them, but then figured if he was immortal, so were his teeth. Convenient. I didn't think there were any dentists in Sheol.

"Can you die?" The thought was suddenly devastating. "Beloch wanted to destroy you. Can he actually kill you?"

He shoved the hood back, turning to look at me. The houses were thinning out now, what looked like a forest of great trees visible in the distance.

"It's damned hard to kill an angel. Only another immortal can do it."

"But I'm not immortal, am I?"

"No."

"Then what good is it, being a god?" I demanded, really annoyed. "If you're telling me I put up with that awful childhood only to get stuck in a new sort of prison, and I have no magic powers as far as I can see, and I'm not even immortal, then that just sucks dead toads."

"Sucks dead toads?" he echoed, faintly horrified.

"Big-time. So if you know for sure that I'm not immortal, do you happen to know when I'm supposed to die?"

Silence. Of course. His short period of talkativeness was over.

"All right, if you won't tell me that, at least tell me where we're going." I glanced in the tiny rearview mirror as the sepia city faded behind us.

"Apparently we're leaving the Dark City. Where are we going?"

"The Darkness."

I wasn't sure if I wanted to laugh or cry. "Tell you what," I said, trying to keep my voice cheerful. "Let's get out of the car, you pick me up, and we'll just fly out of here. Easy peasy, no harm, no foul."

"I can't."

"If you give me one more monosyllabic answer, I'm going to scream."

"That's not monosyllabic. Two syllables: I. Can't. Stop complaining. I just don't talk a lot."

"Make an effort," I ground out.

He glanced at me out of his midnight-dark eyes. "Beloch has placed an impenetrable net over the Dark City. No one can fly in or out. I was lucky enough to get here just before he put it in place."

"I don't think luck had anything to do with it. I think he waited until he captured you. He's far more interested in you than he is in me."

"Indeed. Two syllables," he added.

"And how do we get out?"

"I told you. The Darkness surrounds the Dark City. If we can find our way in there and survive long enough, then we should be able to fly out, assuming I can find the place where the veil is thin."

"Why doesn't that sound like a very encouraging plan?"

"It's not. You may not even survive the transition

into the Darkness. Once there, leaving might prove difficult."

"So what is the Darkness? If the Dark City is heaven, then the Darkness is hell?"

"Not exactly. The Darkness is chaos. Most of the Fallen have survived the Dark City. No one survives the Darkness."

"So you're taking me to certain death? Gee, thanks."

He glanced over at me. "No one has survived the Darkness but me, and I have every intention of keeping you safe."

I considered this. "Why are you the only one to survive?"

He didn't answer. Of course. I persevered. "What happens to us if we die?"

He looked at me incredulously. "If we die, we die."

"I mean, what happens to the battle with the Armies of Heaven? The one you brought me for."

"Without me to lead them, they'll be defeated," he said flatly.

"Then why the hell did you endanger yourself and the future of the Fallen by coming after me?"

"Is there a chance in hell you'll stop asking that question?"

"Is there a chance in hell you'll answer it?" I shot back.

He slammed on the brakes and I went hurtling toward the windshield. His long arm shot out and caught me a moment before I went face-first into the glass. "No seat belts, remember?" he said.

It took a moment for me to catch my breath. "Well?" I said, still pushing.

"We'll go through the Portal into the Darkness," he said finally, "and find a place to recover. I'll tell you then."

"Recover?" I said, not liking the sound of that.

"If we survive," he added, just to make things even more cheerful.

For once I was lost for words. We couldn't stay here—there was no escape from this world within the Dark City, and no fallen angels would be getting in and out. Even if we managed to avoid Beloch, the Truth Breakers, and the Nightmen, just how long could we survive on the road?

I felt sick, dizzy, disoriented, and belatedly I remembered food. I'd always had a healthy appreciation for food, and I worked hard enough that I could eat what I wanted without having to worry about it showing up on my hips.

"I need to eat," I said.

"You won't starve."

"I haven't eaten anything since I left Sheol, and I don't remember when I ate there. I'm so hungry I feel like I'm going to pass out, and if you don't feed me soon I'm not going to be any good to anybody." I waited for him to take the cheap shot, to say I was already of no use, but he resisted it nobly.

"Didn't Beloch feed you? He gave you that strumpet dress—clearly he was priming you for something."

"Strumpet?" I echoed. "Who uses a word like *strumpet* nowadays?" The moment the words were out of my mouth, I realized how stupid they were. "Never mind. He offered me Earl Grey and cookies. I didn't trust him."

"He was hardly going to go to all that trouble to poison you. If he wanted you dead, he could simply smite you."

"Then why didn't he smite you?"

"I'm not as easy to smite."

I slid down farther in my seat. "This is a ridiculous conversation. Wake me up when you find me food." I didn't really expect to sleep. I just didn't want to argue with him any longer. "Just stop at a gas station and get me a bag of chips."

"There are no gas stations."

This roused me from my sulks. "What do the cars run on, then?"

"Beloch."

He really was the most annoying man.

TO MY SURPRISE, I did sleep. When I awoke, night had fallen, a dark, moonless sky overhead, and I was alone in the old car. I clamped down on my initial panic. I knew perfectly well Michael hadn't abandoned me, no matter how much I managed to annoy him. He'd be back, and all I had to do was stay put and wait for him.

That is, he'd be back if Beloch hadn't managed to track us down and kill him.

Michael wasn't dead. I would know if he were. I didn't want to analyze why that was so. The ramifications were too disturbing. I simply dwelled on the comforting knowledge that he was alive, unhurt, and not far away.

How the hell did I know that? Hunger was making me delusional, I decided. My stomach had long ago stopped its ominous rumbling and now was simply a hard ache.

And I didn't even want to think about how thirsty I was. I used to know the formula—you could live two days without water and two weeks without food. Even if I managed to find water, I was never going to make it two weeks.

I probably didn't need to worry. Beloch would kill us both long before then.

The rap at my window was so unexpected that I shrieked, then clapped my hands over my traitorous mouth as Michael yanked the door open, reaching in to haul me out.

"You want to scream a little louder, Victoria Bellona?" he said, back to his usual cranky self. "I'm not certain everyone in the Dark City heard you."

I didn't bother trying to defend myself. I knew I was in the wrong. We seemed to be in the middle of a forest, with tall trees all around us, and in the distance I could see a large square building dark against the sky.

"I don't suppose you found me any food?"

He took my arm and began hauling me deeper into the woods. "I didn't have any choice," he grumbled. "If I didn't, I'd have to listen to you whining and I'd end up strangling you."

"I don't whine!" I snapped. "And where are you taking me? Is this the Darkness?"

He snorted. His hand was tight on my wrist, and I decided I should start wearing some kind of wrist guard. I was going to have calluses at this rate.

"Not likely," he said. "You'll know when we reach the Darkness. It won't be like anything you've ever encountered before."

"So this is only the slightly-darker-than-the-Dark-City. What do we call this—the Grayness?"

"We call this a place to spend the night."

"Why?" I was immediately suspicious.

"Because I've barely slept in the last forty-eight hours, and you're exhausting. You can eat and I'll sleep and we'll both be happy."

"Where?" I was getting this monosyllabic thing down myself.

"There's a deserted barn up ahead with lots of nice, comfortable hay bales. You can keep watch while I sleep."

I stuck my tongue out at his back. While on the one hand I wanted to get as far away as I could from this wretched place, on the other I think if I'd had to spend another hour in that car I would have screamed.

Well, I already had, hadn't I? From now on I wasn't going to breathe a word about food, rest stops, or questions he refused to answer, which was pretty much all of them.

Which meant the rest of our time together would be conducted in dead silence. But if he could manage it, so could I.

The barn was farther away than it had looked, and I was barefoot. I bit my lip and said nothing when I stubbed my toe on a rock. I kept moving as roots and twigs dug into the soles of my feet. The very last thing I was going to do was complain.

Apparently I wasn't moving fast enough for His Royal Holiness. He yanked, and I tripped, barely managing to right myself and avoid crashing into his body.

"Can't you keep up?" he demanded sourly.

"Doing the best I can, Your Saintliness," I replied. I didn't want him thinking I was a whiner or a shrieker. A smart-ass was perfectly all right with me, and accurate to boot.

He turned back abruptly, and this time I did plow into him, slamming up against his iron-hard body.

A mistake. I didn't want either of us remembering the effect he had on me. He was used to sex, even if he'd abstained for the last century. This was simple biology to him. It was everything to me. If I looked at him I felt hot. The sound of his voice, even when he was being deliberately rude, made me melt. The memory of his hard, naked body made me shivery and wet. Maybe it was simple biology for me as well. But it went way beyond the merely physical.

I could come up with any number of perfectly logical explanations for my obsession. With one relatively straightforward act of coitus, he'd managed to jump-start my delayed libido, and now six or seven years of unfulfilled lust had finally broken through, making me look at Michael with insatiable desire.

Well, not strictly insatiable. The other night he'd managed to sate me pretty damned well. The problem was, the more I thought about it, the more I wanted it. Wanted him.

"Don't call me that," he growled.

"Don't call me Victoria Bellona. It sounds like a luncheon meat."

"It's your name."

"My name is Tory. Use it."

He was standing too close to me, and we were both simmering with temper. "And if I don't?"

"Then I'll start calling you Mikey, Your Saintliness."

He was still holding my wrist, too firmly, and he slid his hand up my arm, drawing me closer. "You'll find that it's not wise to wake the sleeping dragon."

We were almost touching. I could change that. I could take a step closer, press my body against his, put my mouth against his hard one. I wanted to, so badly.

I could take one step back, break the spell. I didn't move.

And then the moment passed. He released me, turning away, and I wondered if he was going to abandon me in the night.

"We're here."

I looked up. The barn loomed out of the inky darkness, its shape barely discernible from twenty feet away.

By the time I caught up with him, he'd managed to open one of the doors. There was a hole in the roof and I could see the pale light of the few stars. What kind of sky was I looking at? Was I even still on earth, or was it out there, winking at me? Had Sheol been on the same planet as the *castello*?

"If you're so hungry, what are you waiting for?" Michael's irascible voice came out of the darkness. I couldn't see him, but I moved toward the sound, only to be brought up short by a strong arm blocking me.

"Sit. You aren't going to be happy if you trample your food. And eat slowly or you'll end up making yourself sick."

I sank down where I stood, ignoring the fact that I slid past the front of his jeans. I could only see shadows, but full light right now wouldn't have helped, since everything was gray. My eager hands found a cold bottle of what I assumed was water, a loaf of bread, some kind of grapes, cheeses, and what was most definitely an apple.

"God, I love you," I breathed, and then froze, cursing my heedless tongue. I quickly scrambled for safety. "Of course, I'd be in love with Jack the Ripper if he brought me food like this."

There was a long silence in the darkness, and I would have given anything, short of the food he'd brought me, to see his face. "You love me or you are in love with me? Make up your mind."

"It depends whether you brought me wine or Diet Coke." My hands were still busy discovering things.

"You don't like Diet Coke," he said flatly. How the hell did he know that? "I brought wine and chocolate."

In for a penny, in for a pound. "In love it is, then," I said, my hands finding a chocolate bar. And then I managed to forget all about him as I ate in blissed-out silence while he roamed around in the darkness.

Eventually even I grew sated, and I reluctantly paced myself. "Aren't you going to eat anything?"

"I don't have to eat as often as you do."

"What's that supposed to mean?"

"Stop looking for trouble. The Fallen don't need food and drink as often as their—as the others."

What was he going to call me? His wife? His mate? His girlfriend? "Does that mean I get all the chocolate?" It was dark chocolate with pieces of crystallized ginger in it, and sheer heaven, but I was finally feeling pleasantly stuffed for the first time in what seemed like weeks. If I ate any more, I'd be sick.

His hand closed around mine, plucking the half-finished bar out of my fingers, and I realized he'd been able to see me as I'd been wolfing down the food.

"Just how good is your night vision?" I demanded.

"Better than yours. I've changed my mind—you can sleep for the first shift. I've made you a bed over in the corner. I suppose you need me to guide you to it."

Why wasn't the starlight brighter? The last thing I wanted was the Archangel Michael leading me to bed. And leaving me there, alone.

"Just point me in the right direction and I'll run into it." I rose and his hands settled on my shoulders.

I held my breath, wanting to savor his touch. For a moment he simply held me, and then he gave me a little push, releasing me as I walked.

It was a pile of hay bales with my discarded Truth Breaker robe on top, protecting me from the scratchiness of the straw. He'd piled them fairly high and I climbed up, stretching out on the cloth and staring up through the broken roof. The stars twinkled down on me, letting in the faintest light. Not enough to see him, just enough to let me know there was still a world out there.

I shouldn't be sleepy. I'd slept in the car, I'd slept in Michael's arms, I'd slept in Beloch's room. With Michael so close by, I couldn't believe I could sleep again.

But I did.

CHAPTER
TWENTY

ICHAEL STEPPED AWAY FROM her, trying to ignore the almost inaudible sounds of pleasure as she made herself comfortable on the hay bales. It had been bad enough watching her eat. He cursed his excellent night vision. He'd observed the sensuous pleasure on her face as she bit into the cheese, swallowing it with a rapturous delight. She'd licked her lips, and he'd wanted her tongue on him. Licking his lips. Licking his body.

He wanted to curse, but he had no idea who to blame. Who was responsible for deciding who was his mate and who wasn't? He'd survived two centuries with only one mate, and that was for a very brief time. Once he'd worked through his intense sexual discovery, perhaps fifty years of screwing any willing female, he had recognized the emptiness of it, and celibacy had been an easy choice. He had no illusions that it made him stronger. Sex was a healthy animal activity. If his desire had been great enough, he would have broken his fast. But no one had tempted him.

Until he set eyes on Victoria Bellona. *Tory*, he corrected himself with a faint grin. Her recent habit of calling him "Your Holiness" and "Your Saintliness" amused him, though he wasn't about to let her see it. He didn't want her to have any idea how she affected him. How much he wanted her. Longed for her. Ached for her.

He couldn't blame that short episode in his bed. He'd been filled with ridiculous, powerful lust since she'd first entered the contessa's drawing room, her hair dressed like a vestal virgin's, her body slim and strong in that skimpy black dress.

He'd ignored it. Fought it. It kept coming back, and walking away from her in the workout room, after she lost her bet, had been a Herculean effort. Finding her in his bed had been too much even for him.

He could smell her skin. Hear the strong beat of her heart that grew faster when he got closer. Sense the fullness of her pulses, and he wanted to taste, to drink.

He couldn't. He'd taken a taste, a sip, just enough to appease whatever sadistic overlord was pulling the strings. But if he took her fully, she would be destroyed.

He wasn't going to give in to that craving. If she died, part of him would die with her. He didn't want to consider why; he simply accepted it as the truth.

He would keep his distance, at least from her blood. *Blood-eater.* The phrase echoed in his head, but his habitual aversion seemed to have faded. Disappeared, in fact.

He could sense her desire—the heat of it touched his skin, pushed at his arousal. He'd taken what she'd offered, her lithe, strong body, and managed to survive. In truth, he felt even stronger. He'd lost nothing, gained everything when he'd climaxed.

And he wanted it again.

She turned on the makeshift bed, drifting into troubled sleep, and he wondered if he could ignore that burning need. He hadn't been strictly truthful—he didn't need to sleep right now. Wasn't sure that he could, particularly since the last time he'd slept, she'd been stolen and taken to the Dark City. If he slept again, would Beloch find her? Take her?

He built a pallet for himself on the far side of the barn and threw himself down on it. He wasn't going to touch her.

But he could sense her dreams. The restless way she shifted, the pounding of her heart.

Would it make any difference if he took what he needed? She would still die. Would he be the cause?

It would still trouble him, whether he ever touched her again or not.

She sighed. Just a soft susurration, but it went directly to his groin, and he stifled an answering groan. If it went on like this, he was never going to make it through the night.

He had no clear idea how they were going to get the hell out of this accursed place. No idea what kind of toll the Darkness would demand.

He could die tomorrow. As a soldier he'd lived with that truth for his entire existence. It had never bothered him—it was his fate. And it didn't bother him now.

Except . . . if he was going to die tomorrow, then he was going to have her one last time.

Not her blood. Never her blood. But he could bring her pleasure, lose himself in the tight sweetness of her body. He could have her. And if death came for him in the Darkness, he would meet it head-on, knowing at least some level of completion.

She stirred again, and he thought of her gorgeous mouth. Beloch had hurt her, in the clever ways he could, leaving his victims confused and uncertain. She kept denying anything was wrong, but he'd looked into her green eyes and knew. If he took her, touched her as he so desperately needed, would he hurt her too? Or would he ease some of the longing and frustration that threaded through her body? He closed his eyes, and he could see the fantasy that played in her slumbering brain. Him. Going down on her.

He wouldn't have thought his cock could get any harder. If he just continued to listen in on her sleeping fantasies, he could bring himself off with a couple of quick jerks. But she still moved on the pallet, her hips rising to an unseen mouth, and he gave up fighting. He crossed the midnight-dark room to look down at her.

He hated that dress. Garnet red and low-cut, it was a whore's dress, a message from Beloch. It was no surprise that Michael wanted her out of it.

He closed his eyes, breathing in her desire, and her fantasy came to him with riveting clarity. His long fingers cradling her hips as he tasted her, drank from her, made her explode. . . .

A tiny shiver shook her body, just the merest tease of a climax, and it was the last straw. She deserved better than that, better than a sleeping twinge of satisfaction when he could give her so much more and ease that ache inside him as well.

Her feet were bare. He frowned. For some reason he hadn't realized that. Stumbling through tunnels and along forest paths must have hurt like hell. She hadn't complained.

In fact, she never complained. She demanded food when she needed it, answers that he couldn't give. But she never said she was in pain, or that she was tired. In truth, she was brave, strong, the kind of woman who was more than a match for him. The kind of woman—hell, *the* woman he longed for. And could never, ever have.

He couldn't stay there and not touch her. The air was cool and clear, and it called to him. With one last glance at her restless, sleeping form, he stepped out into the night.

CHAPTER
TWENTY-ONE

I WOKE IN THE DARKNESS. I WAS ALONE in the barn. I knew it, even if I couldn't see it. The stars overhead had blinked out, and I could see nothing. I'd dreamed about him putting his hands on my restless, aching body. Instead, he'd left. I hated this world of unending darkness, darkness without him. Hated His Holiness, the Archangel Michael, hated my own love-starved, traitorous body.

Even dawn in this dark, dismal world was barely a change in light. It started slowly, shadows in the corner of the old barn resolving themselves into piles of hay, an antique tractor, a thick pyramid of milking cans. Did people really farm here? Did they live normal lives, eat and drink and work and play?

They were dead, Michael had told me. Dead people didn't do any of those things, did they?

The lack of color hit me anew as dim light began

to pour through the roof and the doors. In the darkness I'd forgotten about the black-and-white world.

I moved my head, looking down at my body. Still in glorious color, when I felt drab and empty.

I didn't hear him come in. I looked up and saw him, standing motionless, looking at me out of hooded eyes, and I couldn't read his expression.

"Time to go," he said. "We'll reach the edge of the Darkness in a couple of hours." He held out his hand to me. "Come."

I ignored it, of course, sliding off the platform of hay bales on the far side. I shook my skirts free and turned to face him. "I'm ready," I said, somewhat needlessly.

He dropped his hand without another word, turning his back on me, and I watched him, my mournful anger at being abandoned vanishing for one brief moment. That angel-beauty was so devastating, so perfect, that even his tall, strong back took my breath away. Not to mention his gorgeous, tight ass and long, long legs.

It wasn't just his astonishing physical beauty. It was his reluctant honor, his determination to lead his people to victory, the way he risked everything to come after me. The way he kissed me, his infrequent smiles, the intensity in his dark eyes, the sense that no matter how hard he fought it, he couldn't stop caring about me. Even if he wouldn't touch me.

I didn't have the same self-control. If he wanted

me, he could have me, to my everlasting shame. But he didn't. Not enough.

If he could fight it, so could I. If His Fucking Holiness could resist me, then I could ignore him. I was just as strong, just as determined, as he was.

I followed him out into the tepid daylight.

MICHAEL BLESSED THE silence of the morning drive. He'd brought the grapes and cheese she'd missed the night before, but she'd simply set them on the backseat, ignoring him.

It had taken everything he had to keep from going to her last night. He'd seen her dreams, her need, and he'd wanted her so badly he'd been ready to explode. But if he hadn't kept his distance, he would have taken her blood. His willpower was only so strong.

Blood-eater.

He could hear the pumping of her heart, the soft pulse of blood through her veins. When he looked over at her, he could see the artery in her neck, smooth and plump and tempting.

He'd never wanted blood before. He had taken it from the Source without thought, like someone drinking a tonic. Now, suddenly, he was obsessed with Tory's blood. He didn't dare allow his mouth anywhere near her neck or he'd take her.

She was angry with him, though he wasn't quite sure why. He didn't care. It was easier that way for both of them. If they made it through the Portal, made it through the Darkness, she would still be furious with him if he continued to do his best to goad her. It was a good plan. It should have filled him with relief.

He could hear the sound of rushing water up ahead, and for the first time in his existence he felt a prick of apprehension. Not for himself. He was incapable of feeling any fear—except when it came to Tory.

There was no room for fear on the battlefield. Caring about her weakened him, when he couldn't afford weakness.

He brought the car to a stop, pulling out the brake. The river ran fast and deep, the color dark and ominous beneath the lacy froth of bubbles.

He said nothing, just looked at the depths, waiting. She had said nothing since they'd left the barn, not a word. But he could outwait her. He had eternal patience. He wasn't in any hurry to face death.

It took a full ten minutes by his estimation, though he'd expected her to last longer. "All right, I give up," she said in a cool voice. "Why are we here?"

He nodded toward the swift-flowing river. "That's the way to the Portal."

She screwed up her eyes. "There's no boat, and with that current we can hardly swim across. We'd be dragged downstream."

"We're not going across. We're going under."

I didn't know how to swim. It embarrassed me, and I'd done what I could about it. I'd followed swimming lessons on the Internet, practicing while

I lay on the floor: the backstroke, sidestroke, crawl. I suspected that if someone dropped me into a calm, shallow pool, I could manage just fine, and wading into the ocean had felt strangely normal.

But the idea of submerging myself in that angry river terrified me. "No."

He'd already started to climb out of the car, and he walked around behind it to my side. "There's no choice." He opened the door before I could think to lock it.

"It wouldn't have done any good," he added. "I could've ripped the door off its hinges."

I wasn't sure what angered me more, the fact that he had read my mind, or that he'd hidden just how strong he really was. I'd never had a chance in hell of beating him.

"Stop reading my thoughts!" I snapped. "I don't know how you do it, but just stop."

"I don't need magic or bonding skills, Victoria Bellona. Your face is very expressive."

"And does my face express how much it annoys me when you call me that, Your Magnificent Angelness?"

"I already know," he said tranquilly. "Get out of the car. Putting it off doesn't help matters."

"I'm not going in that water. I'll drown."

"Maybe."

Incensed, I looked up at his golden beauty, his dark, intense eyes. "Are you trying to kill me?"

"Don't be irrational. I could have simply left you

to Beloch's tender mercies. Or I could have snapped your neck at any point since we left the *castello*. When you die, it won't be by my hand."

Trickles of uneasiness danced around the solid core of terror that had pinned me to the car seat. "Why do you say *when*? Do you know something I don't know?"

"I know a great deal you don't know," he said. "If I had a few hundred years, I'd enlighten you. But you're mortal."

"And you're an asshole," I said. "If you think it would take hundreds of years to enlighten me about your brilliance, then you're sadly mistaken."

"Out of the car, Tory."

Okay, calling me by my name was an improvement, but not enough to get me out of that car. "I can't swim," I said sullenly.

"It doesn't matter. We won't be swimming. The only way to get to the Portal is to let the river take us." He reached in and scooped me up before I realized what he was doing.

I fought like a wildcat, hitting, scratching, but he was impervious as he carried me toward that river of death. "Don't do this!" I begged.

"There is no choice."

A moment later I went flying through the air, screaming at the top of my lungs. And then the cold, dark water closed over my head, and I sank like a stone, down, down, as the rushing current caught me in its icy grip. I couldn't see, couldn't breathe, as water filled my mouth and nose, weighed down my skirts. I kicked desperately, but I was at the mercy of the powerful river. I could feel thick muck at my feet, and I tried to look upward, but I was down so deep there was no light at all above me, and my feet were stuck fast. I strained upward, where fresh air had to lie, but it was as if my bare feet were encased in cement. Even the powerful current couldn't free me. I was going to die, and I wasn't ready.

And then a strong arm went around my waist, pulling me free, and his mouth covered mine, breathing air into my lungs. I clung to him, not fighting, letting him take me with the deep, dark current, letting go, falling, falling into darkness.

Something hurt. Like a dagger in my chest, sharp, burning pain, and light was filtering down from above. A moment later we broke through into the light, into the fresh, sweet air.

He shoved me up onto the riverbank and we both lay in the grass, gasping for breath. I could still feel the deathly pressure on my lungs, still taste the water in my mouth and nose. Still taste the air he'd breathed into me as he pulled me free.

He moved before I did, sitting up, and reluctantly I glanced at him. The water plastered his shirt to his chest, and I could see the line of tattoos snaking along one arm, twisting, turning in the fitful sunlight. He looked gilded, blessed by the light. "Your tattoos are moving," I said, my voice raspy from all the water

I'd swallowed. Near death had taken the starch out of me, and my hurt and anger faded.

"Yes," he said.

He didn't release my wrist. His hold was surprisingly gentle, and I had no idea if I could break it. I didn't try. Something was happening between us, moving, like the ink-dark lines on his body, and I felt my stomach clench.

Don't be kind, I thought miserably. *Don't be nice to me. Don't make me fall in love with you.*

But this time he didn't read my mind. Instead he looked at me, his dark, dark eyes so deep I felt myself begin to drift, lost in his gaze. Mesmerized. And then he dipped his head toward mine.

CHAPTER
TWENTY-TWO

H E KISSED ME. I TRIED TO PULL back, but the grip on my wrists was relentless, and even though I jerked my head away he held me tightly.

"Why are you kissing me?" I said in a deliberately cranky voice, hoping that would mask the pain. "You don't even like me."

For a moment his blinding smile lit his face, and just that quickly all my resistance vanished. He shifted his grip so that he held me captive with one strong hand, while the other reached up to cup my face, so that I had no choice but to look into his eyes again. Fall into them.

"Such a foolish little goddess," he whispered. Before his mouth caught mine once more.

It wasn't a mercy kiss. It was hard and wet and full of carnal demand. His long fingers pulled my mouth open, and he pushed his tongue into me, demanding a response that I was helpless to refuse. I fell back into that dangerous world, throwing pride and caution to the winds, kissing him, lost in the sensual delight he wove around me with merely a look. I started to move closer, press up against him, but our hands were in the way.

And then he wrenched himself away, and we stared at each other, breathing heavily. "Did you ever stop to consider there might be a reason I keep myself as far from you as I can?" he said in a soft undertone. "I want you. I want everything about you, including your blood."

"But you don't care about . . . blood." I hated even to say the word. It confused me, frightened me, horrified me. The thought of someone drinking my blood, swallowing it, was disturbing. And yet, beneath my horror and aversion ran a thread of arousal that made no sense.

He brushed his mouth across my lips, my cheeks, my eyelids. "I want yours," he said, moving his mouth to the side of my neck, just beneath my jaw. I felt him inhale deeply, and his tongue danced across my veins. And then he pulled away, still holding my hands. "We have to go."

I stared at him, bemused, once more lost in his darkened gaze. "Go where?"

He jerked his head over his shoulder, and for the first time I looked around me.

The river rushed beside us, though we were now

on the opposite bank. Such as it was—the brown-toned landscape looked odd, unfinished, and then my eyes focused behind his head, and I froze.

It was as if someone had painted a watercolor of browns and grays and then left it out in the rain. Walls of viscous light pulsed and throbbed like living things, and I skittered away in fear. "What the hell is that?" I demanded in horror. But I already knew the answer.

"The Darkness." His voice was flat, implacable.

Panic sliced through me, and I tried to yank my wrists free. "I don't—"

He held me, refusing to let me go. "We don't have a choice."

Man up, Tory, I told myself. I wasn't used to being afraid. Then again, all the real danger I'd faced had been human, normal. I'd never faced anything with the malevolent force of this liquid wall of power, and it shook me to the bone.

But I had never been a coward and I wasn't about to start now. "Are we going to make it through?"

I was hoping for reassurance, but His Saintliness wasn't one for meaningless lies. "Maybe," he said. "I can help."

"How?"

"Trust me."

Those were notoriously dangerous words. I said nothing. The dismal truth was that I did trust him, and the last thing I wanted to do was tell him so. He already held too much power over me.

"Good," he said, and I wanted to snarl.

"Don't make assumptions!"

His smile was faint, devastating. "I told you, everything you think shows on your face. You'd be a terrible poker player."

"I don't believe it's that simple." He saw things too clearly for it all to be a matter of an educated guess.

"We can argue about it when we get back," he said. "In the meantime, we have to deal with the Portal and then the Darkness. Time passes differently in this world than it does in Sheol, and we have to get back before it's too late. We need to concentrate on that." He separated my wrists, holding each hand out from my body. "Don't fight this," he said.

"Fight what?"

I had deliberately kept my eyes averted from his beautiful chest, but something drew my gaze. The tattoos were shifting, sliding across his golden skin slowly, sinuously. I wanted to touch them with my mouth, lick the slowly moving marks, but he held himself too far away.

"Hold still."

As if he were giving me any choice. His grip was merciless, and I watched as the line of tattoos twined across his chest, coming down the middle and swirling upward again in mirrored lines, up to his strong shoulders. They curled around his biceps, gliding down to circle his forearms, his wrists, and then across the hands and fingers that held me.

I felt the first touch of them as a faint caress, almost a tickle, and I gasped, looking down as the marks slid up my own arms.

It felt like a hundred butterflies dancing in my veins. They ran upward, disappearing beneath the short sleeves of the ruby dress, and then began to swirl across my neck and shoulders, dipping down beneath the gown to caress my breasts, and I let out an involuntary moan of pleasure.

"There," he said in a muffled voice, and released me.

I fell back, but he caught me, easing me down. I lay in the grass, staring up at the colorless sky, and felt the strength fill my body. After a moment I managed to sit up.

"That was amazing," I breathed. "Better than sex."

There was no missing his wry smile. "It's less work."

"Fuck you," I said genially, twisting my arms to admire the sinuous tattoos. They moved on my skin as well, and the sensation was delicious. Empowering.

"We've put this off too long," he said abruptly, rising to his feet and reaching for his discarded shirt. My own dress had dried with surprising quickness, and wet denim no longer cupped his butt.

I scrambled to my feet too. "What will these do?"

I lifted my skirt halfway up my legs and saw them move across my thighs as well, a soft caress.

"They'll make you infinitely stronger," he said, turning his back on me as he fastened his shirt. "They'll make the pain more bearable, give you a fighting chance." He turned back, taking my hand in his. "Come."

Something felt wrong. I had no idea what it was, but something had shifted, and despite my new strength I felt frightened as he drew me forward toward that malevolent, shimmering cloud.

"What if we don't make it?"

He looked down. "You will," he said, and pulled me into the cloud.

I'd been expecting a veil, a thin wall that would hurt like hell and then be over, but it was thick, impenetrable, like Jell-O.

And then the pain hit, like a thousand shards of glass slicing deep into my skin, and I cried out, shocked at the harshness of it, gripping Michael's hand so tightly that if it had been anyone else I would have broken his bones. I tried to breathe my way through the shattering pain, remembering the movie scenes of childbirth, and I clung to Michael even more tightly, not sure if I could stand it.

And then his words came back to me. "You will," he'd said. Not "We will." *I* would survive.

But what about the archangel? He was stronger, he was immortal, nothing could touch him. But he'd said, "*You* will."

The pain grew, a living thing, the knives of glass digging deep inside, into my organs, my stomach, my heart, my womb, and I began to sink, losing this epic battle, and he was wrong, I wouldn't—

I was pulled up against a hard, strong body, but it was trembling, shaking, as he vibrated with pain.

"Michael!" I screamed in sudden terror, and I felt something wrap around me like a blanket of feathers, shielding me, protecting me, and I stopped fighting, sinking against him, letting go.

And then it was over. Silence, thick and deep, flooded my brain, filling it with marshmallow fluff. I didn't move, feeling those magic butterflies dance through my body, healing, soothing, and I drifted, absurdly happy, wrapped in Michael's strong arms.

It took me a long time to realize that something was wrong. The skin beneath my head was cold, almost clammy. My head was against his chest, and his heartbeat, usually so strong, was faint, thready.

Light blinded me as the protective blanket withdrew. He released me, and I realized his wings had been around me, protecting me, cradling me. That same feathery softness had covered us when we'd made love in his room. Blessing, protection. Love.

But his arms had fallen away, his wings had vanished, and he lay still on the ground.

A faint glow emanated from Michael's body, a much stronger one than mine. I looked down at Michael, and I knew he was dying.

His eyes were closed, his color pale beneath the

cuts and bruises that hadn't been there before. His shirt was shredded, and I gazed at him in horror.

The tattoos were gone from his body—all the marks that had danced across his golden skin. The wards and protections had vanished, and I knew that the Portal hadn't taken them. They still danced across my arms. He had given them all to me, and had gone into the Portal with no protection at all.

"You idiot!" I screamed at him. "Take them back."

His dark eyes fluttered open, but they were dull, fading. "Can't," he said, his voice barely audible. "Takes . . . too . . . much."

"Don't you dare die on me, you asshole!" I said. "You can't live for millennia and then die because of my stupidity."

"Not . . . stupid, Victoria Bellona." It was just the trace of a smile on his battered face and I knew he was doing it simply to annoy me. Even as he was dying, he was still trying to irritate me.

"I'm not letting you die," I cried, my hands gripping his strong shoulders. They were cold to the touch—his life force was slipping away.

"Nothing you can do."

I wanted to howl, to scream, to cry. He couldn't do this. Not just to me, but to the Fallen. To the world.

I tried to shake him, but he was too heavy. "Don't leave me." I don't know where those words came from, and I didn't care. "I lo—" Before I could finish the damning sentence, he reached out and caught my hand with the last ounce of his strength, pulling me down to kiss me.

Then his mouth went slack beneath mine as he let go of life, abandoning me in the malevolent world of the Darkness.

CHAPTER
TWENTY-THREE

I KNELT IN THE GRASS BESIDE HIS LIFE-
less body, and for the briefest of moments
I wanted to scream and cry and rail at
whatever God he supposedly served. But only for a
moment.

"No," I said flatly, calmly. I had no idea what to
do, and I could act only on instinct. Do what my
heart told me. What my blood told me.

I had nothing with which to rip my flesh, but if
it came to it I would tear the skin on my wrist open
with my teeth. And then I remembered the thin
piece of metal I had hidden in the folds of my dress.

It took precious moments to shove my hands
through the cloth to find it, praying as I did that I
hadn't lost it in the car, the barn, the river. I slashed
it across my wrist, and blood welled up. Ignoring my
queasiness, I put my wrist against his lips, forcing my
blood there.

He didn't move. I pulled him partway into my lap, cradling him against my breast as I smeared his beautiful mouth with my bright red blood.

His eyes were closed. All life seemed to have left him, yet I felt a faint stirring in the body I held so tightly, a quickening.

I caught my wrist in my other hand and tried to squeeze it, like wringing juice from an orange, but the steady drips weren't enough.

I reached up to my neck, feeling for my artery. Could I cut into that and still survive? I'd heard that if you nicked an artery, you automatically bled out and died. Of course, that was in a world without vampires or angels who drank blood.

Last resort, I decided. I was willing to die to save him, simply because I couldn't stand the thought of living without him. I refused to consider why; I only knew that the world would be unbearable without his rare, blinding smile. I wouldn't let him die.

I looked down at my body. I wasn't endowed with much extra flesh, but the pale swell above my breast was reachable. I allowed myself a faint whimper of anticipation and then drew the metal across my skin.

The reward was so much blood my hands were sticky with it. Using all my strength, I pulled his comatose body up against me, pressing his mouth against my torn skin, willing him to live.

"Drink, you stupid jerk," I hissed, stroking the bruised skin on his face. I let my fingers push through his short brown curls tenderly, like a mother, as I slowly began to feel the suck of his mouth against my skin.

I could feel the slow beat of his heart growing stronger, and he caught me, holding me still as he drank from me, drank life. He didn't need to know I was giving him everything I could give. How long had I known him? It didn't matter. The last few days had held an eternity, and they were all that mattered.

I was dreamy, only half-aware, as we slowly shifted; I was no longer cradling him, he was holding me in his arms, sucking at me with a slow intensity that was . . . arousing. I knew I was growing weaker, but it didn't matter. I was in his arms, I loved him, and feeding him, saving him, was an even closer bond than the sex we had shared so far. I closed my eyes and dreamed, welcoming death.

STUPID GIRL! THE stupid, foolish creature! Michael slowly released his grip on her, easing her down in the grass as he licked the last of her blood off his mouth. She had done this for him, and he was furious. Her chance of survival, always tenuous, had now vanished completely.

He'd been dead, and she'd given him her blood, brought him back. And she would pay for that with her own life when they faced the Armies of Heaven. Unless he'd already killed her.

Under any other circumstances she'd be dead

or dying, past saving. But he had marked her with his wards to ensure she made it through the Portal, and those marks had kept her alive. Even now she was recovering her color, that horrifying ashen white returning to the soft blush he'd gotten used to. She was healing, thank God.

He glanced down at his body. Most of his wards were back, transferred by her blood. And they were fading from her skin, almost invisible now.

He hadn't even known if it would work. There'd been no time to think—he'd acted on instinct, and only now could he sit back and berate himself.

His death would have jeopardized the survival of the Fallen. And now she would die anyway.

He looked up at the bright, deceptive sun that shone down so fiercely, so oddly in the Darkness. Night would come soon, and the Wraiths would be out. He needed to find shelter.

He scooped her up in his arms, holding her tightly against his chest, and rose. He couldn't afford to wait.

FIRST THINGS FIRST: I wasn't dead. That was as good a way to start the day as any I could think of, and I lay still in the darkness, drinking it in.

I had absolutely no idea where I was. I seemed to be lying on a narrow bed pressed up against a wall, and the air was cold and damp. Light filtered in from a small window. Sudden panic filled me. Had I somehow ended up back in the cell in the Dark City? I managed to move my head, and relief flooded me. This was a different place, though I had yet to find out if it was safer.

If I didn't know better, I'd have said I was in the basement of an American house. I'd seen them in the movies, usually filled with washing machines and furnaces and monsters. None of those were visible, including the monsters, thank God. Unless you counted the one I'd married.

Memory was coming back along with my strength, slowly, and I reached up to touch the upper swell of my breast. I'd slashed myself to save his life, and he had taken my blood, had cradled me in his arms and put his hungry mouth against the gash. I'd felt my life slipping away, and I had been happy. I had been loved.

Ha! Almost killed was more like it. I'd managed to survive after all, probably no thanks to him.

A horrible thought struck me. After he'd almost drained me, had he returned the favor? Poured blood down my throat? Eww.

I licked my teeth, searching for the taste of copper, but there was nothing but a distant tang that took me a moment to recognize. Orange juice. Where the hell had he found orange juice? Just like the Red Cross, had he given me a cookie too as a reward for my donation?

My lip curled, but the thought of cookies made me suddenly ravenous. Wherever the hell we were, I needed food.

The Darkness. That was where we were supposed to be. Apparently this legendary place of terror was a suburban basement. Who knew?

I moved my head lazily, and then I saw him. He was sitting on the cement floor, back against the wall, hidden in shadows, and I wondered if he was asleep.

"How are you feeling?"

Apparently not. His voice was its usual cool, musical enticement, though there was a thread of something beneath it that I didn't recognize.

"Like I got hit by a truck. You didn't feed me blood, did you?" I needed to get my primal fear out of the way.

"No. If I gave you my blood, you would die."

"Well, technically, it would have been my blood. Why would I die?"

"It is forbidden for mates to drink blood. It can cause . . . problems."

"What sorts of problems? Do people grow two heads or something?"

"Why are you so interested, Victoria Bellona? Do you have a craving for my blood?"

Damn, he just loved to annoy me. We were back on track. "No, Your Angelic Idiocy, I don't. I want real food like eggs, ham, maybe a croissant or two."

"This isn't Sheol. Food doesn't arrive simply because you desire it."

"Sometime you're going to have to explain to me how that works," I said, momentarily distracted. "And I know very well we're not in Sheol. Do you want to tell me why the so-scary Darkness looks like a suburban basement?"

He glanced around him. "The Darkness is composed of many different worlds, all seemingly harmless, all of them dangerous. Don't be deceived by it." He rose, moving toward the light that was now pouring in from the window, and I could see him clearly. He was shirtless, having lost the tattered rag that had made it through the maelstrom, and his beautiful chest was once again swirled with those gorgeous, slow-moving tattoos. The cuts and bruises had disappeared, leaving him beautiful and untouched. Perfect, as an angel should be.

I lifted my own arm to look at it. The marks were gone, leaving my pale skin unmarred. "Where are my tattoos?"

"You gave them back to me when you gave me your blood. There was just enough power in them to save you from my rapacious appetite." His tone was wry, mocking, but I knew he was mocking himself. "So tell me, why the hell did you do such a stupid thing after I'd gone to all that trouble to keep you alive? Did you have no idea what all that fresh blood would do to me?"

"Pardon me, but I've never met a vampire before. I'm unaware of the protocol." My voice was cool. I'd saved his life, damn it. Why was he mad at me?

"I'm not a vampire," he snapped.

"Well, you drink blood to live and you have retractable fangs just like your wings. I'd say that makes you a vampire." I thought for a moment. "Or a Venezuelan fruit bat."

Michael was not amused. "If you need food, we will have to leave this place, but you aren't looking very energetic. Why don't you stop annoying me and concentrate on getting stronger? It shouldn't be more than half an hour before you're at full capacity again."

I was momentarily distracted. "Cool. Will this happen every time I get hurt?"

There was an odd look on his face, one that on anyone else I would have said was stricken, and I had to say something. "Look, don't feel so guilty about drinking my blood. It was my idea."

"Why?"

Oh, damn. I should have known that question would come. "You were dying."

"I was dead. Why did you decide to bring me back?"

"Why the hell did you give me your tattoos and go through the Portal without them? Why did you die for me?"

He moved toward me, and I struggled to sit up. This closeness made me uneasy, as always. To my shock he reached out and cupped my face with one hand, his thumb gently brushing against my parted lips.

"An error in judgment," he said in a whisper.

I opened my mouth and took his thumb inside, sucking gently on it, the sensation rocketing to my core. I grew wet immediately. I wanted him, all of him, and this was the only piece he had given me.

He looked down at me out of dark, unreadable eyes as he slowly, deliberately moved his thumb in and out of my mouth, and I wanted more, I wanted his entire beautiful body as my playground, and I sucked on him as he slid his thumb past my lips, and his eyes glittered.

He pulled away so abruptly that I couldn't still my cry of loss, but he was already across the basement, out of my reach. As always.

"Let's agree that we both did stupid things for incomprehensible reasons and leave it at that." The cool, distant archangel was back in place. He glanced toward the bright pool of light, an unreadable expression on his face. "If this looks like a suburban basement to you, then there should be an upstairs complete with food and fresh clothes. Are you going to loll on that bed all day or are you going to get your pretty little ass up?"

I decided to concentrate on the fact that he thought my ass was pretty and little, which wasn't strictly true, and not on the fact that two minutes ago he'd told me to stay in bed and rest. His Holiness was in a snit.

I pushed away from the cement wall, swinging my long legs over the side of the bed. My skirts were hiked midway up my thighs, and I caught him looking. He realized it and turned away abruptly, and I felt a sudden, erotic jolt.

So many contrasting emotions were flooding me that I felt dizzy. Lust and irritation went without saying. But . . . he'd come for me. He'd died for me. He had my blood inside him, making him strong. He had me inside him.

And in willingly giving him my blood, my life force, I was afraid I'd given him more than that. I had given him love.

CHAPTER
TWENTY-FOUR

I WOULD HAVE LIKED TO BE THE ONE TO follow him up the wooden stairs, more to keep him from looking too closely at my bedraggled self than for a chance to admire *his* pretty little ass. My hands felt sticky, and I looked down and shuddered. They were covered with dried blood. My blood.

So was the exposed part of my chest, though I didn't seem to have any gaping wound. For all I knew, the red dress was soaked with my blood as well.

He pushed me ahead of him, his hands now impersonal, and I climbed the stairs, holding my skirts up.

I stopped dead when I opened the door at the top of the stairs and half-expected Michael to barrel into me, but he must have been suspecting something of the sort, because he paused, easily looking over my shoulder from one step below me.

It looked like a kitchen out of the 1950s, a perfect ranch house with orange counters and avocado appliances. And they were in color. Not just color— the hues were blindingly bright.

"What is this place?" I breathed.

"I told you. It's the Darkness."

"This doesn't look like any dark I've seen."

He gave me a little push, and I stumbled into the room. "There's probably food here," he said. "Why don't you eat something while I see if I can find us some clothes."

I held up my bloody hands. "Speaking of eating," I replied with no tact at all, "I'd really like to wash before I do anything else. Unless you'd like to lick it off me?" Oh, God, where the hell had *that* come from?

Something flared in his eyes, and I couldn't tell if it was hunger or irritation. Whichever it was, it was dangerous.

"I would suggest you tread carefully with me, Victoria Bellona," he said in a deceptively mild voice.

I wasn't about to let him see how he affected me. "Yes, Your Angelness."

"That isn't even a word."

"I'm creative."

He heaved a long-suffering sigh. "I'm sure you'll find exactly what you need here."

I went wandering, just as happy to get away from him as he was to be rid of me. There were two bathrooms, both with pink tile and fixtures and fish murals on the walls. No freestanding shower, but I turned on the water in the tub and it not only worked, it was hot.

I washed my hands in the pink sink, thinking that the advent of color wasn't necessarily a good thing. I had no idea why these hues were so bright—perhaps I was simply reacting to a couple of days of sepia and gray. Nevertheless, a little pink went a long way. And I would have been just as happy not to see the brownish-red stains on my hands, the colors swirling down the sink like the shower scene in *Psycho*. Though, come to think of it, that movie had been in black-and-white as well.

I checked what appeared to be the master bedroom. I knew instinctively that no one had ever lived here, ever *would* live here, so I felt no compunction about raiding the closet. There wasn't much to raid. Several cheery dresses, the kind you wore with heels and pearls to do your vacuuming, and a fluffy pink evening gown.

I settled for a strange sort of skirt that wrapped around my waist and reached below my knees and a white T-shirt that clearly belonged to the man of the nonexistent family. I bypassed the girdle but resigned myself to the industrial-size panties. I was ignoring the pointy bras altogether. The archangel already spent too much time looking at my breasts, and at least my smaller ones could get lost in the white cotton, rather than poking in his face. Much as I'd like to seduce him, for the moment I figured it was a lost cause.

But the shower was heavenly, even if the shampoo came in a green tube that looked more like toothpaste. I soaped my body lavishly, then froze. Not all his tattoos had left me. There was a mark on my right hip, one I couldn't begin to decipher. I scrubbed at it, but it didn't fade, and it didn't move, the way Michael's did. Strange. I certainly wasn't going to say anything to Michael about it. He'd probably done it on purpose, and he was waiting to see how long it would take me to mention it. He was going to have a long wait. I deliberately didn't look down, not in the mood to see more dried blood go down the drain. When I finally climbed out of the huge pink tub and wrapped myself in fluffy pink towels, I felt almost human.

Which I wasn't, I reminded myself, turning to stare at my reflection in the mirror. I was an immortal goddess with no powers. Whoopee.

The face that looked back at me was pale as always, my black hair such a mess I wondered if I'd ever tame it. There was a mark above my breast where I had cut myself. It had healed completely, but a thin red line marked the place where he'd put his mouth and drunk deeply. I shivered in reaction, not disgust but something else. Something deeper, more primal.

I pulled on the clothes quickly, not surprised by their perfect fit. Michael was wrong. This was far too much like Sheol. I had little doubt I'd find exactly what I wanted to eat in that ghastly refrigerator.

I was wrong. No Diet Coke; instead there were small, heavy glass bottles of regular Coke, and it tasted even worse than the diet stuff.

There were saltines and cans of tomato soup, milk in glass bottles and bread the consistency of foam rubber. I looked at it all helplessly. I had never cooked in my life, and the stove scared me.

I certainly wasn't going to let Michael know it. The can of soup came with directions, and the stove turned on easily enough, the concentric rings of the burner turning bright red. I poured milk into a saucepan along with the condensed soup, and began to stir with the only implement I could find, a wooden spoon.

It didn't scorch too badly, and I poured some in a pink plastic bowl, only to see Michael watching me from the doorway.

He had taken a shower as well and his short hair was still damp and curly. He'd shaved, an interesting concept—I'd rather liked the stubble that had adorned his too-perfect face. He was wearing a twin to my T-shirt and a pair of baggy khakis. He looked like a man out of time. He looked delicious.

"The soup tastes better if you crumble the saltines into it, rather than have them on the side," he observed, casting a surreptitious glance at the half-filled saucepan.

"Help yourself," I said from my spot at the white metal table. "I left enough for you."

He didn't hesitate, though he frowned at the scorch mark at the bottom of the pan.

"Look, give me a break," I said. "I've never cooked anything before."

He opened one of the square packs of saltines and crushed them in his big hands, dropping them into his bowl and stirring until he ended up with a kind of brick-colored sludge. He took the seat opposite me, digging in with relish. "Never?" he said in disbelief.

"Never. I wasn't allowed out of my room except to train. Of course, I watched years of Julia Child, but while I expect I could butterfly a leg of lamb or whip up a soufflé with a copper bowl and a balloon whisk, Julia never explained the intricacies of opening a can of soup."

"Clearly I married the wrong woman," he muttered beneath his breath.

I reached out to snatch the bowl away from him, but he was too fast, catching my arm before I went in for the kill.

"Your cooking is divine," he said. "And just to prove it, I will generously offer to take your portion off your hands as well, since you'd rather fight with me than eat. My appetites are simple enough since I've fallen. Put food in front of me and I eat. Give me a beautiful woman and I'll have her in bed in twenty-four hours."

In a vain moment I hoped he meant me. I risked complete degradation and said, "It took more than forty-eight hours with me." I waited for him to say something unkind, something crushing.

But for once he smiled at me, such a beautiful smile that my heart sank. Because I loved him, and a smile like that would bring me nothing but grief.

"You were worth the challenge."

I let the words sink in. It was a lie—I had hardly been that interesting a bed partner, particularly to someone who'd explored the breadth and depth of sexuality that Rachel said he had.

I longed for him so badly, and I couldn't have him. The best thing I could do was keep the atmosphere light. "Keep your hands off my tomato soup." I reached for more saltines. He was right, they were delicious mashed into the soup. Who would have thought? "And tell me what your plan is. You do have a plan? You made this place sound like some kind of hell."

"It is." The smile had left his face.

"Hell is 1950s suburbia? I guess I shouldn't be surprised. We're just lucky you happened to find this place."

"Lucky." His expression was unreadable. "Have you looked outside?"

"Actually, no," I said with surprise. I was usually more curious than that. I just happened to be far more interested in looking at him than at the landscape.

"Go to the window and tell me what you see," he said in that voice I was coming to think of as the Archangel Voice.

But I wasn't going to argue. I took the last bite of my cracker sludge and went over to the window. "Just a boring suburban street," I said. "Half a dozen houses, all identical. Perfect lawns, no cars in the driveways, no sign of anybody." I looked back at him, and he nodded, clearly not surprised. "So what happens next?"

For a long time he said nothing, and I wondered if we were back in the "I'm not giving you straight answers" mode.

Finally he spoke, almost reluctantly. "There's a place here where the veil between this world and ours is very thin. We need to find that place, and with luck I can break through and fly us out of here before Uriel's enforcer finds us."

"He's got an enforcer?" I said. As if we didn't have enough challenges.

"Yes."

We were back to monosyllables. "I thought no one knew anything about the Darkness. Come to think of it, Technicolor Suburbia Hell is a better name for it here."

"Too unwieldy. And there's more to the Darkness than suburbia."

A sudden chill shot down my back. "How do you know that?"

But this time he wasn't going to answer. "It won't

be easy," he said instead. "But it's our only way out. If we'd stayed in the Dark City, Beloch would have found us no matter where we hid."

"How?"

"Beloch can always find me." His words were troubling. He glanced out the window. "We can't risk going out now—it's already starting to get dark. Time moves strangely here, and I have no idea how long the daylight will last. It could be a few hours or a few days, but we need to make sure we're not stranded out in the dark. That's when the Wraiths come. Assuming we get past the enforcer."

"Oh, holy Christ, new monsters to deal with?" I had had enough. "Who the hell are the Wraiths?"

He was unimpressed by my temper. "Just what they sound like. The ghosts of creatures who've been sent here."

I digested this. "And what do they do?"

"They suck the light from you, leaving only darkness, despair, and emptiness."

"Just great," I said. "And how do we avoid these Wraiths?"

"Keep in the sunlight and look out for shadows. They can't survive in direct sunlight."

"More vampire wannabes," I grumbled.

"We're not—"

"Yeah, yeah." I dismissed him. "So how long before it gets back to full daylight?"

He shook his head. "Your guess is as good as mine. In the meantime, you ought to try to get some sleep."

"I'm not tired. I don't suppose this place comes with a nice old black-and-white television with *I Love Lucy* on it?"

"What's *I Love Lucy*?"

I shook my head. "Never mind. I'll find something to keep me busy. Maybe I'll just sit around and try to annoy you."

He just looked at me. "There's no 'try' about it. And I could always strangle you."

"No you couldn't," I shot back. "Because then you'd have to put your hands on me, and if you do we'll end up having sex again, and that's the last thing you want." I held my breath, hoping, praying, he'd deny it.

He froze. "We're not having sex again."

I kept my face impassive. "Then don't try to strangle me."

For a long moment he said nothing. Then he pushed back from the table and picked up the empty bowls. "Go find your *I Love Lucy*," he said. "And keep away from me. We're stuck with each other until we get back to Sheol, and in the meantime I need to be alone."

"Ditto," I snapped.

I saw him blink at the word, then place it. "Ditto," he agreed coldly. "Go."

CHAPTER
TWENTY-FIVE

MICHAEL WATCHED HER GO, the skirt swinging around her calves, her breasts moving softly beneath the T-shirt. Damn her. He was having a hard enough time not thinking about her, the taste of her skin, the taste of her blood.

He pushed the thought out of his mind. There was no longer anything keeping him from indulging in every carnal fantasy he'd ever had, but something held him back. He was going to have to watch her die, watch all that humor and vibrant energy be crushed, and he hated the thought. The closer he got to her, the worse it was going to be. He was already having a hard enough time trying to keep his emotions in check. He'd always thought he didn't have any, but he was wrong. At least as far as Tory was concerned.

He glanced around at the plastic kitchen. It was a

stark reminder of who and what he had been. God's enforcer. Which made him Uriel's, delivering justice with a flaming sword, casting souls into the Darkness. Of course he knew more about the Darkness than anyone who'd been there. He was the only one who had ever returned.

The Fallen hadn't even known of its existence until he'd been forced to join them, and he'd always been deliberately vague.

Once Uriel had cast him out, Metatron had probably taken his place. In the short time Metatron had been in Sheol, he'd managed to avoid any substantive conversations with Michael. They both knew the truly terrible things that had been their lot, and to speak of them would only make them more real. The question was, who had taken Metatron's place? Who would be pursuing them through the bizarre worlds that populated the Darkness?

It had been his job to cast people into this. Those who had most displeased Uriel were sentenced to the Darkness, and Michael had brought them there. And if they'd managed to evade the Wraiths, he had come back and hunted them down.

He had always tried to believe that the people he'd hunted had deserved the horror of endless darkness. But Tory didn't deserve it. Tory deserved light and love, joy and happiness and a long life.

Instead she'd gotten a fallen angel who didn't know how to love and a death sentence. And there wasn't a damn thing he could do about it.

He pushed away from the table and headed toward the rectangle of light that Tory saw as a window. It looked as it always looked, a blur of colors that could coalesce into whatever vision of safety and comfort was most likely to lull the hapless quarry into a false sense of security. It made the payoff that much more devastating. And more fun for his previous taskmaster.

There was no question that Uriel took pleasure from the pain of those he punished. And no question that the crimes he'd punished could be relatively minor. Michael had wiped out entire villages, from newborn babies to ancient crones, as punishment for one man's blasphemy, and he'd done so without question.

Questioning had caused his fall from grace. And questioning had caused the fall of the first angel, Lucifer, God's favorite. Michael had been the one to fling Lucifer from heaven, and he'd never regretted it.

He pushed away from the window. Time was passing, much too swiftly. He knew from experience that time moved differently in the Darkness. For all he knew, Uriel would try to keep them there while he sent his armies to destroy Sheol. Michael had to get Tory out of there as quickly as possible.

Night came swiftly. For a moment he feared that Uriel's sadistic mind had given them a false haven, that there would be no lights to keep the monsters at bay. But as the shadows grew longer and he could see the glimmer of the transparent Wraiths waiting for them, the lights came on automatically. He wasn't sure that was a good thing. If they didn't control turning the lights on, then they had no control if something decided to turn things off.

He needed to stay near Tory in case that happened. He wasn't sure what the outcome would be if he were to battle a Wraith. In truth, in the entirety of his existence, he'd never been truly tested by an adversary. He was the Sword of God, and even in a universe where God had disappeared, leaving everything up to a stand-in archangel and the doubtful conscience of mankind, he still held that place. Even Uriel couldn't deny him that, though he could throw him out of heaven.

He moved through the house in search of her. It was easy enough to follow the sweet scent of her skin—even modern soap and shampoo couldn't mask the erotic imprint she'd made on his senses. He would find her wherever she hid.

She was stretched out on an orange and brown sofa, staring fixedly at a paperback book with a lurid cover. She wasn't nearly as aware of him as he was of her—she didn't even notice that he was watching her. He could look his fill at the long legs, her mass of dark hair she tried in vain to control, her breasts . . .

She wasn't wearing a bra, goddamn her. In the artificial light he could see the darkness of her nipples beneath the thin white cotton, and his arousal quickened at the thought of what he'd like to do with those breasts. He'd put his mouth on them and suck, hard, till they came to sharp little points in his hungry mouth, and—

They were already forming hard points. As he watched her, motionless, her nipples hardened, and he reached down and shifted himself in the loose khaki pants he'd found in the bedroom. Not loose enough, apparently.

"Stop staring at my breasts." She hadn't moved, but her voice was caustic. He caught a flash in her eyes, one of the fleeting images that had haunted him for the last few days. She wanted his mouth on her. She wanted everything he did.

"I wasn't looking at your breasts."

"Angels aren't supposed to lie."

"I'm a fallen one, remember? I can lie if I really want to, I can drink, I can fornicate."

She glared at him. "How come when you're talking in the abstract you use a nice polite word like *fornicate*, but when you're talking to me specifically you use a word like *fuck*?"

He shouldn't smile—it would probably infuriate her—but there were times when she was just so damned cute. "Because when I look at you and talk to you, all I think about is fucking. Specifically."

She sat up quickly, her chest rising and falling with temper. Which was particularly nice without the bra. "You're . . . Never mind."

He laughed, and her eyes narrowed. "I'm what?"

She rose, ignoring his question. "I'm going to find

a bed," she said, heading toward him, clearly expecting him to move out of the way.

"Good idea," he said, not moving.

She tried to push past him, a big mistake. The moment he felt her body touch his, his arousal went into overdrive, and he caught her arms so she couldn't run away.

She was barefoot, smaller, and she looked up at him with sudden—it almost looked like fear. Impossible, and the expression vanished immediately, leaving her angry once more.

"Get your hands off me."

He didn't. Not at first. "Is that what you really want?"

It wasn't. He could see the images that flashed through her mind, jumbled, erotic, insistent. He could almost feel her mouth on him, and he wanted to groan.

But she was made of sterner stuff, and she ignored the longing that was suffusing her mind and, by extension, his. "Yes, it is."

He released her, stepping back, and for a moment she didn't move. And then she was gone, her bare feet making a creditable stomping noise as she expressed her displeasure.

Arrogant asshole! Completely egocentric, self-congratulatory son of a bitch of a bloody archangel, thinking I was standing there just trembling for his touch.

It didn't matter if it was true. There was no way he could know it. Unfortunately, he seemed to understand everything I was feeling, whether I'd said something or not. He said I had an expressive face, but I'd been very good at hiding my feelings at the *castello* or from the bad-tempered nuns. Only Michael seemed to be able to read my mind.

Oh, God, that was a horrible idea. Because my mind had been running along X-rated lines, particularly when he was close to me. If he knew what I'd secretly, privately been longing for, then you might as well kill me now.

I hated him. He was probably laughing at me, at my poor, pathetic, love-starved self. He had been willing to fuck me, once—I could use that word too—but since then he'd kept as far away from me as he could. He wouldn't even take the blood he needed so badly, the blood I was foretold to provide. The blood that would keep him strong. No, he would court death rather than drink from me.

Though, come to think of it, why had he given me his tattoos and gone through the Portal unprotected?

Because I was needed. That was why he had come to get me in the first place. The prophecy decreed that I was to come to Sheol and marry the Archangel Michael in order for the Fallen to triumph against the Armies of Heaven. Michael said the Dark City was heaven. If so, did that make Beloch God?

No, I'd forgotten. God had gone on an extended vacation, leaving Uriel in charge. But if that was the case, who the hell was Beloch?

Did I care? Did I care about any of them? The bottom line was that the only kindness and decency I'd experienced had come from the Fallen. No one lied to me in Sheol. No one wanted to smite anyone else; they just wanted to be left alone. The Armies of Heaven were going to attack, not vice versa. The Fallen were doing their best to be ready, but they weren't the aggressors—no one suggested taking the fight to the enemy.

In the end, heaven and hell seemed equally bad, though I hadn't had more than a taste of hell. I would make it through the Darkness, get back to Sheol, and help them fight off their attackers. And then I was getting the hell out of there and getting the first angelic/vampiric quickie divorce I could find.

Next time I was forced to speak to Michael—and I hoped I could wait a good long time—I would assure him that I wasn't about to run off. At least, not until the Bad Guys who thought they were Good Guys were dealt with. He didn't have to pretend, or take pity on any sexual fantasies that spun from my brain. It had nothing to do with him, and everything to do with my wanting to discover life.

I would make sure that wish got granted. In those few short hours in his narrow bed in Sheol, I had discovered a world of sensuality. I had . . . I had become too attached to him, but I would get over it. I'd always been a fast healer, and this was no worse than a broken bone or a case of the flu. I'd survive—I always did.

And the saintly Archangel Michael could go fuck himself.

I stomped into the kitchen, embarrassed and furious. I couldn't even tell him that those fantasies had nothing to do with him. For one thing, the tattoos on his body had played an explicit part in some of them. For another, if I told him to stay the hell out of my mind, we would both have to acknowledge exactly what sort of licentious fantasies had been going on, and it was already humiliating enough. I certainly wasn't going to discuss why I was having such thoughts. Whether it was because he was the first man I'd slept with in more than six years, the first man who knew more than the absolute basics. Or if it had to do with the fact that he was just so damned pretty. Or maybe I was just bored. It had nothing to do with the fact that he fascinated me, infuriated me, touched me in ways I couldn't understand. Or that he'd come after me, rescued me, risked his own life again and again for me.

I opened the cabinet door so forcefully it bounced against the wall and snapped back. I was angry, frustrated, ready to explode, and even though I'd just eaten, I figured I'd better stuff something into my mouth before I screamed again.

Nothing to eat, maybe because the Über-God of

Hell knew I wasn't really hungry. I slammed the cupboard closed again, moving on to the next one.

"Stop having a tantrum." Michael's voice floated in from the living room, rich and seductive like everything else about him.

"Go to hell!" I shouted back. He was right, I was being childish, and I didn't care. I considered myself an intelligent, adaptable, reasonably strong young woman, yet there was a limit to how much I could take, and I had just reached it. I was trapped in this hellish ranch house with a man who turned my knees to water, yet he took me only under duress. He wouldn't answer my questions, he treated me like an idiot, and just when I was ready to give up on him he suddenly started to take notice. There was a term for that, I remembered, combing my memories. Dog in the manger. He had no interest in eating any of the hay placed there, but he wasn't going to make way for those who needed it.

The Archangel Michael had no real interest in me, unless you could count his reaction when I'd shown up in his bed, naked. The memory shamed me—he was more than capable of resisting me. I was never going to put myself in that position again. It didn't matter that I seemed to have developed the equivalent of a teenage crush on him. I wasn't going to offer again. I slammed the cupboard door as hard as I could and yanked open the refrigerator, my hands hot and tingling.

Oops. Stronger than I realized in my blind rage.

The upper hinge broke, leaving the door hanging lopsided.

There was no separate freezer door, only a small compartment in the center. No ice cream, only ice cubes, and while my frustration and fury burned as hot as my hands, I didn't think the cubes were going to help.

"What the hell are you doing in there?" Michael demanded in a muffled roar.

"Venting my frustrations," I snapped, pulling the other hinge free and throwing the refrigerator door across the small kitchen with a satisfying crash.

No sound from the living room. I yanked open another cupboard, grabbed one of the plates, and flung it across the room. Oddly enough, the crash was more satisfying than the heavy sound of the refrigerator door, and I reached for another.

Hands closed over my wrists, yanking me around to face Michael's thunderous expression. I tried to knee him—I was past any sense of fair play—and he sidestepped the crippling blow at the last moment, the flame of fury in his eyes growing hotter. He shook me hard, until I bit my tongue, and in response I smashed my head against his mouth, happy with his muffled cry of pain.

He shook me again, gripping my wrists so tightly that my hands were growing numb. "Had enough?" he demanded furiously.

"Not even close," I snapped back.

And then we both froze. He looked down at me,

bafflement and rage fading from his face. His mouth was bleeding. "Oh, shit," he said.

He released my wrists. I didn't know if he was going to try to pull away, but I wasn't going to give him that chance.

"Oh, shit, indeed," I said, my eyes daring him.

His mouth on mine was hard and angry, and I could taste his blood. It should have horrified me. It didn't. I put my arms around his neck and kissed him back, letting my blood mingle with his, and a moment later he picked me up and set me on the kitchen counter, moving between my legs. His hands slid up under my T-shirt and touched my breasts, and I moaned into his mouth, hot pleasure filling me. I needed this so badly, I needed his body against mine, I needed his fingers squeezing my nipples, I needed the hard bulge of his cock between my legs.

I held on to him tightly, half-afraid he'd pull away, but for now he had given up fighting. He lifted his mouth, and the blood on his lower lip was smeared. "You have blood on your mouth," he said in a rough voice. And he leaned over and licked me, catching it with his tongue.

It was a test, I knew. But it was an easy A. I'd already given him my blood, forced it on him. I felt no squeamish hesitation. In truth, when he had drawn the blood from the cut I'd made in my flesh, the sensation had been disturbingly erotic. I wanted him to do it again.

His hand slid down between us, yanking the skirt

up to my hips. "Shit," he muttered again when he encountered the underwear. And then the panties were gone, sliding down my legs and sailing across the room to land on the discarded refrigerator door with a lot less noise.

I wanted to touch him. I wanted to kiss him, to suck him, to taste him, but things were moving too fast, and when he touched me I burned, hot and sweet, needing more.

"Christ," he swore as I arched against him, and I knew a dazed moment of bemusement. Christianity didn't seem to have anything to do with the Fallen or the strange worlds to which I'd been banished; but then all that left me as he slid his long fingers inside me.

I shattered, letting out a low, keening wail, and he caught the cry from my mouth, drinking it in. Distantly I heard the clang of his belt buckle and the rasp of his zipper, and then he was inside me, sliding deep, pulling my legs around his narrow hips. I was already wet, aroused, my body accepting, and I clung to him, shocked. I felt like a boat on a stormy ocean, adrift in a tempest of sensation so powerful I could focus only on his body and what it was doing to mine. I could feel my nipples contract, almost painfully, as he thrust inside me again and again, and my breath caught, my entire being contracting into a bundle of overpowering sensations.

My head banged against the cupboard above me, and then everything tilted as he picked me up, swinging me away from the Formica so that he supported me entirely in his strong arms. I could move now, levering myself on his cock, and I clutched his shoulders as I slid down on him. I moved with deliberate slowness, teasing him, savoring him now that the first rush of climax was past.

He was cursing, low, guttural sounds that were even more arousing, and I tightened my legs around him, tightened my core around him, and he turned again, falling back against the opposite counter, bracing himself.

I could sense the ripples of pleasure building, building, and I felt a flash of fear. This was too much; I was giving away too much power. I would lose everything, I would die. I couldn't—

He lifted his head and his black eyes bored down into mine, and I knew what he needed, what I needed, when he would have denied us both. Everything coalesced, and the fear vanished. I threw my head back, exposing my neck to his mouth. "Take my blood."

This time there was no hesitation. The sharp, sweet sting as he broke the skin was a triumph, and that was my last conscious thought as I shattered, and he followed, his seed filling me, my blood filling him, giving, taking, life and death, a climax so powerful that the world seemed to blank out. Next thing I knew we were both lying in a tangle on the linoleum flooring of the horrible kitchen I'd tried to destroy, a kitchen I'd suddenly grown to love.

I lay sprawled across Michael's body, my heart still racing God knew how long after. I'd lost my skirt somewhere along the way and the T-shirt was rucked up under my arms. He must have kicked off the khakis at some point, and I could hear his heart beating just as furiously beneath my head.

I wasn't sure what to do. What I wanted was to burst into noisy sobs and tell him I loved him. For all I knew, I'd done exactly that in the last few moments, but I had postcoital amnesia. I simply let myself drift in the feathery soft cocoon of his wings wrapped around us.

Slowly his heartbeat returned to normal, a little before mine did, and his wings retracted and vanished. I felt cold, exposed. I needed to pull myself together. "So," I said, and there was nothing I could do about how raw my voice was, "are we lying on shards of broken china?"

For a long moment he seemed to hold his breath, and then he let it out, and I told myself I was relieved. "You're a brat," he said.

"Yes." He picked me up, and I pressed my tear-damp face against his chest.

"Where are we going?" I always seemed to be asking that question.

But this time the Archangel Michael answered. "To find a bed."

CHAPTER
TWENTY-SIX

MARTHA HATED CHAOS. HER life before she came to Sheol had been full of drama and disaster, with an alcoholic mother, younger siblings who needed constant supervision, and so many responsibilities that she'd felt old by the time she was sixteen. It was little wonder she'd taken one look at Thomas's kindly face and fallen into his arms.

Sheol was in chaos right now. The Source was suffering from an indisposition that no one wanted to name, though Martha knew as well as Rachel what troubled Allie. She was suffused with sorrow and longing for the baby that no Fallen had sired, and the blood that she gave the angels left them mournful as well. So she stayed in bed and wept when no one was watching.

Martha had brought her ginger tea to soothe her troubled stomach, and Allie had managed to drink half the cup, albeit under duress. In the other room Raziel was meeting with some of his chief advisors, and his angry voice carried into the bedroom where Martha and Rachel sat, keeping Allie company.

"Go tell them to shut up, would you, Martha?" Rachel said absently, holding Allie's hands. "I'm working on something."

Martha wanted to protest. She hated anger and confrontation, and the leadership of the Fallen consisted of nothing but anger right now. But Rachel's mysterious gifts were far too beneficial. Martha could offer the grief-stricken Source ginger tea. Rachel could offer healing.

She closed the bedroom door behind her as she stepped into the colorful living room, taking a deep breath, but no one noticed her. Metatron and Azazel were glaring at each other—in Michael's absence, Metatron had taken his place, though his training methods had managed to offend more than a few warriors. Asbel was there—a surprise, when he was usually so unassuming, but Martha was glad of it. Asbel was calm, restrained among so many hotheads. He could keep things in line.

Raziel was deep in conversation with Tamlel, but the Alpha lifted his head, focusing his intent gaze on Martha's face. "Is my wife all right?" he demanded in a rough voice.

"Yes, my lord," she said hurriedly. "Rachel is working with her, helping her to feel better. Her stomach is troubled."

"Her heart is troubled," Asbel said softly, and Martha frowned. Raziel had enough to deal with right now. He didn't need guilt and worry compounding things.

"She'll be fine," she said firmly. "Just give her a little time and things should right themselves."

Raziel nodded, looking unconvinced, and she turned away, secure that voices had lowered when they were reminded Allie was nearby, but Raziel's voice stopped her.

"Had any good visions lately?" he asked in his cool, cynical tone.

She shook her head, reaching for the door handle.

"Because we need to know where the hell Michael and his wife are." His voice exploded with frustration. "We have two weeks before the Armies of Heaven attack—that is, if your previous vision is to be believed—and the most important people on our side have disappeared. We're just lucky Michael thinks people work better on their own, or we'd be in deep shit. I'm not convinced we're not. What are our chances of surviving if Michael and Victoria Bellona don't return in time?"

She didn't waste time trying to scour her mind for a vision that never came when summoned. "I don't know, my lord. My vision said they would both be here."

"But things can change, can't they? According to Rachel and Asbel, the goddess was kidnapped, and Michael went after her. Couldn't that kidnap-

ping have thrown the preordained future into dis-
array?"

"Possibly." Her voice was cautious. "But I have
yet to see any change of vision. I think that if things
had altered that drastically, I would see something."

"Are you sure?" Raziel barked.

She wanted to growl herself, but she remembered
that she never lost her temper. Certainly not with the
lord of the Fallen. "No, my lord," she said. "I'm not
sure of anything. I can only tell you what I believe to
the best of my ability."

Raziel made a derisive sound, dismissing her as
he turned back to the others. "We have to come up
with some kind of alternate plan in case they don't
return in time."

Azazel glanced over at Martha, then back to
Raziel. "I believe he will. I believe they both will."

"And then the goddess will be destroyed," Asbel
said. "Sad, but unavoidable. The future of all the
Fallen is more important than the life of one girl."

"That remains to be seen," Raziel snapped.
Clearly he didn't find Asbel all that soothing. "And
we aren't all the Fallen. There are a few more of us
scattered all over the world."

Asbel looked abashed, his pale eyes lowering. "I
don't believe there's anything we can do. Either they
will return or they won't."

"Brilliant," Azazel muttered, and Martha remembered suddenly that Azazel didn't like Asbel any
more than he liked Metatron.

Raziel rose, looking at her as she tried to make her escape back to the Source's bedroom. "Is there anything more we can do?" he demanded, glowering.

She met his gaze fearlessly. "We can pray, my lord."

MICHAEL LAY AWAKE in the small bed, holding her. She was curled up against him, sleeping, trusting, and he was holding his rampant lust in check. They'd had sex again when they got in bed, this time slowly, deliciously. She'd lain beneath him, accepting, looking up into his eyes as he thrust into her with fierce deliberation, pushing her, slowly, slowly, letting it build until she was shivering and gasping, until he couldn't keep from letting go, holding still inside her, spilling into her as the tight walls of her sex spasmed with climax. His wings wrapped around them, cradling them, and he fell back against her, exhausted, replete. He hadn't taken her blood this time, though he could smell it, feel it dancing beneath her skin, longed for it. He couldn't understand it. He seemed to want her blood as much as he wanted her body wrapped around his. He'd never been at the mercy of his appetites before, and it disturbed him. He craved her, body and blood, like an addict.

And because he'd taken her blood, she was going to die.

He moved slightly, resting his chin against her tousled hair, holding her loosely so she wouldn't wake up. They had to get out of here. He had no idea how fast time was progressing—it moved differently in the Darkness. All he knew was that they had to get back. He had to save Sheol even if he couldn't save Tory.

He had no idea how long the night would last here in the Darkness. It was random, though he'd once known how to control it. He had lost that ability when he'd fallen, but he still understood more about this terrible place than anyone still living, even Uriel. Uriel, who had never been to this place he ruled, leaving it to his enforcer, the Flaming Sword.

If it were up to him, the night could last forever. But the Armies of Heaven would attack whether he was there or not, and if he left the Fallen alone with no one to lead them into battle, they would be defeated. Destroyed.

He couldn't do that. He had been created for war, and the upcoming battle was a righteous one. He couldn't throw away his duty and honor for the sake of the girl curled up in his arms. He was surprised he even wanted to.

But everything about her surprised him, not least his reaction to her. She was a warrior like he was, but she felt fragile when she lay in his arms, and he was filled with the need to protect her. Which was ridiculous—she could make mincemeat of anyone who came near her, with the lone exception of himself. He still marveled at the refrigerator door she'd torn off. He'd never been so turned on in his existence.

But dawn was coming and fate was making its demands. The war was coming, and he was made to lead. It was time to go.

HE WOKE ME with the gentlest kiss on my temple, his lips near my ear. "We have to go." And if he felt any reluctance as he pulled away from me, I couldn't sense it.

My body ached in places I didn't know I could ache. My womb felt battered. My breasts ached and my thighs still trembled.

For some reason my shoulders and arms hurt, and then I remembered why. I had torn the refrigerator door off its hinges in my blind fury. In retrospect, that both shocked and impressed me. I seldom lost my temper, and I hadn't been that furious since I found out Johann had betrayed me.

I was stronger than I'd been at eighteen. I was someone to contend with, and I found that thought curiously soothing.

Michael came back into the room, naked, and I jerked my eyes away from below his waist. He was enticingly beautiful enough, an angel-succubus, and I didn't need further temptation.

"You have just enough time to clean up." His voice was cool and matter-of-fact, as if we'd spent the night playing checkers, and the tentative smile on my face died before it was born. "If you want to wash, you'd better hurry."

He began pulling on his clothes—going commando, I couldn't fail to notice. Damn it. He'd set the tone of the day, but I could play it too.

"Give me fifteen minutes and I'll be ready." I didn't want to get out of the bed in front of him. After last night I would have thought I'd be entirely comfortable with nudity, but apparently I was wrong.

"Make it ten, or I'll haul your ass out naked," he said, forever the gentle lover.

Asshole, I thought, sitting up with only a slight wince, holding the sheet up. "Then go away and let me get ready in private."

I should have known I was playing with fire. He looked at me for a long moment, then crossed the room, yanked the sheet out of my hands, and scooped me up, ignoring my furious flailing as he carried me into that lurid pink bathroom. He dumped me feet-first into the tub, turned on the water, and left.

The first blast was icy and I shrieked, reaching for the knobs. The shower here was wretched, I'd discovered earlier, the hot and cold taps separated, and there was no way to regulate the water properly. It was either frigid or scalding, and I started to believe this was hell after all.

I worked quickly. When I stepped from the bath I would be renewed, the slate wiped clean. Michael wanted to act like it had never happened, and that was fine with me. I could ignore how my body tightened when I thought of him. I could control the way my very blood seemed to cry out for him. I could control my temper, control my longing.

I just couldn't control him.

The mark was still there, low on my hip, indecipherable. I stared at it—what did it mean? Why had it remained? I couldn't ask Michael. To show him I would have to shove down my pants, and that was the last thing I wanted. The tender lover from the dark hours had disappeared, as well as the demanding one from the kitchen. We were back at square one.

"Time's up." Locked doors weren't about to stop His Scum-Sucking Holiness. He slammed it open while I was still dressing. I was about to snarl at him when I saw he was carrying a pair of plain white sneakers in his other hand. For shoes I would forgive just about anything.

I grabbed them away from him, pulling free. "Socks?" I said, in an effort to hide my gratitude.

"Do without."

I trailed after him, hopping on one foot, then the other, as I pulled the sneakers on. Of course they fit. I followed him out into the brilliant sunshine casting its glow on bright, colorful suburban lawns and homes. Hell, I reminded myself. But inside that house, for a few short hours, it had felt like heaven.

He was trying to make it hard to keep up with him, probably so he didn't have to talk to me. I wasn't sure there was much I wanted to say either.

We passed more than a dozen seemingly deserted cars parked in the driveways. "Aren't we going to steal one of them?" I managed to ask, catching up with him.

"They don't work," he said briefly.

"How do you know?"

"They were put here as part of the illusion, as a way to torment those who thought they could escape."

"Yes, but why do *you* know?"

He ignored me, his long legs eating up the distance. I gave myself permission to admire his tight butt before hurrying to catch up with him. I marched along in silence, making up for his long strides with my own speed, concentrating so hard on my pace that I failed to notice where we were going.

He stopped short, and my head snapped up, alert. The warren of suburban roads stretching ahead of us ended abruptly in a wall of impenetrable shadow. And someone, something, stood in the way.

He was huge, as big as Metatron or even larger. He had legs like tree trunks, biceps as large as my waist, hands like clubs. He was dressed in leather armor, and he carried a huge sword, glistening with blue flame. His face was brutal, almost ugly for an angel, and angel he was, with pure white wings spread out behind him.

"Theron." Michael's voice was expressionless. "I wondered who Uriel would choose when Metatron fell."

"Metatron didn't fall. He was vanquished, and he chose dishonor." The creature's voice was strange, eerie. Like his face, it should have held the unearthly beauty that was so intrinsic to the Fallen. But despite its musical warmth, the sound grated on my backbone, and I felt my hands began to heat.

"He chose life, rather than serving death. You could do the same."

The angel called Theron laughed, and the sound was ugly. "I am not so foolish as to question my creator."

"'Creator'?" Michael scoffed. "Has Uriel managed to convince you of that? No matter how much power he wields, he has never had the power to create life."

"You think I would listen to your lies, Michael? I have been warned. You and the goddess will get no further. But I will be more merciful than you ever were. I will give you the choice. Go back to the house, stay there in your bed of lust, spend your wickedness within her soft flesh."

I wasn't liking this discussion of my soft flesh, and I moved from behind Michael. "I'm sorry, we haven't been introduced," I said in cheerful, brittle tones. "I'm Victoria Bellona, Goddess of War, and I believe you're in my way."

Michael hissed. He grabbed my arm, hauling me back. "Leave this to me," he growled.

But it was too late. Theron lifted the flaming sword, and I stared at it, mesmerized. "For this you turn your back on Uriel?" he scoffed, annoying me even further. "You are a fool."

"Listen, buddy," I began, but Michael caught my arm in a grip that was bruising, silencing.

"Keep still, woman," he snapped.

"That's better," Theron purred. "This is between men. You have no business even speaking to me."

The heat was spreading up my arms, past my elbows, and I felt the veins inside me vibrate with it.

"She has nothing to do with anything," Michael said, pushing me behind him. "She is a fuck, nothing more."

"I do not understand such things, but I know the uselessness of womankind. They are a weakness for those who have fallen. But that is over. There is nothing you can do for your brethren anymore. The Armies of Heaven have vanquished Sheol, and the abomination of the Fallen is no more. But I will grant you a boon, since you are so unwisely vulnerable. Once I defeat you, I will end her life quickly. The sword of justice cuts smooth and clean."

"My sword," Michael said.

Theron's smile was terrible. "Not any longer. You may try to take it from me, of course. Or you may bow to the inevitable and get to your knees, and I will finish you quickly as well."

"I would say 'Go to hell,'" Michael murmured, "but you're already there." And then, to my horror, he charged the creature, unarmed, six inches shorter than the angel's towering height, outstripped by those massive muscles.

I slapped my hands over my mouth, stifling my scream. I couldn't risk distracting him. To my astonishment, Michael managed to get in under Theron's upraised sword arm, moving so quickly he took the angel unawares, and the two of them went down, the sword skittering away.

I ran to grab it, but when I reached for the golden hilt, it spat sparks. I picked it up anyway, but the pain was searing, and I was forced to drop it, turning as Michael and Theron rolled on the ground. Theron had a knife, and Michael was bleeding from several shallow gashes, but he'd managed to get a grip on that wrist, keeping the deadly blade away from him. Then Theron's powerful frame twisted and Michael went down beneath him, his head smashing into the ground.

He lay there, stunned, unmoving, as Theron straddled him, and I saw the knife in his upraised hand, the sun flashing on the bright metal blade as it slashed down toward Michael's throat.

I screamed, not in fear, but in pure animal rage. And I flung out my arms, my icy, burning hands, instinct driving me.

Theron jerked, dropping the knife, turning toward me with a look of shock and indescribable pain, and I could have stopped, but I didn't. I slashed my hands at him again, and he twisted, knocked away from Michael. I could smell ozone in the air and the crackle of burning skin, and I took another step toward him, blind in my fury, and slashed my hands down again.

The power sizzled through the air. Theron flew backward, his face contorted, and then lay still, his skin beginning to burn from within, the smell of scorched feathers in the air, his white wings crumpled beneath him.

I stared at the body, unmoving, as the heat began to drain from my arms, and I started to tremble in aftershock. I hadn't even realized Michael had risen until I saw him standing over the body of the angel. He prodded him with his foot, but Theron was gone. What was that saying? "Elvis has left the building"? Theron was somewhere with Elvis now, I thought, wanting to laugh hysterically at the notion.

I felt Michael's eyes on me, but I couldn't say anything. My teeth were chattering, and I was so cold. So very cold.

A moment later he'd pulled me against his solid, warm body, wrapping his arms around me. There was a slash in the white T-shirt and he was bleeding, but it had already slowed, and I stopped worrying, closing my eyes and letting my head rest against him.

We stood that way for a long time. I listened to the beating of his heart as my own eventually slowed to normal, and my body began to regain its natural warmth. He must have sensed it, because he released me the moment I was able to stand on my own, walked away to pick up the discarded sword.

It had been a beautiful weapon, with blue flames dancing along the slender metal blade. When he picked it up, it roared into life. He stared at it. "I never thought to see this again," he murmured, half to himself. He moved over to Theron's body and without mercy stripped the scabbard off him, fastening it around his own hips before shoving the blade back in. And then he finally turned to look at me.

"It appears you have powers after all," he said mildly enough.

"Y-yes." There was only the faintest trace of a stammer in my voice. "Who was that?"

"I thought you'd figured it out. Uriel's current right-hand man." He glanced over at the body. "Or should I say, his late right-hand man."

"What was he doing with your sword?"

"That is the question, isn't it?" he said, infuriating as always. He caught sight of the abandoned knife, retrieved it, and tossed it at me. I reached out and caught it effortlessly. "At least we're armed. And we need to get going."

I didn't move. "He said it was too late. That the armies had already attacked."

Michael's eyes slid over me, an unreadable expression in them. "He lied. Come along, Victoria Bellona. We have to find our way back to Sheol before it really is too late."

He turned his back and started forward, expecting me to follow. I looked down at my hands as if I'd never seen them before. They looked the same, long fingers, narrow wrists, yet they were somehow foreign. I thought I had lost any doubt long ago, but it wasn't true. Only now did I believe for certain. I was a goddess of war and death.

I followed the warrior angel into the Darkness.

THE WALL ROSE up before us, a moving mass of impenetrable shadows. I stopped short. "What is this? Not another Portal?" I asked. "Because if it is, I'm not sure either of us will survive."

He glanced back at me. "It's just illusion. The Darkness is made up of worlds, but most people don't realize they can move between them."

"What's on the other side of this one?" I said, wondering if it was going to be more like a traditional hell.

"Luck of the draw."

To my surprise, he reached out and took my hand, wrapping his long fingers around mine. And then he pulled me forward into the shadows and beyond.

He was right, it didn't even hurt. He let go of my hand the moment we were on the other side, and I looked around me in amazement.

I'd always had mixed feelings about the Willy Wonka movies, though it was hard to dispute how amazing the cinematography was. This was like Willy Wonka gone haywire.

The colors were so dazzling I wanted to close my eyes. The smells were amazing—sugar and chocolate, butterscotch and lemon. It was a Candy Land, with confections growing from trees, begging to be picked. It was the most astonishingly beautiful place I'd ever seen, and happiness surged through me, a joy so overwhelming that I knew it was manufactured, an illusion, just like the candy trees and chocolate flowers.

"Shit," said His Holiness. "We're in deep trouble."

MICHAEL LOOKED DOWN at his companion, though he'd been doing his best to keep from doing just that, and felt the painful emotions fill him. He was having a hard enough time integrating the sudden appearance of her powers with his view of her. She was no longer in need of his protection, and the thought rankled, even as it shamed him. He looked around. "I hate Candy Land."

"Is that what you call it?" she breathed, already entranced. He told himself he should be happy her lust was for something other than himself, but it would be a lie. "What's not to like?" she added, starting forward.

He took her shoulder to stop her, and felt her instant surge of desire. Apparently she had enough lust for both him and the chocolate. "Wait."

She looked up at him, and he could see the thought in her eyes—her body, nude, covered with chocolate that he was licking off her. He cursed his immediate reaction, determined to break the spell.

"I don't like chocolate," he lied.

It jerked her out of her sensuous reverie, and the flush mounted to her cheekbones. Then she glanced around uneasily, not totally certain he'd seen her vision. "There are other kinds of candy you could try."

Damn her. Immediately she started imagining butterscotch on her nipples, and he wanted to shake her.

"You can't eat any of it," he said flatly. "No matter how much you want to, no matter how euphoric you feel."

She made a face. "So I take it this sudden surge of well-being is fake?"

"Completely."

She glanced at him. "That's a good thing. I don't know if I could handle you being euphoric. Even a smile might be too much to handle."

"I smile!" he snapped.

"Haven't seen it," she said, and he knew she lied. He could remember the few times she'd coaxed a smile out of him. Remembered her reaction. "And for God's sake, don't start smiling now. I'm not sure my heart could stand it." She paused, coloring. "I mean, the shock might give me a heart attack, not that I'm falling in love with you. I'm not likely to be that stupid."

Just like that he knew the truth, and it had nothing to do with the giddiness that was battering at the tightly closed doors of his soul. It was something he understood with the kind of assuredness that went with everything he knew to be true. This whole crazy thing had nothing to do with duty, with protecting Sheol, with honor and doing what was right. He cared about her. She mattered to him. She always had, in fact, even before she'd walked into that cold, elegant room in the *castello*. It wasn't a matter of need, of lust, of blood that bound, though all those things certainly existed.

No, his heart called to her. A heart he'd spent his entire existence ignoring. She was annoying, argumentative, powerful, vulnerable. She mocked him, holding nothing sacred. Sex with her sent him to places he had never known existed, and the sweet taste of her blood had washed away centuries of determination not to give in to his curse. And when he was deep inside her and he drank in her rich essence, he was glad of it, reveled in his curse, because it had brought him Tory.

He knew she loved him, of course. He could practically taste her longing. It didn't matter that her experience was just about nil. She could have been in love a dozen times before meeting his gaze in that room, and he would have known.

He was past railing at the unfairness of the universe that the Ultimate Power had abandoned to work things out on its own. He never bothered with self-pity—it was for Tory alone that he had raged. She would die, all too soon.

She was ignoring him, moving through Uriel's latest illusion with the pleasure the place always stimulated.

"Don't eat anything," he warned again, going after her.

"Yeah, yeah," she said dismissively, practically skipping.

"And try to fight the euphoria," he added, ignoring his own pleasure in watching her. He'd been watching her for days—there was no reason to feel such ridiculous longing. Just because he was doomed to care what happened to her, and it did feel like doom, didn't mean she wasn't still highly annoying.

He could blame the world-induced euphoria. Or perhaps his long-delayed acceptance that she meant something to him, that he didn't have to fight that particular truth. Though maybe it was as elemental as how turned on he'd been when he'd seen her sizzle Theron with lightning bolts.

"Yeah, I know," she said airily, glancing back at him. "I'm not allowed to feel good."

"It's safer not to." He followed her broodingly. This nauseating world was as dangerous as the Wraiths, which still threatened them. While the ghost-hunters sucked the light and life from those who ended up in the Darkness, the euphoria of this world assaulted sanity another way, stripping away common sense and judgment and leaving nothing but unreasonable hope and joy, so that Uriel could smash it more effectively. But she wasn't listening to his warnings. He was afraid he wasn't either.

He followed her. She practically danced down the pathways, humming, as he maintained a stony silence. There was always the chance they could get through this world. He still had a few tricks left.

He fought his reaction, keeping his head down. It was only when he realized he no longer heard her humming that he looked up.

To discover that she had vanished.

CHAPTER
TWENTY-SEVEN

I KNEW I WAS BEING SILLY. THE CALM, careful part of me stood right outside my body, telling me this was an illusion, a trick of some cosmic sadist. It was as if someone had pumped happy drugs into the atmosphere, and I was trying so hard to fight it.

But I felt glorious. I felt even stronger, I felt beautiful, I felt blessed. I would live forever; anything I wanted would be mine. Including the dour creature who was following me at a distance.

I smiled to myself. He was doing a better job at fighting this joyfulness, but in the end he wouldn't succeed. It was too powerful, too seductive. It wasn't telling me anything I didn't already know. It was just enforcing it, making it too powerful to ignore.

He wanted me; he would love me if I simply did the right thing, said the right thing. How many women had thought that over the years? But this time it was true. I had fallen, fighting all the way, fallen like the angels who were his people, and apparently mine as well nowadays. He would fall as well, reluctantly, just as he'd served heaven for far longer than the others. He would fall at my feet, and I would take him. Forever. I felt sure of it.

I glanced back to see him walking after me, head down, finding his feet and the pathway of supreme interest. I grinned. I was too much temptation for him, and that knowledge brought me great joy. He was slipping, and I would have him.

The smell of sugar and chocolate had faded so that it barely tempted me. I had a strong and enduring attachment to chocolate, but my interest in Michael trumped it. He was the one I wanted to lick and bite. And swallow.

I wanted to laugh at the salacious thought. I was getting dizzy with the whirlwind of emotions that had swept over me in the past twenty-four hours. The raw passion in the kitchen, the tenderness in the bedroom. The terror of watching him die, the rage at Theron's brutality. The shock of finding the unexpected power that had lain hidden inside me. And, most shattering of all, the ridiculous, unnecessary, unexpected love that was consuming me for the man trailing behind me.

I needed to rein in my burgeoning feelings.

But why? the drugged part of me demanded. It felt wonderful to want, to know that I could *have*. That everything could be mine.

Illusion, I reminded myself sternly. And then I laughed. What was wrong with a little illusion every now and then? As long as I realized that was what it was.

Up ahead the path forked. To the left it led through a bamboo thicket of giant strawberry Twizzlers, never my favorite food. To the right was nothing less than a gingerbread cottage, with child-shaped cookies adorning it. I hoped to God the illusion wasn't so strong that those were real children. No, I decided, testing my own powerful instinct that even Uriel-induced happiness couldn't ruin. There were no children in any way, shape, or form around here.

I glanced behind me. Michael had fallen back even more, and a wicked thought struck me. I could surprise him, jump on him, and he'd be unable to resist. I slipped into the gingerbread house, hiding behind its thick, spicy walls.

It was an odd little room, with a large oven and child-size cages made of pretzel sticks. I shivered. That was carrying the fantasy a little too far. If I opened the oven, would I find a chocolate woman awash in candy-corn flames?

I was about to emerge when I heard him calling my name, sudden panic in his voice. It was this place, of course. In a normal world he would never allow panic to show. Not that we'd ever been in a normal world together, I reminded myself. I moved toward the door, planning to jump out and scare him, but I was too late. He was already disappearing into the Twizzler-bamboo forest.

But I don't like Twizzlers, I reminded myself. And that wasn't the right way to go. I emerged into the glaring colors, glad to be away from the cottage. I should go after him. I would follow orders and not touch the tempting foliage and infrastructure, but I was tired and my legs ached, and other parts of me as well. I'd had very little sleep the night before, and we'd been walking for a good long time. I could use a little rest.

I moved away from the disturbing cottage into the forest, where the smell of strawberry was strong. The ground beneath it looked soft and inviting, and I touched it tentatively, afraid if I lay down I'd be covered in icing. But it was springy to the touch— maybe dyed, shredded marshmallows, but at least it wouldn't cling to me. I sat down carefully and waited, kicking off my new sneakers and rubbing my feet. No blisters—apparently such difficulties didn't exist in Confectionary Hell. I felt a burble of happiness inside me and I tried to tear it out. It was too stubborn.

It was a beautiful day and I was in love. Of course I was happy.

I lay back on the marshmallow moss, staring up into the sky. Thick white clouds against a bright blue backdrop, and those looked like marshmallows as well. They probably were. I closed my eyes and let my senses speak to me. I let my mind wander up my legs, which had trembled as he held them while he thrust into me . . . my sex, still swollen and sensitive, which tightened with longing when I thought of him . . . . my breasts, still feeling his touch, the suck of his mouth, the dance of his teeth . . . my neck, as I remembered his mouth pressed against it, drinking from me as he filled me.

Arousal swamped me at the memory, and my hands were shaking with it. I knew I should do something to stop it, but instead my hand moved across my belly in a slow, languorous caress. Up to my breasts, flicking the nipples with my fingers, but the touch wasn't the same. One hand reached my neck, and my fingers caressed the spot, now invisible, where he had fed, as my other hand moved lower, starting to slide beneath the aqua capris that apparently were the height of fashion in midcentury America.

"What the hell are you doing?" Michael roared, and I opened my eyes lazily, smiling at him. He was doing a better job of fighting the insidious effects of this world. But I thought he was losing the battle.

"What do you think I'm doing?" I murmured happily. "Reliving last night."

He caught the hand that was about to move beneath my pants and pulled me upright. "It's the euphoria," he said tightly. "It's not real. You need to fight it."

"There was no candy-induced insanity last night. And this morning," I added judiciously.

"Don't."

I smiled at him. "Come here, Your Angelness. I want to be kissed."

He shook his head. "You don't know—"

"Of course I know. This world is infused with something very dangerous. It makes people happy, and I don't care. It's not making me feel anything I haven't been feeling already. It's just getting rid of my fears. Come here and kiss me."

"Fears can be a good thing," he said stubbornly.

I put out my hand and beckoned. "Not this time."

"No." He didn't move, and some of my happiness faded. His will was too strong; it couldn't be crushed by Uriel's tricks or my dubious charms.

"I can't read you here," he said, "but I can guess. You're thinking I can resist you, even with all the temptation thick in the air, because I don't really want you. And you'd be wrong."

"There's another reason why you can resist me?"

He shook his head. "No. Fuck the magic atmosphere and the euphoria and the way it can strip away common sense. I can fight that." He came closer.

I just looked at him, waiting for a mortal blow and hoping that here in the land of happiness it wouldn't hurt too much.

"The one thing I can't fight," he said, moving closer still, so close I could look into his obsidian eyes and see myself reflected there, small and vulnerable, "is how much I want you."

He kissed me then, just his mouth touching mine,

keeping his hands at his sides. I did the same, letting only our mouths blend, tasting his lips, opening my mouth when his tongue pressed against my lips, feeling the slide of his tongue, and my legs felt shivery, weak. It was then he caught me, pulling me against him, but his kisses were slow and lazy, as if we had all the time in the world.

"What's on the ground?" he whispered.

"Marshmallows. Very soft."

"Pillows or fluff?"

"Shredded and dried."

"Good." He pulled me down onto the cushiony bed, his hand running down to catch my hip possessively. Exactly where his tattoo lay deep in my skin. Another wave of desire shimmered through my body. I wanted his mark on me. I could feel the strength, the connection between us, and I reveled in the idea.

I could do this forever, float in this dream of sexuality. The bright colors, the euphoria, the smell of chocolate, wiped out any doubt I should have had, and I let go of any last trace of wisdom, giving myself to his mouth, his hands. He held me there, brushing his lips across my face, feathering my eyelids, my neck, the hollow of my throat. I didn't have to see his beautiful hands to picture them as he pushed the virginal blouse out of the way, and then, oh, God, he was kissing my breasts, and I was going to climax simply from his mouth on me. He did things I hadn't imagined, sucking and then blowing cool air on them, using his teeth, even his fangs, and the sensation was shocking as tiny orgasms teased at me. I thrashed my legs in demand, but he simply stroked my body, as if to calm a skittish horse, until the screaming desire faded back into a vibrating need, and he laughed softly.

"We can't do it here," he said. "Too much innocence."

I looked at him, startled. "We can't?"

He shook his head. "Just another trick of Uriel's. Either you'll have a regrown steel hymen, or my erection will immediately disappear. But I can do this . . ." He stroked me, slowly, and I wanted to purr with delight.

"I love you," I said happily. I knew he would freeze at my artless words, and I didn't care.

He was leaning over me, the brightly painted sky behind him. "I love you too," he murmured, brushing his mouth against mine. "But once we're out of here, I'll deny I ever said it."

"That's okay," I said tranquilly. "Just tell me now so I can enjoy myself."

He laughed again, and there was no mocking tang to it. "I'm in love with you, Victoria Bellona, Goddess of War, pain in the butt extraordinaire, wielder of lightning bolts, slayer of good intentions and angel-enforcers. I've tried to fight it—I don't do love, but it's too strong. The moment we leave here I'll tell you you imagined it, but I'm tired of fighting everything, particularly myself. I love you, no matter how much you annoy me."

This was nice, I thought happily as his large, clever hand kept tracing circular patterns on my stomach. It was the euphoria, of course. He didn't mean a word of it. But I could pretend, and his caveat made it more believable. A sudden thought struck me. "You're not just telling me because I backed you into a corner?"

"No."

"It's not because I'm going to die of some tragic, beautiful disease and you want to make my last weeks happy ones?" He jerked uncomfortably, which struck me as odd, but I went on. "No, that's not the Archangel Michael. If I were about to die, he'd be practical and move on. He wouldn't waste time with a lost cause."

"You forget," he said in an almost dreamy voice as his eyes followed his hand, stroking, stroking. "My job *is* lost causes."

"I thought that was Saint Jude."

"Don't be picky." He slid his hand up to cup my chin, and I looked up into his dark, dark eyes as he slowly rubbed his thumb across my lips. "We need to go. We have to get back to Sheol. Theron may have been lying about the battle, but he's right about one thing. We don't know how much time has passed, and if Uriel has anything to say about it, our time is running out."

I smiled at him, happy to do anything he wanted. It didn't matter if some distant, critical self knew I was being an idiot. Nothing mattered besides the fact that for now the euphoria was telling me that he loved me. I let him pull me to my feet, ignoring the weakness in my knees. "Can the magic here make you nice?" I said, allowing just a hint of worry in.

He smiled wryly. "It's not magic. It's the wrath of God. Besides, I'm nice. When I want to be." He put his hand on mine, holding me beside him. "We have to keep moving."

"I'm ready. If you'll talk to me."

I saw the battle raging in his eyes, a battle he'd already lost. "I'll talk to you," he said.

"Good." I curved my body against his, savoring his warmth. "Then tell me what you're hiding from me."

THE ARCHANGEL MICHAEL looked down at the woman beside him, tucked so comfortably within his arm like she belonged there. The damnable thing was that she *did* belong there. She fit perfectly, and he wanted to pull her into his arms completely and sink down on the marshmallow grass. He started walking, pulling her with him, fighting the need to open himself to her, the terrible desire to expose his soul to whatever she wanted to know.

No matter what, he wouldn't tell her she was going to die. Nothing could force him to do that. He had been tortured, he had gone through every kind of hell Uriel and mankind could come up with, and he hadn't broken. He wouldn't break for her.

He brushed a kiss against her lips, wishing to God

they were in any other of Uriel's treacherous worlds. A world where he wasn't overcome with the need to love her, a world where he could simply shove her against a wall and lose himself in her flesh while she shattered around him. But this was one of Uriel's games, and he had to keep her moving. "No," he said. "We don't want to talk about the past, do we?"

"You're right," she said happily, and he would have reveled in her docile manner if he didn't know it was not the real Victoria Bellona. Tory would argue about everything, drive him mad. It was one of the things he loved about her, even as he wanted to wring her neck. In all his existence he didn't remember anyone able to break through his control. To infuriate him, to make him feel. He hated her for it. He loved her for it. And damn this world for making him love. "Do we have to leave?" she added.

"We can't have sex while we're here," he reminded her.

She looked up at him, a mischievous expression on her face. "Let's hurry." Sudden worry flashed in her eyes. "You'll still want me when we leave here, even if you won't admit it?"

He fought the words, but he said them anyway. This was the one place he could, with the excuse of the euphoria ripping away his armor. He looked down at her. "I'll always want you. Throughout time and space, I will love you."

She grinned at him. "A good thing. It's not wise to piss off the goddess of war."

She was ridiculous, infuriating, adorable, and he leaned down to kiss her, wrapping his arms around her and pulling her against him. He was hard as a rock, and he was wondering whether Uriel's edict against sex in this level of hell was simply another lie among so many lies, when he felt the sudden darkness. He lifted his head and swore.

Her eyes followed his as the shadows began to grow around them. "We need to hurry," he said, taking her hand and starting to run.

"There's a gingerbread cottage back down the path," she said, but he shook his head.

"That's a trap." He could see the Wraiths starting to congregate at the muddy outlines of this fairy-tale world, shimmering like the phantoms they were.

How could he have been so stupid, wrapped up in the halcyon illusion Uriel had forced down his throat? If they didn't make it through this world, it would be his fault.

But they would. He was determined. If Uriel wanted to play some kind of celestial game, then Michael would play, and triumph in the end. He was an expert at snatching victory out of the jaws of defeat. And he had Victoria Bellona by his side.

He glanced down at her, hoping she wouldn't see the Wraiths. But the almost drunken happiness had faded from her face, and she was looking at the ghostly apparitions moving to block their way.

"We're in deep shit, aren't we?" she said in a conversational voice.

It made him laugh. That was Tory, unfazed by anything. She couldn't fight these. Lightning bolts would pass through them; sheer strength would be useless. They were screwed, and it didn't matter, because they were together.

"Yes," he said. "We are."

CHAPTER
TWENTY-EIGHT

I HAD NEVER LIKED HORROR MOVIES. Now, suddenly I was faced with the physical incarnation of all the things that had secretly terrorized me, and it was all too real. Theron had been real, physical—something I could touch, something I could fight. These were different, eerie.

They shouldn't have been so frightening, these gray, transparent figures who converged on the path in front of us. The brilliant color around them leached into gray as well, as if they sucked all life from everything they touched, and they would do it to us, leaving us empty husks.

"Get behind me," Michael said in a rough voice as he drew the flaming sword he'd taken from Theron. It glowed in his hand, and it seemed to belong there.

"Hell, no," I shot back, trying to fight the warmth that was still flowing through me. In this Candy Land world, nothing that bad could ever happen to me, could it? Looking at the ghosts, I knew that it could. "That's all right," I added in a softer voice. "If I have to die, at least I get to die with you."

He made an exasperated noise. "That's the euphoria talking. Victoria Bellona isn't going to accept death that easily."

But I was Tory, and I didn't want to fight anymore. I had spent my entire life fighting, and all I wanted to do was curl my body around Michael's beautiful one and let go. I knew it was the effect of Uriel's illusion, and I tried to fight it. With a sigh, I squared my shoulders and said, "If we're fighting, then I'm fighting by your side."

He snarled, and I wanted to laugh. Apparently Happyville couldn't tame the grumpy archangel that much. "If you love me so damned much, you'd listen to me for a change."

"That's not love, that's blind obedience," I shot back. "No false euphoria works that well." In fact, some of the warm, fuzzy feeling was fading. He was still as unrelentingly gorgeous, I was still as unrelentingly tied to him, but I was regaining some perspective. "We fight together."

They were drawing closer, seeming to float just above the ground, and wherever they moved the landscape turned dead and blackened. I could see their ghostly faces now. I'd expected rage and evil, but the empty sorrow there was even more chilling.

"What are they?" I asked, horrified.

"They're what's left of the souls who were flung

into the Darkness. Uriel doesn't believe in short-lived punishment—he likes it to be eternal. Those who are condemned to the Darkness live out eternity sucking the life out of everything that ventures near."

"Great," I muttered, my happy glow vanishing as they drew closer. "And how do we kill them?"

"They're already dead."

"Then how do we stop them?"

For a moment he said nothing. "I don't know. Get the fuck behind me while I try to think of something."

I opened my mouth to protest, but I must have still been feeling the effects of this treacherously sweet world. He caught my arm and shoved me behind him, somehow managing to wrap my arms around his waist and hold me there.

It was an interesting position. To be plastered against him was undeniably wonderful—I could soak in his strength and power, wrap myself around his gorgeous body. On the other hand, he was holding me prisoner, which infuriated me; his grip was so tight I could barely move, and I couldn't see a damned thing.

"I am the Archangel Michael. I have dominion over darkness and evil. Leave us alone."

A thin, wispy voice came back, horrible in its raspiness, as if it were forced through shredded vocal cords. "Archangel Michael, you have dominion over nothing. You cast us into the Darkness, you doomed us to unending torment."

I wanted to close my ears. The voice rose like a shriek on the wind, and I clung to him, shaking, no longer fighting to get free.

"Leave us," Michael thundered again, for some reason not denying the creature's horrible accusation. He should have told them it was Uriel who had thrown them here, doomed them here.

"We cannot." It now seemed as if more than one voice scoured the wind that had picked up around us. They were in ragged unison, the sound as horrid as broken glass scraping against bone. "Give her to us."

I felt Michael's start of surprise. "And what do you want of me?"

"We cannot touch you. Leave the girl and you may return to Sheol."

Oh, shit. Michael had a battle to fight—everything he had done, including coming to fetch me, had been in service to that ultimate demand. He would have no choice.

"It's all right," I said against his strong, unwavering back. "Let me go. You should never have left the Fallen."

"Shut up."

So much for loverlike appreciation of my grand sacrifice, I thought. I tried to break free, then froze as the voices rose on the wind, an eerie chorus of ghostly shrieks: "Give her to us, give her to us," and the sound grew close, closer, until they were almost upon us.

Being unable to see drove me crazy, and I tried to peer around his broad back, but it was impossible, even when a new voice rose above the others, stronger, but with the same shredded violence that told me he was one of them. "Enough!" that empty voice thundered, like a ghostly version of Michael himself.

The chorus stopped instantly, and I thought I could sense them retreating. I began to struggle in earnest when something was thrown over me, like a down blanket, soft but enveloping, shutting out light and life. I felt my heart rate slow, my breathing fade, and I wondered if I was dying. Were they leaching the light out of me? I didn't want to let go, but the feather-soft darkness enveloped me, and the last thing I heard was that new, eerie voice.

"Hello, Michael."

THE ARCHANGEL MICHAEL stood still, releasing Tory's hands. She was wrapped in the cocoon of his wings, safe in a temporary stasis. The Wraiths had no reason to fear his flaming sword, but they had faded, leaving only one Wraith in their place. One shockingly familiar.

"What are you doing here?" he demanded, sounding almost as raw as the apparition had.

"I am not here. The Ultimate Power has seen to that," the flat voice came back as the impossible image floated too close. "I am trapped throughout eternity, remember? You helped see to it."

He felt cold, so cold. "It was a fair fight."

"Indeed. You were the Flaming Sword of Justice, following your path. Cutting down your brother on the word of God."

"You had sinned—"

"I had questioned. But it seems you have gone the same way. Though you stayed far longer, following Uriel's orders, no matter how cruel. That mighty sword of justice has killed a world of innocent people."

At least Tory couldn't hear. She wouldn't know the terrible things he had done. Not until he told her.

He didn't defend himself. "Yes," he said. "My crimes were far worse than yours. There is no way I can atone."

The Wraith's smile was terrible. "And there is no way I can touch you. The only one who could have hurt you was Theron, and the two of you took care of him. I can't come near you until I am released from my imprisonment."

"Where are you? The Fallen search for you. It's you they want to lead them, not me."

"Jealous, Michael?" came the sinuous voice.

He steeled himself against reacting. The angel behind the Wraith had always been good at twisting words, at charm and manipulation. It had been those very traits that had sentenced him to eternal torment.

"I would happily give you charge of them."

"Would you just as happily die at my hands?"

"If it would save the woman. Yes."

The Wraith shook his head, his beautiful face unmarred by the pain the others used like a weapon. "I told you, I cannot harm you. You are impervious to the dangers of the Darkness. Impervious even to the sweet seduction of this world."

Michael jerked, startled. "You're wrong. I am undone by the euphoria like anyone else."

The Wraith's long hair flowed around him as he shook his head. "You are not. You were simply looking for a reason to say the things you were afraid to say. I have been watching you, Michael. You are as besotted as all your brothers, each and every one who fell so long ago for love of a woman."

He wouldn't waste time denying it. "Then it's a good thing I have already fallen. What do you want from me?"

The Wraith hovered, and Michael could feel the malice emanating in waves toward him alone. This was his ancient nemesis, facing him again, all this time after he'd cast him into eternal emptiness. "I plan to show you the way to the cliffs where the veil is thin."

If it was possible to still be shocked after the appearance of the last being he'd expected, this would have done it. "Why?"

There was cool disdain on the ghostly face. "Because we want the same things. Because Victoria Bellona must participate in the battle in order for you to win, and time is running out. You've been here too long—each day is like ten in the world of Sheol.

If you don't return in time and win, Uriel's darkness will cover everything and the Fallen will perish. After that, it is only a matter of time before mankind is wiped off the face of the earth."

"She will die."

"We all die, sooner or later," the Wraith said callously. "At least she will find a better afterlife than the Dark City or this eternal hell. Furl your wings, Michael. I won't tell her your miserable secrets."

"You may tell her anything you want," he snarled back, fury vibrating through him. "You still haven't answered my question. Where are you? How can the Fallen release you?"

Lucifer, the first of the Fallen, the most beloved, the Bringer of Light, his implacable enemy, looked at him. "First they must release my spirit from the Darkness."

"And how do we do that?"

Lucifer's smile was as infuriating as the last day Michael had seen him, when they'd battled sword to sword and Michael himself had flung him from heaven. "God knows." He made a dismissive gesture. "First things first. Release the goddess. We have to get you out of here."

WHEN I WOKE I was still pressed against Michael's back, my arms around his narrow waist. I felt as if I'd taken the most comfortable nap in my entire life; I felt renewed and alive. He was no longer holding me, keeping me trapped, and I knew I had to let go, but I wasn't in any hurry. It felt too good. And then I remembered what had happened just before the night had closed in.

I shoved him away from me. "What the hell?"

I'd forgotten about the Wraiths. Only one remained, insubstantial, beautiful, without the leaching sorrow the others had held. "Who the fuck are you?" I demanded, not in the mood to be polite.

The landscape behind him was winter-dead, drained of all color, the trees black skeletons against the gray sky. The euphoria was gone, vanished, as we stood in a no-man's-land between death and candy.

The Wraith smiled, and I gasped. It was a warm, slow, seductive smile on a ghost, and the effect was . . . enchanting . . . disturbing. "Don't worry, goddess. I mean you and your mate no harm."

I glanced at Michael's stony face. "This is—" he started to say.

"The leader of the rebel Wraiths," the apparition broke in smoothly, and despite the wind whistling through his voice it was curiously warming. "Take your noble lover's hand and I will lead you to freedom."

I glanced up at my "noble lover." Had there been mockery in the Wraith's voice? I held Michael's hand tightly. He didn't look at me.

"How do I know we can trust you?" he demanded of the Wraith.

I wouldn't have trusted his smile farther than Michael could have thrown him, which, given the

Wraith's insubstantial form, wouldn't have been far, but I knew instinctively that he was no threat to me. He might not care much for Michael, but he was on my side.

"Ask the goddess," the Wraith said.

Michael had no choice but to look at me. The magic of illusion had died away, and there was no love, no openness. The cold, hard bastard was back. "We can trust him," I said, giving nothing away. Not the bereavement that tore at my heart, not the anger at being given a gift and then having it stolen away.

"Then come," said the Wraith, reaching out a transparent hand. There was nothing to hold on to, and yet I reached out, one hand still clinging to Michael's.

We followed him, into the wind.

CHAPTER
TWENTY-NINE

WE WERE STANDING ON A WIND-swept plain, a high plateau where no trees grew. There was color, muddy and undefined, and I was still clinging to something that felt like clouds. It was the hand of the Wraith, fully as beautiful as any of the Fallen.

Michael pulled me away from the Wraith abruptly, then dropped my hand, leaving me standing there. "You can go," he told the creature in a rough voice.

That taunting smile, meant for Michael alone, lingered on the ghost's face. "Are you going to tell them about me?"

"Of course," he snapped.

"Are you going to tell *her*?"

Silence.

"Tell me what?" I demanded. There was something going on between the two of them that had nothing to do with me, and I was being used as a pawn. I hated being used as a pawn.

"Tell her what?" Michael echoed, and there was a dangerous edge to his voice. I couldn't imagine what harm he could do to such an ethereal being, but the creature blinked anyway.

"I wish her no harm or pain, Michael," he said softly. "Tell her about you, of course."

"And you think that won't cause her pain?"

"Stop talking about me like I'm not here!" I snapped.

"I wouldn't—" The mocking expression vanished from the Wraith's vivid face, replaced by alarm. "You must get out of here. He's coming."

"Who?" I demanded, but Michael was already hauling me toward the promontory overlooking a vast wasteland, and his grip was painful.

"Going so soon?" A young man stood in front of us, blocking the way, and Michael yanked me to a stop, frozen. The man looked past us to the Wraith, and he should have been no threat, not against Michael's powerful sword, not against the lightning bolts I could feel beginning to form deep within me, but Michael didn't move. "Don't leave us, Bringer of Light," the man continued in a soft voice. "Since you've decided to involve yourself, I'm certain you wish to be here for the grand finale."

I stared at the man, uncomprehending. He sounded like Beloch. If I unfocused my eyes and looked just past him, he even looked like Beloch, instead of the very ordinary young man who blocked our way.

I glanced over at the Wraith, who had frozen as if glued to the spot. Bringer of Light? Why did that sound familiar?

"You've been very adventurous, Michael. I should have known you'd be up to the challenge. But you can't think I'd let you go after all this, can you?" Beloch's smooth, taunting voice came from his young mouth. "I must say I am surprised you managed to best Theron, but I see that you did. Otherwise you wouldn't be here, and you wouldn't have reclaimed your sword."

"I didn't kill Theron. Tory did."

The young man turned to look at me with greater interest. "How extraordinary," he murmured. "Who would have thought it? You have more powers than a relic of an ancient civilization should have."

"One could say the same thing about you, Uriel," Michael said in a voice like ice. "What are you doing here? You never used to bother with the Darkness. You left it up to your enforcers."

The young man's smile should have been charming. It sent shivers down my spine. "Oh, a great deal has changed since your day."

Uriel? The epitome of evil, the monster, the Big Bad? Not this sweet-looking young man!

"You sound like Beloch," I said abruptly.

He laughed. "Smart child. I am many things and take many forms. That is but one of them."

I frowned. Beloch was Uriel? I looked up at Michael, expecting shock on his face, but the classic lines were set in stone. He knew. He had always known.

"I think you should let us go," I said, not in the mood to grovel. "We made it through all your nasty worlds, we found the place where we can fly out. Why don't you accept defeat gracefully?"

His smile was angelic, and I remembered with shock that he too was an archangel. One who reigned in heaven. A heaven that looked like the Dark City, or someplace else? "No one defeats me, my child. And there are many other worlds here. You're almost out of time. Without Michael's talents, you could have wandered for years. After all, this was once his hunting ground."

I froze. "Hunting ground?"

Uriel smiled. "For millennia the Archangel Michael was my right hand, my enforcer. He made certain my decrees were carried out, that villages were razed, that blasphemers and their families were destroyed, that unbelievers suffered. He brought those who belonged into this place, and hunted them while they ran and hid in the illusions. He was brutal and efficient, the angelic equivalent of a mass murderer. How do you like that? No one else has served me as well, though I had hopes for Theron. And Metatron failed me most grievously. I am most displeased."

"Hardly failed you," Michael spoke suddenly. "He delivered Tory to you."

"'Tory'?" Uriel echoed with a warm laugh. "How enchanting. Is it possible the Archangel Michael's stone heart has finally cracked?"

"No."

"Ah, well, that is perhaps for the best. I would hate to think you had any moments of true happiness before you were wiped out of existence," he said. "I must confess, Metatron has proven immune to my blandishments. I had to turn elsewhere for assistance."

Michael had taken my hand again. I tried to yank free, but his grip was unbreakable, and I knew he was the closest thing to an ally I had. If I was to get out of this, it would be with him.

"Who?" Michael demanded, glaring at Uriel.

"Why would I have any desire to assuage your curiosity?" Uriel said softly, then turned to me. "And you, Victoria Bellona, pagan goddess of a degenerate civilization, you look as if you are willing to die with the man you love, despite his past. I think that perhaps you need to know one thing more. The secret he's been keeping from you."

"Uriel, no!" For the first time Michael showed emotion, rage—and something else I couldn't define.

But Uriel had no mercy. "We can't let her go in ignorance, Michael. You've been trapped in my world for almost four weeks, while your followers floundered in their pathetic attempt to prepare for my armies. Tomorrow is her birthday. She needs to know, don't you think? We'll only be anticipating it by one day. She won't be missing much. It might be easier to die knowing she will only miss one day."

"Don't listen to him, Tory," Michael said, a thread of desperation in his voice. "It's all lies."

Pay no attention to the man behind the curtain, I thought dully. But this man was pulling the strings, making the lightning.

"What do you mean?" I managed to keep my voice cool. The heat in my hands and arms had abandoned me. Whatever powers I had must have known they'd be no good against this creature.

"Why, that you are prophesied to die in battle on your twenty-fifth birthday. It was the only way the Fallen could prevail against my armies. Not that it would have been the final battle—just an opening salvo. But if you aren't there, if you don't die, the cause of the Fallen is lost. Michael has always known that. That's why he brought you to Sheol, that is why he consented to mate with you. In the taking of your body and your blood, he did his part to fulfill the prophecy. He only agreed to the marriage because he knew it would be of short duration."

I was already facing imminent death at the hands of what stood for a benevolent God. I shouldn't have felt such lacerating pain, such complete betrayal. "No," I said.

"Tell her, Michael."

I looked up at him, though I didn't want to. "Tell me, Michael."

He was bleak, distant. "You will die on your birthday, on the sands of Sheol. No one can change it."

"And if I don't? If I refuse to go back?"

"Then everyone dies."

"And that," broke in Uriel, "is exactly what is going to happen. Because you won't be there. You will die one day early, and Michael will arrive back in Sheol one day too late, and—"

The wind had picked up, whipping across the top of the plateau, and Uriel broke off, frowning. "This shouldn't happen. You can't—"

I knew who had done it. The Wraith had broken free of whatever had held him in place, and he was moving, the wind moving with him, whipping his long hair around his beautiful face, whipping his loose clothes against his body.

"Run!" he said, his torn voice echoing to the skies, and he threw himself against Uriel.

Into Uriel, disappearing behind his skin, pushing at his body from the inside. Uriel screamed, turning gray, slapping and tearing at himself, horror in the mild brown eyes, and then I couldn't see anything, as Michael started running across the plateau, dragging me after him. Dragging me to my certain death.

I was past fighting. He yanked me into his arms, painfully, as he leapt over the precipice, and I closed my eyes, wondering if the net overhead was really thinner at this spot, or if that was another of Uriel's tricks. I glanced down, but I could only see one figure flailing on the ground as we went higher and higher.

I knew it was very cold, but I didn't feel it. I felt nothing at all. The silly world of candy and euphoria had been an illusion, and nothing Michael had said was the truth. Higher and higher we went, his warm body against mine as the air grew thin. Into the light, and gone.

CHAPTER
THIRTY

MICHAEL LANDED LIGHTLY ON the rocky beach outside the main compound, holding Tory tightly in his arms. It was late afternoon, the light fading, and it took him a moment to remind himself that there were no Wraiths to endanger them in this place. And that the Wraiths had never been any danger to him, except, perhaps, the final one, the one who had saved their lives. He had to let go of her, set her down in the sand, even if he wanted to hold on to her forever.

She fought free of him, pushing him away, and he wondered if she'd throw up. She was pale, sick looking, but she had herself under control, and the look she cast him was filled with such cold contempt that he should have felt relief. Everything between them was gone. She would die hating him. She would have no qualms leaving him or the cruel world he'd brought her to. He would lose nothing.

Someone must have seen them arrive, because the Fallen poured out of the building, running across the lawn to surround them. He saw Tory push past the crowds, ignoring everyone, and he let her go.

There was nothing he could do, not in the twenty-four hours she had left to live. Telling her he loved her would only make it worse. Of course, he already had, when he thought the euphoria would excuse it. But she believed that was a drug-induced lie.

That didn't mean he was going to give up without a fight. She had powers no one had imagined. And he could watch over her. Find others, trustworthy people like Asbel, who could keep an eye on her in the coming battle. He simply wasn't going to let her die.

I STRODE BLINDLY through the crowd, determined to get away from the questions and the curious eyes. Let the archangel deal with it. I had no idea where I was going, only that I needed to be alone, to think, to prepare.

I was going to die. I think I'd always known it, deep in my heart. Not "someday," but that my death was imminent, preordained—which explained why I had been so fearless no matter what dangers I faced or how insurmountable the odds. My death was set in stone, and nothing I did could influence that fact. And Michael had always known.

I felt frozen. Weeping wouldn't help; rage against the cruelty of an indifferent fate was useless. I could despise Michael's betrayal, but that would get me nowhere. I simply had to endure.

I passed more people hurrying toward the beach, but I kept my head down and no one stopped me as I made my way through the main building and into the annex that housed the workout room and my bedroom. And Michael's monastic cell.

For a moment I considered whether there was any revenge I could enact on his room, then dismissed the idea. Chances were he wouldn't even go to his bed tonight, not with a battle on the horizon. He'd train all night.

Unbidden, the memory rose of watching him pour water over his body, how it had sluiced down the lines of muscle and sinew on his lean skin, and I grew hotter. And angrier.

All this time he *knew* I would die and he hadn't told me. No wonder he'd agreed to marry me. One month and he'd be free—it was hardly an onerous task. And even with an end date, he still had been reluctant to bed me, the bastard! I could just imagine the weak excuses he'd come up with. None of them were acceptable.

My room was just as I'd left it. I opened the french doors and took a deep breath of the sea air. When we'd first arrived I'd been too upset to notice, but now I could feel the calm benediction break over me as surely as if I were swimming in the icy surf. I knew the sea healed the Fallen, but it wouldn't heal me. Perhaps I could tell Rachel or even Martha that I wanted to be buried at sea. There were worse places to spend eternity.

I stepped out onto the beach, kicking off my shoes, my toes digging into the sand. I started up the beach, walking until I could no longer see the house or any of the Fallen clustered around Michael. There was a promontory, up high, and I decided to climb, scrambling up the sheer wall fearlessly. After all, there was no way I could fall to my death—I still had twenty-four hours to live.

It took me close to an hour before I collapsed on the shelf of rock that overlooked the ocean. I could see for miles and miles, without a fallen angel in sight, and I felt a curious sense of peace settle over me.

Back in the direction of the house, the Fallen had cleared the beach, probably training for tomorrow's battle. I supposed I should be doing the same thing. Even if the outcome was foretold, I could make a difference.

I'd do what I had to do. Kill if I had to, die when I needed to. It was out of my hands.

I heard the sounds of wings on the air, and I felt hope surge in my heart. I was going to blister him, rip into him and tear him to shreds. I was going to push him off this cliff if he dared sit next to me, I was—

Azazel alighted, carrying Rachel as effortlessly as Michael carried me, and I fought to ignore the searing disappointment. Of course Michael hadn't come after me. I was nothing to him. He'd done what he had to do: brought me here to die. His work was done.

"May I stay?" Rachel asked, stepping free of Azazel's hold.

I looked at her, considering. It was clear she had known of my death as well, yet she had said nothing. She was also the closest thing to a friend I had. "All right," I said grudgingly.

Without a word Azazel soared upward, and I watched, momentarily stunned by the grace and beauty of him. Would any of the Fallen die tomorrow? Oh, God, would Michael die?

I tamped down the fear as I looked at Rachel. Her red hair was tied at the nape of her neck, and she wore the white training clothes that were the default uniform for the army of the Fallen. I, however, was still wearing aqua capris from the ranch house. Absurd.

"I don't suppose you're here to tell me there's a way out of dying," I said caustically.

Rachel shook her head. "I only wish I could. Martha and Allie and I have looked at it in every way possible, but there seems to be no way to change it."

"So be it." I stared out at the sea. "Then why are you here? If you're going to tell me to forgive Michael, you're wasting your time."

"Forgive him for what? For not telling you that you're going to die? That's hardly a crime. What would you have done had you known? How would that have helped things?"

She was being practical and I wasn't in the mood for it. "I would have gotten the hell away from here," I said stonily.

"It wouldn't do any good. You're going to die on our beach. You can't run away from it. If you could, I would help you."

"I had no intention of running away from it." I was thoroughly sulky by this time and wallowing in it. "But at least I would have had a chance to experience life. I wanted . . . I wanted everything. I wanted passion and grand adventure. I wanted sex and devotion and love. . . . " My voice had an annoying tendency to crack on that. "And instead I get His Scum-Sucking Holiness, the asshole Archangel Michael."

"Indeed," Rachel said. "Your prayers were answered."

I jerked around to look at her. "You're kidding."

She shook her head. "Think about it. Think about Michael. Think about what you know to be true."

I pushed that knowledge away, still too angry. "He's been nothing but a pain in the ass."

"That's Michael for you. At least he wasn't trying to kill you, like Azazel was when he came after me. Count your blessings."

That managed to shock me. "He was trying to kill you?"

"Rather than submit to the prophecy that we were going to be married."

"Isn't that a little extreme?" I said sarcastically.

"You've seen Azazel. What do you think?"

I pictured the cool, beautiful man who seldom left Rachel's side. "I assume he changed his mind."

Her small, secret smile twisted my stomach. I wanted to have that kind of smile when I thought about Michael. "He did," she said, and for a moment she seemed lost in reverie. Then she looked back at me. "If attempted murder didn't interfere with our falling in love, then you shouldn't let this interfere with you and Michael. You're running out of time to be happy, Tory."

I glared at her. "Thanks for reminding me. Okay, I forgive him. He was simply being kind. Now go away and leave me alone." I looked around us for Azazel, but for once he was nowhere to be seen.

"I told him to give us some time," she said, correctly reading my glance. "I don't think you want to die filled with rage."

"You know, it's supposed to happen in the middle of a pitched battle. I imagine rage is helpful in such situations."

She laughed. "You'll feel better if you're fighting side by side with him."

"Michael is a man who fights on his own. He may be a genius at military tactics and unstoppable when it comes to hand-to-hand combat, but he doesn't play well with others."

"I think he probably plays very well with you."

I blushed. I could feel my skin heat, and my skin was so fair everything showed on it. "Admittedly, the sex was good," I allowed.

She raised an eyebrow. "Only good?"

I grew hotter. "All right, great. Amazing. Stupendous. Unearthly. Satisfied?"

"It's *your* satisfaction we're talking about, not mine."

"What is it you want from me?" I let out a growl of frustration.

"I want you to forgive Michael."

"So he doesn't have to feel guilty when I bite the bullet?"

"No. I don't know if anything will help Michael when you die. Losing your mate is a traumatic thing, and Michael isn't particularly adaptable. I want you to forgive him for your sake."

"So I can die happy?" I said caustically.

"I can't change your dying, Tory." Rachel's voice was full of pain. "I just don't want your last hours eaten up with anger at the man you love."

"Love?" I sputtered. "You think I love that son of a bitch?"

"Do you deny it?" Her eyes were warm and soothing.

"Of course not. I'm not an idiot."

"Then forgive him."

As if by magic, Azazel appeared overhead, alighting on the promontory once more. I looked at him, remembering Rachel's words. He looked fully capable of cold-blooded murder. If Rachel could forgive him, I certainly ought to be able to forgive Michael.

"Don't worry," I said airily. "He's forgiven. You can tell him so."

"It would be better if you did."

"There's a limit to what I'm willing to do."

Rachel rose and stepped into Azazel's arms. "Do you want me to send someone to fly you back down? The hill is treacherous—you're the first person who's ever managed to climb it."

I shook my head. "Can't die till tomorrow, remember? I'll be fine. I just need some time alone." No way I was leaving this bluff till I was good and ready.

I watched them soar upward against the sky, incredibly graceful, and fresh pain speared into me. Did Michael and I look like that when he carried me?

The wind was chilly on my bare arms as it blew in across the ocean, and the rock I sat on was growing cold and uncomfortable. It didn't matter. I wasn't going to move until I had made some kind of peace with this.

The sun was sinking toward the horizon, its rays spreading across the rough waters, sending a shaft of orange across the waves. I watched in bemusement as the sun began to set on my last full day, and then everything became crystal clear. I knew what I had to do.

I climbed down the ledge, carefully, despite my assertion that I couldn't be killed. For all I knew, I could end up a crumpled bloody heap at the base of the cliff and not actually expire from my injuries until the next day. I slid once, scraping my hands and ripping the knees of the stupid capri pants, but I finally made it back to the beach in one piece, just as darkness closed in.

It was then I realized I was famished. I seemed to have spent most of my life since I left the *castello* expiring of hunger. I mentally composed a menu for my last supper—every single damned thing I wanted, and to hell with the calories. Pasta quattro formaggio with Gorgonzola. It had to have the bite of the Gorgonzola. Broiled trout with lemon sauce. Chocolate torte, the richer the better, and fresh whipped cream. With perhaps some spinach risotto, a nice white wine with some heft to it, and Moët champagne with the dessert. At that point I figured I'd be so full I'd roll into bed and sleep like the dead. Until it was time to die.

When I stepped into my room, I could smell the lovely scent of chocolate on the air, and the covered trays were waiting on the glass coffee table. I did like Sheol. I wasn't sure just how far the magic extended, but there was no way I was going to eat before I took a shower and changed my clothes.

I looked at the table sternly. "Stay warm," I told it, in the same tone of voice I'd use on a well-trained pet, and disappeared into the shower.

I took my time—even cold, that food would be delicious—and dumped my torn rags into the trash with only the slightest pang. I remembered Michael's hands unfastening the buttons of my blouse, sliding beneath my waistband as the euphoria made him say things he would never say, never believe in this lifetime. It had been glorious while it lasted, but everyone had to wake up eventually. Just as well I only had a short time to deal with the fallout.

The food was still hot and utterly delicious, but for some reason I wasn't in the mood for the impressive pig-out I'd planned. I had some of everything, a few mouthfuls of wine, two bites of chocolate cake with fresh whipped cream dolloped over it. And then I covered the trays and stood, restless.

The wind had picked up, stirring the already turbulent waves, blowing in the open doors. I stretched out on the sofa, letting the breeze blow over me, feeling the emotions rise and the smell and the feel of the ocean reaching into my bones. Looking out, I saw that the moon was almost full, sitting high overhead in the ink-dark sky.

He wasn't coming. Of course he wasn't. He was under no compulsion, no euphoria-induced affection, no orders from the Fallen. The only reason he would come to me was if he wanted to. Needed to.

The only way he'd ever come close had been at my urging. Each time we'd had sex, it had been at my instigation.

I could do it again. Go to him, and he would treat me tenderly, because he felt guilty. He would give me blindingly wonderful sex, because he could. He would pleasure my body, but my heart would feel emptier than ever.

It was the last night of my life, and I wanted to spend it with him.

Just not enough to beg.

I moved through my rooms, turning off the lights. The moon shone in from the beach, filling the place with a silvery light. I went into the bathroom to change, and when I came out the dishes were gone. Magic or miracle? It didn't matter.

The silk nightgown flowed around my body. It had always been there, purportedly for my wedding night. For my valedictory night it would do just fine—I wore it to please myself. It was made of soft, twisted panels of white fabric, and it hugged my body like a caress. I looked in the mirror, and all I needed was a laurel wreath to complete the picture. I looked like the goddess I was. A goddess who could send lightning bolts and destroy angels, but a mortal one, without the power to make one man love her. If I had to be an ancient Roman goddess, why the hell couldn't I have been Venus? I bet she never had trouble with her love life.

No self-pity, I reminded myself, turning off the bathroom light. I pushed back the covers and stretched out on the bed.

I could see the moonlit water from my bed if I put my head at the foot and lay on my stomach. I shifted, staring out into the night, and a curious peace settled over me as I listened to the sound of the surf.

I jerked awake to see him standing in my open

doors with the water rough and wild behind him. He just stood there, watching me out of his dark, fathomless eyes.

"I need to make a confession," he said, his rich, warm voice still able to make my blood dance beneath my skin.

I raised my head, but I didn't move from my hopefully provocative position. "I don't want to hear your confession," I said. "I don't need it."

"What do you need?"

In the end men, even archangels, were simple creatures. They were no good at inferring, guessing, coming to conclusions. They needed to be told. "You," I said.

In the moonlight I could see the slash of white as he smiled. "Good," he said, and came into the room.

I rolled over on my back, looking up at him.

He sat down on the edge of the bed, his fingers catching the folds of the silk nightgown. "Where did this come from?"

"It's always been here," I said, suddenly nervous. "I think it was supposed to be for my wedding night."

"It looks like something Rachel thought of."

"Don't you like it?"

"I like you better out of it."

So should I sit up and struggle out of the complicated bands of the nightdress? Maybe this was a bad idea—

"You know what I think, Victoria Bellona?"

"I have no idea, Your Impeccable Angelic Magnificence."

He choked with laughter. "That's the best so far, but a little unwieldy for sex talk. I was thinking"—his hand slid up my leg, taking the filmy nightgown with it—"that you haven't been properly seduced."

I swallowed. The touch of his hand on my skin was having its usual effect on me. "What are you going to do, bring me flowers and chocolates?"

"I think we're a little past that, don't you? But I'm not sure we're past me convincing you to go to bed with me. You have so many reasons to say no."

I couldn't think of one at that particular moment—but I took his word for it.

"I think," he continued, and his hand reached my thigh, "that I need to work very hard to make sure you don't regret this. I need to show you a very good time."

I shook my head. "I don't want tonight to be about me."

He looked at me for a long moment. "You want it to be about us," he said.

It didn't matter if he'd cheated by reading my mind. Just the fact that he knew without my telling him was enough. "Yes," I whispered.

He cupped my chin, leaning down to kiss me. "You're going to break my heart," he said finally.

I wanted to lessen the tension with a snappy "Are you sure you have one?" but something stopped me. The time for banter was past.

So I said nothing at all, and neither did he, as he slid his other hand behind my head, bringing me to him, his long fingers kneading my scalp, holding me still for his soft, seductive kiss.

It started slow, a soft nibble on my lips, just a taste, almost curious, and when I tried to deepen the kiss he pulled away. "Uh-uh, Victoria Bellona," he said. "You're not rushing this. We're taking our time, and I'm going to savor every square inch of your skin."

I felt my heart stop and then start again, faster. He kissed me again, and I followed his lead, the leisurely discovery of taste and tongue and teeth, and I ran my hands over his close-cropped head, loving the feel of him. He lifted me higher, pulling me into his arms, as the kiss deepened naturally, the slow embers of desire building, building.

He was wearing a shirt, and I wanted it off him. I slid my hands beneath the collar, reveling in the feel of his hot skin, and tried to unfasten the buttons; but my fingers were clumsy, and he laughed. "Wrong shirt?" he said.

I simply yanked it apart. The buttons went flying and he laughed again, shrugging out of it before putting his hands back on me, sliding up my arms to the straps of the gown.

I don't know how he managed to deal with it, but a moment later he'd pushed it down to my waist. "Only fair," he whispered, and lay down beside me, pulling me against him, my bare breasts pressed against his chest, and the feeling was glorious. I moved, rubbing against him, and the arousal was overwhelming. I wanted more, and I didn't know what to do.

"Tory," he whispered in my ear. "You don't have to be frightened. It's just me. Just this body you've already had a time or two. Do what feels good."

My eyes met his, and the last of my uncertainty fell away. He wasn't going to leave me. He wasn't going to betray me. We were past all that. We were going to make love, and I was going to do everything I'd ever dreamed about, and then do it all over again.

I gently pushed him onto his back, and he went easily, his eyes hooded. I slid my hands up his chest, over the muscles that banded his ribs, covering the flat nipples, then moving down over his stomach. He lifted his hand to catch mine, to guide me, and then dropped it. Waiting for me.

I slid my hand down and covered him, and I almost pulled back in blind panic. He was *that* big? He'd already unfastened his jeans, probably not wanting to risk permanent damage from my nervous hands, and I shoved them down his narrow hips. I had never thought a penis was beautiful. I didn't even like the word. But he was gorgeous. Big and hard, pale with blue veins, and I circled him with my hand, loving the feel of him, silken skin over iron.

He was watching me, breathing heavily, but he made no move to push me. And I did what I'd been dreaming about. I put my mouth on him, drawing him in deep.

He arched off the bed, his hands gripping the sheet, and I felt his cock jerk in my mouth. And then I stopped thinking, loving the feel of him in my mouth, the taste of him, the scent of his skin, the pounding of his heart, the absolute fierceness of his arousal that was for me and me alone. I tried to take more, and more, but he was too big, and I started to shake with need, when he finally reached down and lifted me off him. "Next time," he whispered. "I want to come inside you tonight."

I started to lie down on the mattress, but he moved, turning me so that I was on my knees on the bed, and he stripped the nightgown off me entirely, kicking off his jeans. He held me in place, coming up behind me, his hands on my hips.

"Put your hands on the bed," he whispered.

I did it immediately and felt him against me, against my sex, sliding against the wetness between my legs. "Do you want this?" he whispered.

I nodded, unable to speak, and he pushed forward, into me, sliding into the soft folds of my sex, and the angle was exquisite, shocking, wonderful. He was slow, inexorable, even bigger from this position, filling me inch by inch until I wanted to cry out. I put my face down in the sheets to stifle the noise I wanted to make, and the angle made his invasion easier, so that he slid the last bit, up against my womb.

He began to move, and I sobbed with need, shivering beneath him. I wanted this to go on forever, I wanted my sex to grip him and never let go. He moved one hand down over my stomach, between my legs, and touched me as he surged inside, and I shrieked as the first powerful climax hit me like a lightning bolt.

I felt my entire body ignite. He continued to thrust, slow and steady, as he caressed me, and no sooner did I start to come down than I shot to the stars again with that same driving force. I buried my face in the sheets, clutching them, sobbing, thrashing. I could hear my voice from a distance, begging him, begging him not to stop.

And then it became too much. It frightened me, the darkness he was drawing me into; it was the death I was facing, and I wanted to tell him no, but he kept moving, and my mouth was filled with nothing but needy sobs as we went deeper and deeper into a place I hadn't imagined existed, and the fear mixed with an incredulous joy as the last inhibition shattered, and there was nothing left but Michael and me.

He thrust, so hard he was shaking the bed, pounding into me, and I reveled in it, in the pleasure-pain of it. He froze, and I felt his climax inside me as a final paroxysm shook me, and I lifted my face and screamed.

We fell together, his body wrapped around mine, holding me tightly as a blanket of feathers enclosed us, and I reveled in Michael's black wings, impossibly, feathery soft, wrapping us in the aftermath of our lovemaking, and then I stopped thinking anything at all.

We didn't talk for a long time. He stroked me, brushing the tears off my cheeks, and I turned my head for his long, sweet kiss before settling back against him. I had never felt so safe, so loved, in my entire life. This was Michael, my bonded mate, my lover. He was mine, for as long as I lived.

I reached up sleepily, pushing my hair away from my neck, exposing my vein to him. I wanted him to drink from me, to take from me, but I didn't know if he would. A moment later I felt the slight sting as he broke the skin, and then the slow, seductive suck of his mouth against me, and I drifted off in blissful arousal.

If I had known, I would still choose this. Choose him. The world I had wanted to discover lay within him and me, and even if there wasn't enough time, there was more than enough love.

I was content.

CHAPTER
THIRTY-ONE

ALLIE LAY IN BED, AFRAID TO MOVE. She would throw up again, she was certain of it. No one seemed to have the vaguest idea what to do about her stomach bug. She'd been sick for weeks now, barely able to keep anything down, and yet, despite Sarah's promises that no one ever changed in Sheol, she seemed to be gaining weight.

She needed to get up. Today was the day they had dreaded, the day they knew would come. Uriel would send the Armies of Heaven against them, and the Fallen would prevail. After disappearing for weeks, Michael had returned in time, bringing the goddess of war with him.

And she would die.

Michael was in love with the girl. Allie had needed only one look at him, as he watched Tory run from him on the beach, to know that the impossible had happened. The Archangel Michael, always so determined to keep aloof from life, had fallen for good, embracing the humanity he'd always avoided so assiduously.

He'd taken her blood as well, when he'd sworn never to drink any more than the little the Source offered. In the end it would make no difference, Martha said. Whether he'd taken Tory or not, her death on the bloody sands was assured. At least this way there was some joy before the inevitable parting.

It was a good thing he wouldn't be looking to the Source—she had been called upon so often in the last few weeks that she figured that must be partly to blame for her constant sleepiness. To be sure, none of the unattached angels drank much. And Allie did her best to eat spinach and liver, though she really shouldn't be anemic. Women in Sheol didn't have periods, because their bodies didn't change, and there were no babies to be had.

And she wasn't going to think about that. She'd let it go. She couldn't spend the rest of her life mourning the inevitable. It distressed Raziel. It distressed them all.

She'd already made peace with that. Loving Raziel as she did, she decided it would be enough for her. And for years it had been enough.

It wasn't as if she even had a biological clock ticking. While the other women in Sheol lived out long but normal lives, there was a good chance she'd make it several hundred years or more, thanks to the blood Raziel had given her when she had been dying from a sword thrust. Such gifts were strictly forbidden, and it was a lucky thing that Allie hadn't died from the cure. Instead it had saved her, made her stronger, surer, more powerful.

She'd never touched his blood again. He would take hers, and if she felt a strange sort of longing she ignored it, finding enough sensuous satisfaction in the giving of blood. After all, she was ostensibly still human, even if it was up in the air whether she was technically alive or not, having been whisked away to Sheol after her fatal encounter with a bus but before being cast into the afterlife Uriel had planned for her. Humans couldn't digest blood—she'd looked it up on the Internet once in that previous life when she'd considered writing a book about biblical vampires. Little had she known how close that was to the truth.

Funny, but she didn't miss the Internet, or television. She still had books, and she wrote. Anything worth doing was worth doing for love, and there was something freeing about not having to worry about sales and marketing. She could just write, and no one would look over her shoulder.

Except Raziel, who would snort in disbelief and then make her act out the love scenes in bed. Which was perfectly fine with her. As long as this intermittent nausea wasn't plaguing her.

Raziel wasn't going to die today. She refused to consider that possibility. Besides, she would know, and if that were the case she would drug him and tie him up and hide him until the danger passed. There was no way in hell she was going to let him die, no matter how mad he got. To hell with honor and duty. She was keeping her man safe.

But her Spidey-senses told her he'd be fine. Even so, she couldn't loll around in bed while the Fallen were risking their lives. She needed to be there, for moral support if nothing more. She wasn't sure she could wield a sword at this point, though maybe she could throw up on someone.

She sat up slowly. Raziel had already left the bed, though he'd held her in his arms all night long. It was just past dawn, and the Fallen would be assembling on the beach, awaiting the first wave of Uriel's armies.

And, damn it, she was going to be there too.

CHAPTER
THIRTY-TWO

I T WAS AN EXQUISITELY BEAUTIFUL morning. I walked out into the dawn-lit sky, listening to the gulls as they cried, watching their graceful swoop and dive. Was there such a thing as reincarnation? If so, I might want to come back as a seagull, here in Sheol. The fish were plentiful, the ocean would surround me, and I could watch over Michael to my heart's content.

But I wasn't going to think about that now. There was a job to be done, and it was a good day to die. I would die cleanly, bravely, with the minimum of fuss. I just hoped it would be at the end of the day, when victory was assured, and not at the very start of the battle.

Michael held my hand, his grip a little too firm. I felt almost tender. It would be worse, much worse, if he really loved me the way the euphoria had forced him to profess. He cared about me, I knew it. He did love me, just a little, though he was still fighting it. And he would grieve, I had no doubt.

But he would get over it. He had been alive since the dawn of time; he had done horrific things and wondrous ones. During the small, quiet hours of the morning he'd confessed, driven by some need, and I'd heard it all, holding him in my arms. And when it was over I'd kissed him, and I felt his grief. He would be alive for millennia more, time enough to make amends for all the harm he'd done at Uriel's behest, if he felt the need to. I wouldn't be there. He might even forget all about me. I was a mere blip on the endless timeline of his life.

I smiled up at him. His face was carved in granite, his eyes like obsidian. He was a man with everything held firmly in check. A soldier ready for battle.

I was trussed in lightweight armor at his insistence. I humored him, though I knew it would do no good. He'd had far longer to get used to the inevitable, but clearly he wasn't able to let go. If I could accept it, so could he.

I looked up at him and a little part of me melted as I relived the feel of him, the taste of him, the sweet joy of giving and taking. I would die with his seed inside me, with the marks of his lovemaking on my breasts, on my thighs. I would die happy.

We were a ragtag group, I thought, glancing down the line. Everyone was on the beach, more than I could begin to count, the Fallen and their wives and a few widows, armed with every sort of weapon.

No guns, thank God. Guns were too impersonal. If someone was going to kill me, I wanted to see his face.

It was after 6 a.m., almost full daylight, and the ocean had calmed, as if it knew all the drama was going to be played out on the sand. Rachel stood beside Azazel, both of them calm and determined. I could see others whose faces I knew but whose names were unfamiliar. Raziel paced before everyone, but there was no sign of Allie. I glanced back and saw her standing at the main entrance of the house, watching over everyone. She looked pale but composed, and there was a strange light emanating from her. I gazed at her, and felt an irrational hope for the future.

"We're all glad you're back, Victoria Bellona," Asbel's soft voice intruded, and I jumped, startled. I hadn't noticed him so close to us, his sword drawn, waiting with the others.

I summoned a smile. "Wouldn't miss it for the world," I said lightly.

The sun was shining cheerfully, glinting off the ocean, sparkling in the sand. It made the sudden darkness so much more startling as the sky was filled with shadows, and we all looked up, into a heaven filled with what seemed like a thousand winged creatures all heading toward us, blotting out the sun.

I tried to pull my hand free of Michael's, but he held on tightly, and I yanked at it till he turned to look at me. I gave him a warm smile. "You can't hold on forever, Your Saintliness," I said lightly. "We have a battle to win."

For a moment I thought he wouldn't release me. The first wave of angel-soldiers had landed on the beach, the first clash of metal on metal resounding through the early-morning air.

"I'll look out for her," Asbel said.

"No one's looking out for me," I said firmly. "You will look out for yourselves."

Michael didn't move, and in his dark, dark eyes I read love. "I need to tell you one thing," he said, drawing his sword with his other hand.

"Okay."

"I'm immune to euphoria." He brought my hand up to his mouth and kissed it, hard, before releasing it. And then, with a furious roar, he drew his flaming sword and charged into battle.

I had never been in a war before. The movies had it wrong—there was no glory, no courage, no sense. Just noise and blood and sweat as we slashed our way through Uriel's army.

There were so many of them, faceless angels, their wings stark white, a strange contrast to the deep hues of the Fallen, Raziel's iridescent blue, Azazel's jet black, the deep, burnished darkness of Michael's wings that had felt so soft around us. Wave after wave they came, dressed in armor, wielding swords.

The energy burned through my body, down my arms, and I flung it at the angels overhead, hearing their screams as they caught fire and plummeted to the ground. Over and over I sent the punishing bolts of energy into their midst, until the battle came to me, and I had no choice but to draw my own sword and fight hand-to-hand. I couldn't count, but the ground was thick with them, and more were coming. I hacked and slashed my way through, ignoring the cries of pain, ignoring the blows that hit me. There was no way any of us would come out of this—we were outmanned, outmaneuvered. It didn't matter that Michael had spent the time between arriving back in Sheol and coming to my bed involved in feverish planning. Even the most brilliant tactician couldn't succeed against such insurmountable odds.

It didn't matter. I couldn't think about outcome or survivors; all I could do was fight my way through this faceless crush of warriors, angels, friend, and foe, and push them back toward the sea. Rachel had told me the sea healed the Fallen. I had no idea why we were driving our enemies toward it, but I followed orders without question. In a moment I knew.

As each wave of angels landed, their blindingly white wings furled, disappearing and leaving no sign on their strong backs as they charged into battle.

But the moment their feet touched the water the wings unfurled, large and unwieldy, dragging in the seawater, soaking in it, until they were dragged down, helpless beneath their own murderous weight, and I felt hope burst in my heart. I didn't have time to think of right or wrong, or the horror of taking joy in another's death. This war was not of our choosing, and if we didn't stop the invaders they would bring that war to the world, destroying humankind as if they were locusts. I pushed, forcing another into the sea, ignoring the blood that splattered me, ignoring the cries and howls of fury, ignoring everything but what I must do.

I had to get as far from Michael as I could. Three times I saw him leave what he was doing to slash at someone heading my way, his vicious, flaming sword a beacon in the bright sunlight. I knew he was still trying to protect me. Didn't he know it didn't matter? He loved me. The foolish, tender things he'd told me in that sickly-sweet land hadn't been brought out by euphoria; they had been real. He loved me, and that would be enough. Even if our time together was short, it had been glorious.

More angels were descending, but the beach was filled with fighting men and bodies strewn about, and there was no place to alight. Many attempted to land on the edge of the surf, only to be pulled immediately into the water's depths. Others tried to drop down atop the broken bodies of their comrades, but lost their balance and had to face the fury of the Fallen. Wave after wave, till the beach was soaked with blood and the water ran red, till the cries of the wounded and dying filled the air. In the distance I saw Metatron, fighting with a ferocity matched only by Michael's, and I knew a moment's confusion.

One of the invading angels struck me in the side, the blow partially deflected by the armor Michael had insisted I wear, and I fell to one knee, the breath knocked out of me. My enemy moved in, his blade held high to bring down a killing stroke.

I shoved my sword up into his throat and felt his hot blood spray me before he pitched forward into the sand. I rolled out of the way just in time, springing to my feet again as more of the enemy landed.

Time lost its meaning. The noise faded into silence as the battle raged around me, and I continued to fight like a creature possessed. I couldn't worry about when my own fatal blow would land. I had accepted that it would, and that I would fight until it came. I fought until my arms were numb, until my skin was stiff with blood splatter.

They were dying all around me, and I reveled in it, as tears ran down my face. I killed, I wept, I triumphed. I fought as my feet slid in gore and blood-soaked sand, I fought until I knew I could fight no more, and I kept going, knowing my strength, my precious strength, was beginning to fail me.

I looked up as the sky darkened once more, and my heart sank in despair. A huge cadre of our enemy had appeared in the sky, so thick with sharp white wings that they blocked out the sun. I wanted to drop my sword and send what fierce punishment I could into the sky, but the fighting was too thick around me, and I knew we were all going to die, and I would go down fighting.

There was no place for them to land on the bloody beach, and they hovered, a phalanx of death. Then I saw Rachel in the distance, bloody, fierce, throwing her hands toward the sky.

If she could do it, I could. I thrust my sword into the sand. I was going to die anyway; I might at least die trying. I could feel the heat rush through my body, down my arms, and I raised them and flung the bolts of energy directly into the enemy's midst.

The angels veered, trying to avoid it, just as a fierce wind caught them, and they plummeted, miscalculating, into the sea, pulled to their deaths in the beautiful ocean.

And then, suddenly, there were no more to kill.

I looked around me in blind exhaustion and disbelief. The fighting was winding down and I knew that, at least for now, we had prevailed.

And I still lived. It made no sense, but I lived.

I looked across the body-strewn beach, trying to see whom I could recognize among the dead and dying. In the distance I saw Michael, his massive sword ablaze, still fighting the few remaining soldiers, unable to stop until the last enemy was vanquished; if I hadn't been numb, I would have smiled. But something was wrong.

Someone jostled me and I spun, arms raised defensively, only to see Asbel, curiously unmarred by the bloody war, standing there with his sword drawn. "It's you," I said with relief. And then that relief vanished as I stopped and focused. And remembered the smell of him, cinnamon, just before I'd been knocked unconscious and delivered to Beloch. "It's you," I said again, a world of meaning in my voice.

He glanced around him. "Sorry, goddess. Just following orders." His sword glinted bright in the sunlight, and I tried to block him, but I was just too tired. I'd dropped my sword, my arms were numb, and I was frozen to the spot.

It didn't hurt. I felt the slash of his sword ripping through me, and the heat of my blood poured out. I put up my hands, trying to catch it, knowing it shouldn't be wasted, as I sank to my knees in the sand. I could hear Michael's roar of fury, and Asbel's face turned white as he realized he'd been seen. It didn't matter, I wanted to tell him. This was all preordained. Nothing could change it.

My eyes were open long enough to see Asbel's head spin from his body beneath Michael's sword. I felt Michael fall to his knees beside me, pulling me into his arms, and I tried to smile up at him, to tell him it was all right, but my muscles were weak, my voice locked.

All I could do was close my eyes and die.

CHAPTER
THIRTY-THREE

MICHAEL ROSE, CRADLING HIS wife's body against his. She was covered with blood, but this time it held no erotic allure. This time she was dying, the blood that had defined her draining away, and he wanted to scream in rage and denial.

The survivors moved out of his way, silence all around them as he started toward the house. He had no idea where he was taking her, but he refused to leave her body with all the others, broken and torn. He pulled her against him as if he could contain the very last flicker of life before it went out entirely, and he knew this was one battle he couldn't win. Seawater wouldn't heal her—she wasn't an angel. Already the wounded were wading in past the bodies floating in the water, white wings sodden and outstretched. But he couldn't waste time worrying about his army, not now. All that mattered was Tory.

He carried her up the lawn toward the wide front opening of the house, where the Source waited for them. He slipped, going down on one knee, and realized with shock that he was weeping. Angels didn't weep.

But he was weeping for Tory.

"Put her down, Michael."

He heard Allie's voice from a distance, but he ignored her. As long as he held Tory she wasn't gone, and it would take an army to pry her away from him.

He felt a cool, soothing hand on his bloody shoulder. "Put her down, Michael," Allie said again. "She needs to let go."

He wanted to scream at her, but he knew it was useless. He would break Tory's bones if he continued to grip her like this, and she deserved to be as beautiful in death as she had been in life. Slowly he loosened his hold, setting her down on the grass.

The sound of her final breath leaving her was so quiet it was almost inaudible, and yet it thundered through his soul. He needed to put back his head and roar out his pain, but Allie knelt on one side of him, Martha on the other. Martha, with her fucking visions of death.

"She's gone," Allie said. "She died on her birthday, yes, Martha?"

"Yes."

He wanted to tell them to leave him alone to mourn, to weep, but Martha had put her strong hands on his other arm.

"You can save her," Allie said.

Raziel's ragged voice broke through. "Allie, no!"

She ignored her husband. "At least you can try. Give her your blood, Michael."

He stared at her blankly.

"It will kill her," Azazel said flatly.

Allie shot him a glance. "She's already dead. There's a chance he can save her."

"It's forbidden," one of the other Fallen insisted.

"It's never been done."

"It shouldn't be done."

"It's been done," Raziel said finally. "It saved Allie, years ago, after Sammael attacked her."

Silence fell. Michael had lost his weapons along the way, sending his flaming blade spinning into the air after he decapitated the traitor Asbel. He held out a bloody hand to Raziel. "Give me a knife."

He thought Raziel would hesitate. He didn't. The curved blade was clean, no enemy blood tainting it, and he ripped away his leather armor to draw the blade across his chest. Blood welled, and he realized he'd cut himself just as Tory had slashed her own chest in an effort to save him.

"Don't," Tamlel cried. "It could kill you!"

He ignored the warning. Scooping Tory up, he put her mouth against the bloody wound, pushing the warm, coppery liquid into her mouth, massaging her throat to make her swallow.

The first flutter of movement was so slight he thought he'd imagined it. It grew stronger, a pulse of life slowly beginning to glow, and he tucked her against him carefully as she drank.

He knew when she'd had enough. Her heartbeat had grown strong and clear, and she began to choke. He pulled her away, looking down into her pale face, her dazed green eyes, his blood on her mouth almost unbearably erotic. "What . . . the fuck . . . are you doing?" she choked out.

He laughed. For the first time in his endless existence, he felt such joy that he thought he might die from it. But that was no way to deal with joy. "Saving your life, Victoria Bellona."

She screwed up her face in expected annoyance. "You better not be turning me into a vampire, Your Saintliness." She was still weak, the words barely audible, but he could see that the hideous wound on her body had already begun to heal. She would live.

He managed a shrug. He had a gash across his back that would need stitches, he could do with a dip in the ocean if he could fight his way through the bodies, and they needed to count their losses and review their triumph. This had been only the first battle in a war that had been a long time coming.

He was doing none of that. He was going to hold on to Tory until his arms went numb and she yelled at him to go away, which she would, sooner or later. But for now she was his, and he was never going to let her go.

EPILOGUE

MARTHA CLIMBED THE END-less stairs of the big house, a basket looped over one arm. Allie and Raziel still lived on the very top floor instead of in the traditional quarters for the Alpha and the Source, which made visiting a pain in the butt. She didn't mind. Rachel would already be there, and she didn't want to wait.

It had been a very long day. By now the bodies of the dead had vanished, by Uriel's hand or by those of the Fallen. Their own casualties had been very light, but each loss was heartbreak. Gabriel was alone now, his wife dead in the sand. Tobias and Gadrael were gone as well, and others were grievously injured.

But Tory lived again, safe in the archangel's arms. Never in her life had Martha so wanted a prophecy to be proven wrong. In the end it hadn't mattered.

Allie had held the secret of life. In more ways than one.

It was a hard day, reminding her of the day she'd lost her Thomas, cut down by the Nephilim. She still bore scars across her own body. But Tory's triumph was somehow a triumph for them all, a reassurance that perhaps it could be all right in the end.

Martha never wanted a vision again in her life. In truth, she'd been trying to keep herself awake so she wouldn't dream, hoping that would be enough to keep the worst of them at bay, but for a few short hours this afternoon she'd drifted off as she waited by Tory's bed, holding the girl's hand while someone worked on stitching up Michael's back. She'd seen him then, the black angel who was coming, and she'd been filled with apprehension. There was no room for newcomers in Sheol. They didn't need any more trouble, and this man, she could tell, was nothing but trouble. She knew his name, though she wasn't sure how.

Cain.

She could only hope it would be years before he arrived. But her dreams were never in the distant future. Once envisioned, they came true far too quickly. A decent gift would give them time to plan, time to adjust. A decent gift would give clear answers.

She finally reached the top floor, premonitions sweeping through her. Everything was about to change.

Rachel let her in, a conspiratorial smile on her face. "She's in bed."

"Is she all right?" Martha demanded, worried.

"She's fine. Just a little sick."

Martha couldn't resist asking. "Do you have any sense that something might be wrong? I don't, but it might be wishful thinking on my part. She's wanted this for so long. We've all wanted this."

"She's fine," Rachel said again. "I know these things. I've looked after womankind for most of my existence."

Martha took a deep breath. "All right," she said, and marched into the bedroom like someone going before a firing squad. "Hi, Allie. How are you doing?"

"Fine," she said weakly. "I just wish I knew what was wrong with me. I'm feeling weird, bloated, and so damned tired." She looked up at Rachel pleadingly. "I don't want to die."

"You won't," Rachel said, sitting on the bed and taking her hand.

Allie looked up at her warily. "I'm dying, aren't I? Martha's seen a vision. You've come to tell me I'm going to die, and this time Raziel's blood won't save me."

"You were very bad," Rachel said. "Azazel told me it was a very dangerous thing to do."

"Not when it's a question of life and death."

"And you've never had his blood since?"

Allie shook her head. "No. We were afraid that the next time it might be lethal."

"Perhaps," Martha said meditatively. "There have been many lies spun as truth over the years. Men like to control things, and the Fallen are, unfortunately, still men."

Rachel snorted. "You go, girl. Just don't let Raziel hear you talking like that. He gets offended."

"He can handle it," Allie said. "But if I'm not dying, then what's wrong with me?"

Martha put the basket in front of her and pulled back the heavy holland cover that had protected the delicate things for so long. Allie just looked down into the basket blankly.

"Doll clothes?" she demanded. "Aren't I a little old to be playing with baby dolls?"

"Not doll clothes, dear Allie," Rachel said softly. "Baby clothes. You're going to have a baby."

EVERYTHING STILL HURT, including my stomach, but I didn't care. I was strong enough to walk on the beach, now that the heavy rains had washed the blood away, strong enough to walk beside Michael. It was a beautiful day now that the storms had passed, and Martha's prophecy had come true after all. I had died. And I lived again, strength flowing through me. Michael's blood flowing through me.

There was no sign of the carnage that had filled this beach, filled the ocean three short days ago. All was peaceful, the smell of the ocean filling my lungs. I smiled up at Michael.

"Last one in is a rotten egg," I said, and sprinted into the surf.

He caught me before I was waist-deep, and we fell together, tumbling in the cool, healing water. I wrapped my arms around him, my legs around him, and let him take me wherever he wanted. I was whole, I was his.

And I would live forever.

Can't get enough Kristina Douglas?
Turn the page
for a sneak peek
at her next sizzling Fallen book

REBEL

Available June 2013 from Pocket Books

I COULD FEEL IT COMING OVER me, and I was frozen with dread. Not now. Not again. I fought it, struggling, the entangling sheets trapping my body, and I ended up on the hard stone floor as pale mist filled the small confines of my room, and my heart clenched in dread. Could it be Thomas? Darling Thomas, dead for so many years, coming back to give me another, unwanted warning? He had always watched me a little too closely.

I could hear soft whimpering, and knew it came from me. No, it wasn't my dead husband. This was nothing more than the mist that always shrouded Sheol, keeping it safe from the ordinary world. Like Thomas, there was no malice in it, but it brought the visions that plagued me, and I curled up in a corner on the floor, wrapping my arms around my legs, burying my face against my knees.

It wouldn't stop the visions. Nothing would. I couldn't control them, couldn't understand them— months could go by without anything, and then I'd end up on my knees, sobbing.

No one knew. Life in a world of fallen angels was never easy for a mortal, particularly one who'd lost her mate. If they had any idea the pain my visions cause me they would want to help, and I couldn't bear the thought of it. Whether I embraced them or not, the visions came, and the best way to get through them was to keep them private. Otherwise there were too many questions, too many demands, for clarity that was maddeningly out of reach. I needed quiet to make sense of the bits and pieces that came to me like shards of glass, piercing my battered soul.

I huddled in the darkness like a miserable coward, trying to calm my thundering heart. I was covered with a cold sweat, even though the room was warm, and I forced myself to take slow, steadying breaths. Letting it in.

He was coming. The Dark Man, who brought disruption and destruction. The name had been clear in my mind for months now, but I had said nothing to the others. I knew nothing. Only his name.

Cain.

And he was coming for me.

I should get up. I had no idea whether it was this day or another, but soon. Soon he would come and everything would be chaos. It was little wonder I hadn't told Raziel. As leader of the Fallen he had more than enough to deal with, and now, with the astounding miracle of his wife's pregnancy, he had no time to worry about half-formed visions that meant nothing. I'd hoped to wait until later, until I knew more about the prophecy.

But later was now.

My fears were absurd, of course. I knew it intellectually, but my heart still pounded. What disaster awaited the Fallen? What disaster awaited me?

In the hierarchy of the Fallen, I was nothing but a vestigial organ, neither angel nor mate. Thomas had plucked me from the chaos of my human life. He'd been watching over me, he'd said. I told him once he had been a pretty ineffective guardian angel, and he'd been offended. Thomas hadn't had much of a sense of humor about things. I was so young when he'd brought me here, only seventeen, but he had given me love and safety and a peace I had craved and never known, and for ten years I was happy.

And then the monstrous Nephilim had broken through, and he had died, and the visions had begun.

At first I welcomed those visions. Raziel had offered to send me back to the human world, my mind wiped clean of any memory of my life in Sheol, but I had refused. Why would I choose to return to hell after living with the angels, albeit fallen ones? Raziel had promised me that I would always be welcome among the Fallen, but trust had always been one of my failings. I'd been terrified he might change his mind, see me as useless.

The visions gave me a purpose, a role in the world of the Fallen. While the angels had varying abilities to see the future, none were nearly as good as my own, imperfect dreams. As incomplete and frustrating as they were, they gave me a reason to stay in Sheol, one I welcomed despite the pain.

So why should the Dark Man be coming for me?

The next vision hit me like a knife, and I jerked, moaning, horrified by the vision. It was raw, embarrassing, a vision of sexual intimacy that made me close my eyes, trying to shut it out, but it wouldn't stop. I didn't want to see this, I didn't want the sensual reaction that spread beneath my skin like the fire that poisoned the Fallen.

But the visions never listened. Closing my eyes only brought the pictures into clearer focus; running didn't help. I curled in on myself and endured, as the couple moved on the bed. I could see the man's face, angelically beautiful, devilishly wicked, as he slowly thrust into the woman beneath him. She looked up into his face, and it was my body he was pleasuring. The dream-Martha tried to move, but her hands were tied above her head with a soft, silk scarf. There was no coercion; this was play, and I watched it in fascinated horror. I wanted to say something, to stop the power of the dream, but all I could hear was a moan coming from my throat as the visions sliced through me, the pain ripping at me. Yet this time that pain was mixed with deep, forbidden pleasure.

It vanished. One moment I was writhing in sexual ecstasy beneath the dark angel, the next I was alone in my room, huddled and shaking on the hard floor, early-morning sunlight streaking the room. The mist was gone with the vision, leaving me incomplete, my body still tingling with a shameful, absurd arousal. I had learned nothing new, nothing helpful. Only that a dark angel was coming.

And he was coming for me.

I pushed to my feet, using the wall to steady myself. I was shaking, my heart pounding, my head aching, but I had long since trained myself to ignore it. I straightened the dream-tossed bedding on my narrow cot before heading into the utilitarian bathroom. The hot shower helped, easing some of the tension from my muscles, beating against my oddly sensitized skin. It was as if I could still feel his touch. And my own arousal. I shook my head, wiping the moisture from the mirror, and looked at myself dispassionately.

The bonded mates of the Fallen aged differently than they would have in the human world they'd left. I was thirty-one, and looked ten years younger. I would live to the century mark and well beyond, if the violence inherent in the lives of the Fallen didn't kill me first. I looked normal, calm; my short curly brown hair fluffed around my narrow face, my changeable eyes a calm sea-green today. I had bitten my lip during the vision, though I couldn't remember when, and my mouth looked bee-stung, as if I'd been thoroughly, relentlessly kissed. But if anyone looked at me they would never know I'd spent the last hour wrapped in pain. Wrapped in sex.

Then again, no one ever looked at me too closely. In Sheol, as in the human world, widows were invisible. My dubious gifts were valued, my presence welcomed and cared for. But, in the end, I mattered to no one.

The ominous rumble of thunder broke through my brief flash of self-pity, a welcome distraction. I shoved my fingers through my hair, then went to dress as the thunder grew louder.

I heard the sizzle of lightning, followed by a crash that seemed to shake the earth, and an eerie blue light speared into my room. I froze, panic filling me. He was coming *now*, and I had to warn them.

Not bothering with shoes, I raced along the corridor, dodging the sleepy inhabitants who'd emerged from their rooms to observe the storm. I had to get to Raziel as fast as I could, to give him a belated warning.

I raced around a corridor, almost slamming into the Archangel Michael, but one look from his dark eyes and I slowed to a brisk walk. Panic wouldn't help anyone.

"Where is Raziel?" I resisted the impulse to grab his shirt and force an answer as another bolt of lightning slammed down, followed by a roar of thunder.

"On the beach," he said shortly. "It's dangerous out there—if you can wait, you'd be safer. Unless . . . do you know anything about this?"

Suspicion and annoyance were in his voice, and I couldn't blame him. He had already been a victim of my half-assed visions, and even if it brought him Tory, he still held a grudge. "I don't," I said, semi-truthfully. Because I didn't know. I could only guess.

People were moving now, heading out onto the beach in the midst of the lightning storm, an act of utter insanity. Few things could kill fallen angels, usually only other unearthly creatures or the open flames that poisoned them. But what about the fierce power of lightning? And what would it do to the human wives who moved out into the storm?

"It can't wait," I said. If it brought an end to my existence, then so be it. I pushed past him, moving through the open doors, out onto the beach, searching for Raziel's tall form among so many.

The moment I set foot on the beach all hell broke loose, as if the storm had released its final restraint. It crashed down with the ferocity of a caged monster who finally broke its chains. The sky turned black, roiling with angry clouds, the only light the almost constant bolts of lightning slamming into the ground, into the sea, shaking the very pillars of the earth. The roar of the wind battled with the constant, deafening thunder, and I felt the wind catch my loose clothes and plaster them against my body. I stood and watched the end of the world.

Raziel loomed up out of the chaos, fury vibrating through him. "Do you know anything about this?" he demanded, somehow being heard over the noise.

Time to face the music, I thought miserably. Raziel needed any information I had, as insubstantial as it was. "Someone's coming."

The wind caught my voice and whipped it away, but he heard anyhow. "Who?" he shouted.

I shook my head. "I don't know. I'm not sure."

"Who?" he repeated.

I heard the sizzle, and my ears popped, my face burnt with the sudden heat, and in the midst of the beach something burst into flames. Flames that could consume the Fallen, destroy them.

People scattered in panic, some heading into the healing safety of the furious sea, some running toward the house. I stood transfixed, staring at the column of flame, Raziel motionless by my side, as the form of a man appeared in the midst of the blaze.

Not a man—an angel. I could see the wings outlined against the orange-red glow, and I stifled my horrified cry. I had seen the agonizing devastation fire could wreak on the angels, even a spark, and this poor angel was consumed by it.

I watched, unable to turn away, expecting him to disintegrate into ash. No one moved to help him, no one could. They all stared at the culmination of their worst nightmares come to fruition.

He didn't scream. Didn't thrash or struggle. Instead, he stepped forward, out of the flame, and it dissolved behind him, leaving him standing there, untouched, his deep-hued wings spread out behind him as he surveyed the people around him.

And then the angel smiled, the most devilish, charming, diabolical smile, as he snapped his fingers. The fire vanished. The sky cleared instantly, the wind dropped, the thunder and lightning gone as if it had never consumed their universe. He looked around him at the shocked faces, almost benevolently.

"I always did know how to make an entrance," he said.

I could feel the fury vibrating through Raziel, so fierce and powerful it reached into me as well. "Cain," he said in tones of utter loathing. "I should have known."

See where it all began in . . .

THE FALLEN: RAZIEL

The first book in Kristina Douglas's
sexy, exciting fallen angel series

I WAS RUNNING LATE, WHICH was no surprise. I always seemed to be in a rush—there was a meeting with my editors halfway across Manhattan, I had a deposit to make before the end of the business day, my shoes were killing me, and I was so hungry I could have eaten the glass and metal desk I'd been allotted at my temp job at the Pitt Foundation.

"Shouldn't you be heading out, Allie?" Elena, my overworked supervisor, glanced over at me. "You won't have time to get to the bank if you don't leave now."

Crap. Two months and already Elena had pegged me as someone chronically late. "I won't be back," I called out as I hobbled toward the elevator. Elena waved absently good-bye, and moments later I was alone in the elevator, starting the sixty-three-floor descent.

It was a cool October afternoon, with Halloween only a few days off. The sidewalks were busy as usual, and the bank was across the street. I could always walk and eat a hot dog at the same time, I thought, heading over to the luncheon cart. I'd done it often enough.

With my luck there had to be a line. I bounced nervously, shifting my weight, and the man in front of me turned around.

I'd lived in New York long enough to make it a habit not to look at people on the street. Here in midtown, most of the women were taller, thinner, and better dressed than I was, and I didn't like feeling inadequate. I never made eye contact with anyone, not even with Harvey the hot-dog man, who'd served me daily for the last two months.

So why was I looking up, way up, into a pair of eyes that were . . . God, what color were they? A strange shade between black and gray, shot with striations of light so that they almost looked silver. I was probably making a fool of myself, but I couldn't help it. Never in my life had I seen eyes that color, though that shouldn't surprise me since I avoided looking in the first place.

But even more astonishing, those eyes were watching me thoughtfully. Beautiful eyes in a beautiful face, I realized belatedly. I didn't like men who were too attractive, and that term was mild when it came to the man looking down at me, despite my four-inch heels.

He was almost angelically handsome, with his high cheekbones, his aquiline nose, his streaked brown and golden hair. It was precisely the tawny shade I'd tried to get my colorist to replicate, and she'd always fallen woefully short.

"Who does your hair?" I blurted out, trying to startle him out of his abstraction.

"I am as God made me," he said, and his voice was as beautiful as his face. Low-pitched and musical, the kind of voice to seduce a saint. "With a few modifications," he added, with a twist of dark humor I couldn't understand.

His gorgeous hair was too long—I hated long hair on men. On him it looked perfect, as did the dark leather jacket, the black jeans, the dark shirt.

To hell with the hot dog—my best bet was to get away from this too-attractive stranger, drop off the deposit, and hope to God I could find a taxi to get me across town to my meeting. I was already ten minutes late. I stepped out into the street, which was momentarily free of traffic.

It happened in slow motion, it happened in the blink of an eye. One of my high heels snapped, my ankle twisted, and the sudden rain was turning the garbage on the street into a river of filth. I slipped, going down on one knee, and I could feel my stockings shred, my skirt rip, my carefully arranged hair plastered limp and wet around my ears.

I looked up, and there it was, a crosstown bus ready to smack into me. Another crack of thunder, the bright white sizzle of lightning, and everything went calm and still. Just for a moment.

And then it was a blur of noise and action. I could hear people screaming, and to my astonishment money was floating through the air like autumn leaves, swirling downward in the heavy rain. The bus had come to a stop, slanted across the street, and horns were honking, people were cursing, and in the distance I could hear the scream of sirens. Pretty damned fast response for New York, I thought absently.

The man was standing beside me, the beautiful one from the hot-dog stand. He was just finishing a chili dog, entirely at ease, and I remembered I was famished. If I was going to get held up by a bus accident, I might as well get a chili dog. But for some reason, I didn't want to turn around.

"What happened?" I asked him. He was tall enough to see over the crowds of people clustered around the front of the bus. "Did someone get hurt?"

"Yes," he said in that rich, luscious voice. "Someone was killed."

I started toward the crowd, curious, but he caught my arm. "You don't want to go there," he said. "There's no need to go through that."

I glanced back up at the rain-drenched accident scene in front of me, and I thought I caught a glimpse of the victim—just the brief sight of *my* leg, wearing *my* shoe, the heel broken off.

"No," said the man beside me, and he put a hand on my arm before I could move away.

The bright light was blinding, dazzling, and I was in a tunnel, light whizzing past me, the only sound the whoosh of space moving at a dizzying speed. *Space Mountain*, I thought, but this was no Disney ride.

It stopped as abruptly as it had begun, and I felt

sick. I was disoriented and out of breath; I looked around me, trying to get my bearings.

The man still held my arm loosely, and I yanked it free, stumbling away from him. We were in the woods, in some sort of clearing at the base of a cliff, and it was already growing dark. The sick feeling in my stomach began to spread to the rest of my body.

I fought my way through the mists of confusion— my mind felt as if it were filled with cotton candy. Something was wrong. Something was very wrong.

"Don't struggle," the man beside me said in a remote voice. "It only makes it worse. If you've lived a good life, you have nothing to be afraid of."

I looked at him in horror. Lightning split open the sky, followed by thunder that shook the earth. The solid rock face in front of us began to groan, a deep, rending sound that echoed to the heavens. It started to crack apart, and I remembered something from Christian theology about stones moving and Christ rising from the dead.

"The bus," I said flatly. "I got hit by the bus. I'm dead, aren't I?"

"Yes."

I sure as hell wasn't going quietly. "Are you an angel?" I demanded. He didn't feel like one. He felt like a man, a distinctly real man, and why the hell was I suddenly feeling alert, alive, aroused, when according to him I was dead?

His eyes were oblique, half-closed. "Among other things."

Kicking him in the shin and running like hell

seemed an excellent plan, but I was barefoot and my body wasn't feeling cooperative. As angry and desperate as I was, I still seemed to want him to touch me, even when I knew he had nothing good in mind. Angels didn't have sex, did they? They didn't even have sexual organs, according to the movie *Dogma*. I found myself glancing at his crotch, then quickly pulled my gaze away. What the hell was I doing checking out an angel's package when I was about to die?

Oh, yeah, I'd forgotten—I was already dead. And all my will seemed to have vanished. He drew me toward the crack in the wall, and I knew with sudden clarity it would close behind me like something out of a cheesy movie, leaving no trace that I'd ever lived. Once I went through, it would all be over.

"This is as far as I go," he said, his rich, warm voice like music. And with a gentle tug on my arm, he propelled me forward, pushing me into the chasm.